Slow
Burn

Slow Burn

ANNE MARSH

BRAVA

KENSINGTON PUBLISHING CORP.
www.kensingtonbooks.com

BRAVA BOOKS are published by

Kensington Publishing Corp.
119 West 40th Street
New York, NY 10018

All Kensington titles, imprints, and distributed lines are available at special quantity discounts for bulk purchases for sales promotions, premiums, fund-raising, educational, or institutional use.

Special book excerpts or customized printings can also be created to fit specific needs. For details, write or phone the office of the Kensington special sales manager: Kensington Publishing Corp., 119 West 40th Street, New York, NY 10018, attn: Special Sales Department; phone 1-800-221-2647.

ISBN-13: 978-0-7582-8786-1
ISBN-10: 0-7582-8786-0

First Kensington Trade Paperback Printing: April 2013

10 9 8 7 6 5 4 3 2 1

Printed in the United States of America

Chapter One

The vintage Corvette Faye Duncan had mortgaged her life to buy took the curve sweet as apple pie—and landed her straight in hell. The mountain slope plunged away from the car's left, a two-thousand-foot drop just beyond the battered steel guardrail. The drop was bad, but the brush fire licking over the road and up the side of the mountain on her right worried her more. There shouldn't be flames on the road.

She hit the accelerator, because it was too damned late to stop. If she came to a screeching halt now, she'd be barbecue. The Corvette shot through the flames and smoke, and she braked hard, loose gravel pinging against the car's undercarriage.

Her ex-husband would have laughed at her nerves, but, then, Mike Thomas didn't think twice about plunging into a burning L.A. high-rise. He lived for the next fire call, the ride out on the truck, and the chance to pit himself against the flames in the company of his boys.

She didn't. Carefully, she pulled off onto the narrow shoulder. She'd left L.A. five hundred miles behind her, but this wasn't the adventure she'd been looking for.

The road was still on fire.

She grabbed the cell from her purse on the front seat, but dialing 911 didn't seem particularly helpful. After all, she didn't know precisely where she was. A quick glance at the dashboard warned her that the brush fire wasn't her only problem. The Corvette was almost out of gas, and the engine—or some other, unidentified part of her very new car—had been making strange noises for the last forty miles. The 425-horsepower, big-block engine that had practically melted the Daytona Speedway when it was first introduced and that the ad copy had promised her would deliver speed, speed, speed.

She'd traded in her 401K and all of her spare cash for this car.

Of course, she knew better than to believe everything she read in a glossy catalog. She made a living taking photographs for similar catalogs, and she knew that pretty perfection was staged. The tableware and picture frames she shot appeared on pages that were the empty sets for someone else's imagined life. Pretty, but impersonal, the catalogs promised stories waiting to happen when people bought the stuff and shed the boxes. She and Mike had been given an entire set of silver wedding frames.

Those frames were empty now, packed in a box in storage.

The fire contracted, then leapt forward, a little whirling hop of a dance that had her inching the Corvette ahead to put another handful of yards between her and the flames. From her new vantage point, right around the hairpin turn, she spotted a pickup with a dust-covered firehouse logo on its side. The local fire department was already on the scene. Thank God.

Rolling down the window, she hollered over at her savior. "You got this? Need me to call it in?"

The firefighter gave her a quick thumbs-up and started shoveling dirt onto the flames dancing along the edges of the asphalt and whipping up the mountainside. Thank God. He'd take care of the problem. Maybe he was a volunteer with the fire department she'd been hired to photograph for a local color piece.

She watched him for a minute, catching her breath before she grabbed her camera from the front seat. Why not? Bracing her arms on the window edge, she snapped a few shots. The firefighter had his back to her, thin flames whipping around his boots as he worked the shovel. The powerful muscles of his tanned forearms flexed as he did his thing, rescuing her and the mountain from imminent immolation. He'd pulled a bandana over most of his face and jammed a baseball cap down low on his forehead, making it impossible to see him clearly through the smoke, but he certainly filled out a pair of jeans nicely. *Jesus.* Maybe she had something here, something she could use. They didn't make men like that back in L.A.

Or if they had, she'd been blind.

Which was always possible. This firefighter was whipcord lean and wiry, pure strength taking on the fire single-handed. He could easily star front and center in her magazine piece. Re-covering the lens, she dropped the camera onto the seat. Putting the car back into gear, she lifted a hand in farewell, pulled out, and headed down the road.

When her cell buzzed a few minutes later, she flicked on the hands-free. The number on the screen was all too familiar, unlike the small town coming up fast in her windshield. That had to be Strong. There wasn't an overabundance of small towns up here in the Californian mountains.

"Six plus one," her sister, M.J., said when Faye answered. "You're a single woman again."

Six months and a day. That was how long it took to officially end a marriage that had, emotionally, been over almost before it started. "That's no newsflash."

She'd counted down the days with her sister, finding a

new reason each day for what had happened. The problem had been him. Her. The lack of a *them*. The ultimate betrayal had been his—and that had hurt, impossibly so, finding him in the arms of another woman—but she'd lost Mike long before that last afternoon. Or he'd lost her. They'd slowly drifted apart.

Now she was done. Mike was five hundred miles and 181 days in her past, and she wanted to *live*.

She slowed, the Corvette flashing past a signpost: WELCOME TO STRONG. Ponderosas shaded well-kept buildings lining a main street that a bronze plaque proudly proclaimed *historic*. There were certainly plenty of pastel-paint jobs and storefronts, not that Faye had ever been the shopping type. Still, there was something about the wooden sidewalks and pots of red flowers soaking up the sun that had her smiling.

"Tell me you're out celebrating, doing something memorable," her sister demanded.

"I just hit Strong." *Almost literally.* The car stalled, and she coaxed the engine back to life, her gaze flicking to the dashboard. She needed a gas station and a mechanic. Stat.

"That sounds like fun. Fingers crossed you meet some hunky new firefighters on the job." The other woman's voice sounded hopeful. M.J. wanted her baby sister to get right back on the marital horse, find herself another man—one who wouldn't turn up in bed with a woman he'd initially sworn was "just a good friend."

No more men.

"Where, exactly, is this Strong?" her sister asked, not done with her questions.

And it was a good question. The Corvette shuddered once more and then died silently. The needle on the gas gauge hovered on empty. Like her life.

Guiding the car into an empty parking spot in front of what appeared to be a pretty little general store, Faye considered her options. Which weren't many. Out of gas. In the middle of nowhere. Looking on the bright side, she didn't have anywhere else to be, which had been the whole point of this road trip to take pics for a freelance job. She'd packed up the car and decided to do a Thelma-and-Louise—just drive off into the sunset—but without a Louise, the guns, or the crime spree. Maybe, if luck was on her side, Brad Pitt would put in an appearance for a summer fling. Although, the last time she'd stood in line at an L.A. supermarket, gazing at the tabloids, it had looked as if he was firmly off the market and busy collecting kids.

Instead of getting it on with Brad, she would be spending the night in Strong. The general store's wide plank porch and potted red geraniums made the place postcard pretty. The country shop could have been a set for one of the catalog shoots she'd done.

"Up in the mountains. Maybe fifty miles past Sacramento?" she admitted when the silence on the cell stretched too long. She hadn't been interested in plotting the place on a map—she'd wanted to leave L.A. behind her, and Strong had fit that bill.

There was more silence on the other end, while her sister tried to figure out a tactful way to ask why, before she gave up and asked her question point-blank. "And you chose this spot because?"

"The name is good," Faye hedged. "And I've got a freelance job here, photographing a historic firehouse renovation." Plus, if she was being honest with herself, she'd been running when she left L.A., looking for another chance. A second chance.

Strong was going to be her do-over.

When she got out of the car, the air hit her first, all pine and lavender. One side of the street sported a display of antiques and a flower shop that was apparently the source of the lavender smell—two women were carrying in bundles of the stuff. When she peeked around the corner, however, there was no missing the town's honky-tonk bar. It was a visual assault, all tacky neon signs and promises of a good time. *Ma's*. Perfect.

"I saw Mike the other day." Her sister tossed her ex's name out casually. Faye didn't want to go there again. Six months wasn't enough time to make her willing to talk about what had and hadn't happened in her marriage. The pause on the other end was expectant, then exasperated. "Faye? Did you hear me?"

Yeah, and her sister wasn't going to walk away from the topic. Faye considered ending the call, but M.J. would hit redial. Again and again. So, instead, she went for the platitudes. "How'd he look?"

"Good." Her sister said the word carefully. "He said he hadn't seen you in a couple of months."

That's because we were getting a divorce.

"Are you okay?" The concern in her sister's voice warmed her even as it angered her. M.J. loved her, but she sounded as if she was afraid Faye would break, or break down, when Faye had been the one who'd asked for the divorce in the first place.

"I'm fine," she said again. "Really. Mike's part of the past now. I'm moving on." Mike had been all bona fide hero when she'd first met him, newly returned from a tour of duty in the Middle East and an L.A. fire-department re-cruit. He'd headed out on fire calls, and she'd watched him go, heart in her throat. He'd put himself into danger for others, and he'd been her very own hero. He'd whispered promises to her, vowed to keep her safe.

The firefighter by the side of the road was a hero. Mike was simply her past.

As she headed for the bar, dust covered her shoes. The hot, dry California summer was in full swing up here, but that was July for you. It seemed like only yesterday it had been winter, full of rain and wet.

Six plus one. 181 days. Her divorce was final.

"I'm going to lose you," she warned M.J. "I doubt they get much of a signal inside the bar." Maybe they did, maybe they didn't, but she needed to end this conversation.

"Faye—" Her sister didn't sound ready to hang up, but finally she said, "You be careful now. Don't drink and drive."

"No, ma'am." She eyed the Vette ruefully. "No worries there."

A handful of sentences later, she was a free woman. Shoving open the door to Ma's, she stepped inside. Friday-night noise assaulted her. The locals were getting an early start, *and* it was clearly happy hour. Now she knew she was in the right place.

She'd gas up and find a mechanic in the morning—she'd spotted a gas station down the street—take her pictures, and hit the road again as soon as she could. Find those adventures and that life that had to be out there waiting for her to drive up and say, *Here I am.*

"I need you to look after my wife."

His last jump, Evan Donovan decided, must have been too high, too fast. Maybe his ears weren't working right, because no way he'd heard correctly. Hell, he hadn't even realized Mike Thomas had gone and gotten himself married.

Evan and his crew had just come off a jump. He was tired, and he definitely stank of smoke. The wheels of the DC-3 had barely hit the runway before his cell phone had vibrated with Mike's incoming. The jump team's pilot, Spotted Dick, had set the DC-3 down like she was a newborn, and now the older man was fussing over the gas tanks while the rest of the team lined up to shower in the jump camp's two solar showers. His brothers, Jack and Rio, slapped palms with the others, trading laughing insults. Someone had already dragged out the plastic cooler, brimful of ice and longnecks. A chorus of caps popped as his team celebrated its victory over the day's wildland fire in a familiar, happy refrain. None of them would have dreamed of drinking on the job, but afterward, a cold one waited for every man.

Live for the moment, and live it up. Take in every second of this hot, glorious, goddamn summer because, while there was always another fire, sometimes a man ran out of tomorrows. Evan had walked away when others hadn't. Good people had died fighting fires before, but he'd be back on the DC-3 tomorrow, ready to go up again.

That was how Donovan Brothers, the private fire management company he ran with his brothers, Jack and Rio, operated. Government or private—they worked the fires, traveling whenever and wherever the flames were. Business had been good enough to run multiple teams these last few years, although they'd all come home to Strong this summer because this job was personal.

Mike's business also sounded personal.

He toed his pack aside and waited for Mike to give him deets, cradling his cell between his cheek and shoulder. Daylight was burning. He needed to check his chute, then repack it. And food. He definitely needed food. A shower, too, because he smelled too much of smoke and sweat. After that, he had an appointment with his bed.

He did *not* want to listen to any tale of marital woes.

"Your wife," he repeated carefully into the phone when the silence stretched on for too long. He and Mike had fought together on the other side of the world, done a tour of duty together. The man was a good Marine, and he'd always had Evan's back. They'd stood side by side through firefights and sandstorms and other shit Evan didn't really want to remember right now. Still, they hadn't talked in a year or three. The social hi-how-are-ya wasn't how Evan spent his time.

The silence on the other end now spoke volumes. "My ex," Mike said finally. "The divorce was finalized today." Mike sounded rueful. And regretful? Evan was no psychologist, and he'd never done emotions. Whatever Mike felt or didn't feel was Mike's business. Not Evan's.

"I thought you were down L.A. way, fighting fires."

"I am. Doesn't mean I can't get married. I did, but . . ." Mike paused, clearly unsure how to condense months of backstory into a few sentences. "It didn't work out. I fucked up."

Hell. Putting words together to console a buddy wasn't Evan's thing.

"I'm real sorry," he said finally, because good manners demanded a reply.

"Yeah." The other man sighed. "So am I. So I need you to check up on her, okay? She was headed your way— that's what her sister said. She hit Strong this afternoon. All you have to do is look her up, make sure she's fine."

Evan didn't know why Mike's wife—*ex*-wife—was visiting Strong, but maybe it didn't matter much.

"You sure this can't wait?" he growled.

"Please," Mike said.

Evan cursed silently. That military unit had been family for Evan, so if Mike really wanted this, Evan would do it.

"Where d'you think she is?"

"Her sister mentioned a bar. Place called Ma's."

That worked for him. After Mike's little bombshell, Evan needed a beer.

★　★　★

There was a pixie sitting on top of Ma's jukebox. A sensual, goddamn, sexy pixie of a woman. Evan let the bar door slam shut behind him. The pixie was tone deaf, too, if the country tune she was belting out was any indication. Still, the woman perched on the jukebox was a wake-up call he didn't need or want. She was all legs. Long, long *bare* legs. One leg crossed on top of the other, she sat up there as if the jukebox were some kind of throne and tapped a foot to the beat of the song. The sun-kissed color of those legs made a man think about bikinis and beaches and warm, sleepy afternoons. "Legs" wasn't wearing a bikini, though. She had on some impossibly floaty skirt. The scalloped lace hem stopped at the top of her thighs, and a particularly vigorous beat in the song had the fragile fabric billowing around her.

Christ. This wasn't like him. He didn't stare at strange women—or, worse, *parts* of strange women—and imagine lustful possibilities.

What he did or didn't do didn't seem to matter to his unruly libido, however. He still wanted to smooth his hands up those bare thighs and beneath the gauzy fabric of her skirt. Backlit by the glowing neon bar signs, she looked like an angel. A naughty angel with honey-colored hair and sun-kissed, golden skin.

And she was more than a little the worse for wear.

He counted three empty glasses parked on the jukebox next to her, ice cubes melting into little puddles of wet. Someone or some ones had been buying this angel drinks. He hoped like hell that someone had warned her exactly how lethal Mimi's rum punches were. The bartender's concoctions could knock a grown man onto his ass, and his angel was a little bit of a thing.

Damn. He wanted a shower and his bed. If she was who he suspected—and since hers was the only unfamiliar face in the bar, odds were high that she was Mike Thomas's ex—she'd be emotional. She'd need the kind of rescuing he didn't do. He shoved aside his anger at Mike for getting him into this situation. He'd promised, so he'd do this, and he'd do it fast.

He laid in a course for her.

"Faye?" When he slapped a hand down on the jukebox next to her, her head followed the movement of his hand first, before snapping back to his face. Brown eyes stared up at him. She sure didn't look sad.

She looked pretty. That was his first thought. Real pretty. He could see the soft curve of her jaw and cheek. Not tall, not short, just somewhere comfortably in the middle, where her head would hit his shoulder when he tucked her up against him. Which he wasn't going to do. Honey-colored hair, thick and wavy and cut into layers, framed her face.

"Who wants to know?" The soft, liquid edge of her words was a definite tip-off. The woman holding court on the jukebox wasn't one hundred percent sober.

"Evan Donovan," he drawled. He leaned in closer, but she didn't move away. That could be a good sign, right there. Most people flinched when he got too close. Especially now, when he was jonesing for that shower and had more than his fair share of soot from the fire streaking his face and his clothes. No way she wanted to be close to him.

"I don't know you." Those brown eyes examined him.

"Does it matter?" He could take advantage of the whole halfway-to-drunk thing to get her safely out of there. If he was lucky, she wouldn't even ask too many questions.

She eyed him, clearly considering something. "No," she said finally. "I don't think it does matter. Not tonight. We're singing." She patted the jukebox. "You want to come sing with me, Evan Donovan?"

"No," he said bluntly, and she sucked in a breath. *Way to go, making her feel better.*

"You don't like to sing?" She asked her question as if he'd copped to pulling the wings off butterflies.

"Not really, darlin'," he drawled. He was tempted to tell her exactly what he was interested in—and where he wanted to put his hands—but he was supposed to be watching out for her, not putting the moves on her.

"Oh." She chewed her lower lip. "Can I buy you a drink?"

If she bought him a drink, he'd have to sit down and drink it. Getting in and out quickly was starting to look like pure fantasy on his part.

"Where are you staying?" he asked, ignoring her question. "I'll take you there. You shouldn't be driving."

The big, dark bear of a man had come through the bar's door like some kind of medieval knight. Or a Viking. Faye could definitely imagine Evan Donovan as a helmeted invader, bare-chested and draped in furs. The man was too big and too close, but some primitive, feminine side she didn't recognize had come *alive* when he burst through the door. Her ex hadn't been a small man, either, but this stranger was the largest man she'd ever seen. And Mike had been more pleasant, more charming. Evan Donovan was irritable as hell. He smelled strongly of smoke and the outdoors. Despite some recent attempt at a cleanup that had left his short hair slicked with dampness, he'd clearly scrubbed at his face with one big paw of a hand, because dark streaks of soot painted his jaw.

Definitely not her type, though that too-large build of his promised an adventurous ride a woman wouldn't quickly forget.

You wanted adventure, a familiar voice whispered.

"Come on," he said again.

"Where do you want to go?"

He leaned in closer, the heat of that large body surrounding her. "You can't stay here," he pointed out, annoyingly logical. The smile tugging at his lips did something less logical to her insides. "And it's going to be closing time real soon. You got a plan for tonight, Faye? You need to go home, darlin'."

She didn't have a home to go to and didn't know why he wanted her gone—but it was perfectly clear that he didn't want *her*. Any other man would have seen the opportunity for a pickup, so his lack of interest both hurt and pissed her off. Sure, she wasn't looking for a quick hookup in a no-name bar to break up her road trip. Not really. Not if she was being honest with herself. Which was, she admitted, much easier to do after too many rum punches. But she'd been enjoying the possibility, the fantasy of choosing someone and enjoying a no-holds-barred, no-strings-attached night of pleasure. He could have at least flirted with her.

Played the game a little, because she'd admit he was beautiful in a raw, male way that woke up some part of her she'd buried when her marriage headed south.

"Christ," he said. "Why does this have to be so difficult?"

She snagged her drink and raised the glass to her mouth, wrapping her fingers around the cool, damp sides. Most of the rum punch was gone, leaving just a handful of ice cubes slowly melting, watering down the leftover alcohol. Not bad, though.

His hand came up and carefully tugged the glass away from her. "You want to be careful with those." He shot a warning glare at the leggy blond bartender. "Mimi doesn't pull her punches when it comes to alcohol."

She let him take the glass. She was done with it, anyhow. His fingers were so warm, closed around hers. Did he know what he was doing to her? Should she care that such a simple little touch felt so very, very good?

"It's time for you to get out of here," he said, tugging gently on her hand.

He was right, of course, but she suspected he was used to being right, because he looked like the kind of man who wouldn't open his mouth, wouldn't speak, until he'd thought things through and come to a conclusion. She leaned toward him, staring up at that rugged face of his. Too bad he was in such a rush. "Do you have somewhere to go?"

"I was planning, darlin', on going home. To bed."

"Sounds good to me," she whispered.

Her head hit his chest before her brain could kick into gear. She was too tired, the events of the day—her "six plus one"—pulling her down. She had the sudden urge to let it all go, to fall asleep right where she was, as if she were a baby. Or drunk, she thought, wry humor spiking through her. Too many rum punches in an unfamiliar bar. Dimly, she heard Evan Donovan say something, but sleep was tugging at her eyelids. She'd figure it all out tomorrow. Right now, all that mattered was the solid-and-warm beneath her cheek and the reassuring beat of his heart.

There was a sigh from somewhere up above her, and strong arms closed around her, anchoring her. She let it all go and slipped into sleep.

Well, hell. Just hell.

Mike Thomas's wife—his *ex*-wife—had gone to sleep. On his chest. She slumped against him, all sweet and warm, as if they were spooned up in bed together. Evan carefully closed his arms around her and looked down. This wasn't good, wasn't part of the plan. There was an unwelcome feeling in the pit of his stomach, a sensation he hadn't felt since the last time his steel-toed boots had cleared the jump plane's bay and sent him hurtling out into empty sky, only to discover that the wind had shifted and the drift streamers he'd checked mere minutes before weren't pointing in the same direction anymore. He'd jumped off course that day and hung up in the mother of all ponderosas.

The woman in his arms was pure trouble. And if he hung on to her, he'd be off course *now,* so fast, his head would spin.

Mimi came around the end of the bar, sauntering up to him. All long, jean-covered legs, she looked a bit like an angel, too. One who'd fallen but didn't mind the change in her location one bit. Yeah, she was also trouble, but she wasn't his problem. He liked Mimi, always had, but last time he'd checked, she'd been busy running the bar she'd inherited and giving his younger brother hell. "You got this?" she asked, propping a hip against the bar.

He looked down again at the woman sleeping against him, but Faye clearly wasn't going to be any help. She let out a little mumble and snuggled in. Definitely not going anywhere on her own.

"You can put her on the couch in my office," Mimi offered.

He ignored her. "Hey," he whispered roughly. His mouth brushed Faye's ear, and his dick came alive. That was too close to a kiss, too close to touching her deliberately. And he wasn't. Wouldn't. He was enough of a gentleman to know there were lines a man didn't cross. "Wake up," he growled.

She didn't. She just turned her face farther into his chest with a long sigh.

Tightening his arms around her, he let himself savor the sweet, hot weight of her body against his for one moment. Maybe two. The filmy material of her skirt floated around his legs. She was impossibly feminine and delicate-looking, but he could feel for himself that she wasn't fragile. She was strong, despite the sweet, soft brush of her breasts against his arm that he was trying to ignore.

Sliding his elbow beneath her shoulder, he lifted her until her chest was pressed against his. Another thing that felt too damn good. This was professional, he reminded the unruly part of himself that had other ideas. A routine rescue and nothing to get excited about. Grabbing her right wrist with his left hand, he draped it over his right shoulder. Slipped his right hand between her thighs, on the back of her right leg. After that, it was easy money to lift her over his right shoulder in a fireman's carry and step away from the jukebox.

"She can't sleep here," he said to no one in particular.

Mimi looked at him, and there was no missing the humor in her eyes. "Yeah," she agreed. "This is *so* not a hotel. Although, again, I'm going to point out that I've got a couch in my office. You can put her there."

"And then what?"

Mimi gave him a strange look, almost as if she didn't recognize him, even though he'd been hanging at her bar for years. Not that he was all that much of a drinking man. Sure, he liked a cold one after a long day, but getting drunk off his ass had never appealed to him. Growing up rough the way he had, until Nonna had stepped in and adopted him, he'd known early on that he couldn't afford to lose himself like that. A beer or two at the end of the day, yeah, but never enough to forget who he was or what he was doing.

Mimi was still staring at him.

"When she wakes up"—alone and somewhere unfamiliar, because she wasn't from Strong—"then what?"

Mimi shrugged. "Whatever she wants, if she's okay to drive."

Cheerful shouts from the other end of the bar had her

turning back. "Put her in my office, okay, Evan? It's not like there's a Motel 6 in this town."

He strode down the hall, toward the office, and gave it a once-over. Mimi's couch wasn't going to cut it. No way that plaid monstrosity could be comfortable, even small as Faye was. The cushions looked hard. Plus, there wasn't a blanket.

Maybe, though, the woman in his arms had already solved this problem for herself. Maybe she'd had a plan for the night. Cradling her in one arm, he rummaged quickly through her handbag, looking for answers. Unfortunately, there wasn't much in there. The usual feminine bits and pieces. A package of tissues and a pretty little gold compact with a French name he couldn't pronounce. And a set of car keys. He'd seen her car on the way into Ma's. It was hard to miss a red Corvette, especially when it was parked on Strong's one and only Main Street.

No sign, however, of where she'd planned to lay her head for the night.

The way he saw it, that left him in charge.

He carried his load out Mimi's back door—he'd already hear about this rescue for the rest of the fire season, so there was no need to give anyone a closer look—and got the passenger-side door to his truck open. It was probably a good thing his unexpected passenger was out of it. He eyed the cherry-red Corvette parked haphazardly down the street. After driving a real pretty car like that, she might not like riding in the beast. His truck was a big, mud-splattered behemoth of a Ford that took him where he needed to go, and fire roads were no racetrack—that was damned certain. The beast could eat up asphalt if he needed the speed, but it was tough, too, if he ran out of road and needed to keep going.

Still, the Corvette would be plenty of fun to drive.

He slid her into the seat, dropping her bag at her feet.

Good enough. He buckled her in, careful to avoid the danger zone of her chest. There was no missing that soft rise and fall. She was out real good.

Fine. He'd take her to his place. Mike's request to watch out for her meant he couldn't leave her at Ma's, and, as Mimi had reminded him, Strong was singularly lacking in the rent-a-bed market. There was no motel he could cart her to closer than thirty miles away, which he was too damned tired to do. Plus, she'd want to collect that Corvette of hers in the morning. He damn sure wasn't letting her near any sports car right now. If he did, he'd be fishing her out of the nearest ditch before long. He palmed her keys from her bag and closed the passenger-side door.

Two minutes later, his tires spat gravel, and he tore out of the parking lot as if he was running from something. But he wasn't sure that *something* wasn't sitting right there, in the cab of his truck.

Chapter Two

The need for an Advil reached kill-for-it status, the dull throb behind Faye's eyes a warning last night's adventure had *not* gone as planned. Her headache threatened to spiral out of control.

God. What had she done?

Little flashes of memory teased her, unfortunate reminders she didn't really want. Ma's bar. The positively lethal rum punches the leggy blond bartender had poured. Someone popping a quarter into the jukebox, and who'd've thought this town would still have an old-fashioned jukebox? She'd wanted to dance and sing and laugh.

She'd done the dancing, met a few folks—and then what?

Because she clearly wasn't sleeping it off in the Corvette, as she'd intended. She dug her fingers into the lush softness beneath her. That was one hundred percent mattress. Instead of the Corvette's plush leather, she was lying on cotton sheets.

Hell. She was fairly certain that Strong didn't have a motel and that she couldn't spare the cash even if it did. Hence her whole sleep-in-the-Corvette plan.

The sound of steady breathing behind her had her opening her eyes wide despite another stab of protest from her head. It was still early, the room wrapped in that not-dark-not-quite-light shadow. She was in a cabin of some sort, the dim outline of a bathroom half-visible through a partly open door. From the middle of the enormous bed where she lay, she could also see a stone fireplace. Two easy chairs. The collection of clothes dropped haphazardly on the floor included jeans and a pair of work boots. A man's balled up T-shirt.

No, she definitely wasn't alone.

She looked down. A man's arm was a warm, heavy band around her waist. There was a military tattoo on his wrist, a dangerously sexy swirl of dark ink that branded that too-large, capable hand as the lethal weapon it probably was.

Great. She'd started off her grand adventure by hooking up in a bar. She wanted to think she'd been all bold and luscious, that she'd swept this man, whoever he was, right off his feet. Unfortunately, it was looking as if she'd been the drunk pickup instead, because here she was, parked in his bed, wearing only her panties and an unfamiliar, too-large T-shirt.

At least the panties were good ones—Betsey Johnson and all wicked black mesh with little pink bows. She'd picked them out for a weekend getaway with her husband—now ex—all part of a master plan to rekindle the romance that had somehow gone AWOL from their marriage. Instead, she'd come home that afternoon and found Mike in bed with another woman.

Now *she* was in bed with someone else herself. Rolling over carefully, she took stock. And what a man.

She remembered this version of big, dark, and sexy from the bar all too clearly.

Unfortunately, when his eyes snapped open, on full alert, Evan Donovan didn't look as if he was enjoying this morning-after any more than she was. He looked pissed.

"You're the firefighter from the bar." She couldn't keep the note of accusation out of her voice.

"That shouldn't come as a surprise to you," he grumbled. "The whole damn bar was full of firefighters, darlin'. I'm just the one you happened to fall asleep on."

"I fell asleep?" That didn't seem possible, but he kept right on glaring at her. Still, whatever had happened, he'd brought her here. He'd put her in this bed—she was suddenly damn sure of that—and then he'd put himself right there beside her. So he had no business acting so pissy.

"Yeah," he drawled. "One minute, there you were, perched on top of Mimi's jukebox. The next minute, you'd picked my chest out as your new pillow."

Pieces of memories, pieces of last night, assaulted her. Since the best defense was attack, she forced herself to lean toward him. Plus, that chest of his was something else, all hard muscles and summer-kissed skin. She wouldn't mind starting at the top and working her way down, kissing each tempting ridge.

"You're a big boy," she said coolly. "I don't think you did anything you didn't want to do."

Lying in this unfamiliar bed—in *his* bed—felt deliciously wicked. This high in the mountains, the day wasn't hot yet. Not like it would be later, when the sun climbed right on up the sky and got to work. The cotton sheet felt good. She stretched her legs, working out the aches.

He was so big, and she didn't know him, she reminded herself. God, this was beyond foolish. She should get out of his bed, find her clothes. Leave.

Only, she didn't know where she wanted to go.

And she'd wanted an adventure. Last night, when she'd first laid eyes on him—before he'd opened his mouth— she'd thought he was every big-brute fantasy she'd ever had come to life. If she'd been home, back in L.A., maybe she would have worried. Right now, though, in this sleepy little town, he represented possibility, and she could feel the anticipation building inside her. He didn't know it, but he was going to be hers. Only temporarily, of course, but she was so very tired of not living. Of coming home to an empty house. Of having empty arms.

"What," he growled, "do you think our next step should be?"

He clearly expected her to acknowledge her mistake and get the hell out of his bed. Where he'd put her for some inexplicable reason of his own, undoubtedly tied to those protective instincts so many men seemed to come with. He was a firefighter, and that meant he knew how to protect. To defend. To keep on fighting when all that stood between the flames and others was his body and his determination to defeat the fire.

She sensed he was the last person who would hurt her.

Why *not* ask for what she wanted, explore where this could go? He'd been standoffish last night, but then he'd brought her here. That had to mean something.

She put a hand on his arm, soaking in the warmth of his bare skin. God, he felt so good. *Live in the moment,* she reminded herself.

"You could kiss me," she said boldly.

Faye Duncan was killing him.

"You think this is about sex?" he growled. "Not yet, it isn't."

Evan didn't do relationships. Hell, he barely even had sex anymore. There was no room in a smoke jumper's life for that kind of complication. When a man jumped head over ass into the heart of a wildland fire at a moment's notice, that man wasn't "keeper" material. He never knew when he was coming home or even if he was. Call came in, and he headed out. It didn't matter what time of day, what day of the week, or if he'd had plans. Fire didn't wait.

Home was the hangar and the belly of the plane that spat him out over the day's hot spot, and that left no room for a lover. He certainly didn't want to make the space or the time, but giving this fire season his all wouldn't be possible if he kept staring at the woman in his bed the way he was. *Damn.*

He'd known Faye Duncan was trouble the moment he laid eyes on her.

"Well?" she demanded cheekily instead of answering his question. Her hand stroked his arm as if he was some animal she'd decided to tame.

She needed to learn that he didn't heel.

"You don't want me to kiss you."

There. She sucked a breath in, as if he'd hit her. Now she'd get up and go.

Instead, she simply slid closer. Another handful of inches and they'd be skin to skin, and then she'd know exactly how much she affected him. He'd brought her here because he'd been too damned tired to think straight. Leaving her, alone and vulnerable, in the bar, even on Mimi's couch, hadn't been acceptable. What he should have done, however, was cart her ass to Nonna's. Let his adoptive mother deal with her; Nonna was good at handling strays like Evan and his two brothers.

His erection told him all too clearly, however, why he hadn't taken that saner, wiser course of action. Part of him really, really wanted to get to know Faye Duncan better.

Much better.

"I think you do," she challenged.

Yeah, she was right about that.

Cupping the side of her face, he dragged a thumb along her jaw. She had the softest skin. He'd stripped off her clothes last night, telling himself she couldn't sleep in a skirt and itty-bitty tank top that smelled of smoke and rum punch. Truth was, even though he'd done it quickly in the near dark, he'd wanted to sneak a peek. Yeah. He was definitely a bastard.

He should have thought more about how those memories would stick with him. He'd seen all that pretty skin of hers. Bare. He hadn't touched, though, not more than was necessary. When she woke up, he'd thought, *then* he could touch a little more. Kiss that neck and those shoulders, kiss his way straight on down her body if she'd let him.

She was Mike's ex. She was a woman he'd rescued— *temporarily,* he reminded himself—from a night spent sleeping it off on Mimi's office couch. He needed to get up. He needed to go.

Ignoring the unmistakable dare in her brown eyes, he jackknifed off the bed. His pager picked that moment to go off, and fate handed him an ironclad exit plan. Spotter had seen a fire, and the plane was going up.

"I've got to go." He swiped his clothes from the floor and got ready to bail. Whatever it was she really wanted from him, he'd have to figure out later.

Leaving. Story of his life.

"Fire call?" She rolled over in the bed, taking his sheet with her. She didn't look surprised, but then, she'd been married to a firefighter, hadn't she? He'd bet Mike had left her on more than his fair share of late-night calls. "Or is this how you leave all your women?"

Wordlessly, he tossed her the pager. He wasn't going to argue with her, and he didn't have the time, anyhow. Time was a luxury none of the jump team had. Summer up here might be slow and hot, real quiet—until the fires started, and the plane went up. But once a fire hit its sweet spot, found the fuel and the air to burn like hell, there was nothing slow about it. The men who fought fires knew, when that happened, that they were pure out of time.

She tossed the pager back to him, but not before she eyeballed it. "I was teasing."

Grabbing his jeans, he stepped into them and pulled the

worn denim up his legs. So much for taking another shower this morning.

He could feel her gaze on him, and suddenly it was that much harder to get the denim past his erection. *Hell.*

"I know you all work hard." She sat up, and the sheet fell away. At some point during the night, his favorite T-shirt had tangled around her waist. From where he stood, he could spy a strip of bare, sun-kissed skin peeking out between the bottom of the shirt and her panties. With her hair tangled around her face, she looked like a woman who had been well-kissed. Last night she'd been a stranger. She'd been a name dropped in a phone conversation.

Now she was half-naked in his bed, and Evan knew that this image of her was one he wouldn't soon forget. She wasn't just Mike's anonymous ex anymore; now he had his own damned fantasies about her. He wanted to learn her. Wanted to thread his fingers through that silky hair, memorize the texture and the scent of her. Hold her real close.

Instead, he grabbed a T-shirt and yanked it on. Not too far from the cabin, the powerful throb of a plane's engine kicked to life. His boys were getting business done at the hangar across the runway, and he needed to be there.

"You're a firefighter," she said for the second time when he didn't break the silence but got on with dressing.

"Smoke jumper," he corrected, because as great as his admiration was for the boys who rode the trucks, that wasn't who he was. He jumped.

"I came to Strong to take some pics," she informed him. "Firefighters, smoke jumpers, and progress on the new firehouse here."

He opened his mouth to share Mike's request and closed it.

His brother Jack was revamping the mostly volunteer

fire department in Strong. Strong had been a one-truck town with a single paid fire chief, until Jack bought the old fire station earlier that summer, with visions of adding more trucks and more men. Too bad the place was a run-down piece of crap. Maybe it was an antique and on the historic register, but Evan figured that was shorthand for *fixer-upper* and *money pit*. Ben Cortez had held the place together all these years, whipping his volunteers into shape, but the older man had to be thinking retirement one of these days, and Jack had apparently picked up a vision of something a little bigger and better, along with a fiancée, in Strong.

If Faye Duncan was supposed to be documenting Jack's progress, Jack would be plenty pissed about her current location in Evan's bed. He'd tainted the witness, all right.

It didn't matter that nothing—much—had happened. Jack had drummed into his brothers' heads that sometimes appearances mattered almost as much as facts. And this was clearly one of those times. Jack had been hunting down outside funding sources for Strong's new fire department, and Evan could easily imagine this magazine piece starring front and center in Jack's efforts.

"I'm already impressed by what you and your guys are doing."

"Thanks for the vote of confidence." He sank onto the bed's edge to pull on his socks and steel-toes, because it was the bed or the floor, and his dignity had taken enough of a blow.

"No, I mean it," she said, and maybe she did. Her voice rang with sincerity, and she shifted closer, the mattress dipping beneath their combined weight. "The firefighter at that mountain brush fire yesterday was really spectacular. He was right there, pronto, before I could even phone it in. It's like you guys pop out of the woodwork or something when there's a fire."

Christ. According to the official reports, Evan had been first on the scene of yesterday's only brush fire, pinch-hitting for one of Ben's guys. He hadn't seen any sign of another firefighter—or of Faye or her fancy car. "You saw a brush fire yesterday?"

"Yeah." She tucked the sheet beneath her arms and eyed him. "On my way into Strong. I came around a bend, and there it was. I drove right through it."

"You remember what time that was?" Had there been another fire he hadn't known about?

She shrugged. "Three or four o'clock. Exact time-stamp will be on the pictures." She grinned at him. "Happy hour had already started at Ma's when I got there about twenty minutes later."

Christ. Of course she'd taken pictures.

Her next words were the final nail in the coffin. "I'm sure I can use some of them in the photo spread."

"You work for a magazine." Shit just kept on coming, didn't it? He needed to go, but he also needed to hear what she had to say. His fingers flew up the laces of his steel-toes, but no plan popped ready-made into his head.

"Catalogs mostly, but I'm freelance now. This piece on Strong's volunteer fire department is for a magazine. Show the firefighters doing their thing in a historic firehouse that's being restored."

Jack was definitely going to kill him for getting involved with her.

"We need to talk about that brush fire." He stood up, considering his options. He'd ask Ben to double-check with his team and verify that Evan really had been the first responder. Maybe someone else had put in an unofficial appearance, but something was off here and, until he figured out what, he needed her to stay put, so they could have that conversation. "When I get back."

"Really." Her eyes narrowed.

He'd seen that look of feminine outrage on Lily Cortez's face. His brother's fiancée didn't take orders well, either. He knew he'd stepped in it. Again.

"Look, I appreciate the bed for a night, but now I'm out of here. I need to do my thing. I got some good quotes last night. I'll talk to one or two of the firefighters down at your firehouse. Take a few more pictures. Then I'm hitting the road. All I need is the name of a good mechanic. My car was acting up on the way into town."

"Wait for me," he repeated. "I'll hook you up with a mechanic, if that's what you need, but first you have to talk to Ben Cortez, the local fire chief, and my brothers. Tell them about this brush fire you saw."

"I can't afford a motel," she admitted.

He wanted to pull her toward him, stroke away the pink flush on her cheeks. He'd done things to be ashamed of. He doubted that this woman had.

"You saw my car?" she continued.

"I saw it." It would have been damned hard to miss the cherry-red Corvette, and they both knew it. "It's a real nice car. Fast, too, I'll bet."

"That car," she said simply, "represents the sum total of my life savings. Beyond the change rolling around in the bottom of my purse, that car is all I've got. Whatever your fire chief needs to discuss, I need it to be quick."

This he could fix. "So you need a place to stay."

"Other than in my car? No. I need to take my pics and leave. It's almost too bad," she said, and she smiled her Mona Lisa smile. "There could be a whole lot to like about this Strong of yours." That trick she had of looking up at him from the corners of her eyes was pure sex kitten. But there was something else—someone else—hiding behind those eyes.

He was suddenly sure of that much.

Playbook said kissing her would be a mistake. She'd be

entitled to call a penalty, but he couldn't bring himself to care. He had to taste her, had to find out if she lived up to the promise of those mischievous eyes.

"I'm going to kiss you now," he warned, because giving her fair warning he was taking her up on her earlier offer was the right thing to do.

"That right?" she asked. The words were pure challenge, but she glanced over his shoulder, toward the door and the buzz of noise outside warning him he didn't have much time left. He needed to go.

Still, he'd make this kiss his opening salvo in the battle they were apparently waging.

She didn't say no. He gave her the time, and she stared up at him, impish challenge painted all over her lovely face. "Well," she said, "I guess a guy's got to do what a guy's got to do. So you go off now and save us all from the fires. The incoming. Whatever." She shrugged, and his T-shirt slid down her shoulder in a little tease that had his blood heating right up. That shirt always had been a favorite of his.

"I do need to go. But that's not all I need." The words coming out of his mouth didn't belong to him. The words were smooth, the practiced lines of a player. He'd never been a player. Funny thing was, he meant them. And that was almost enough to send him running for the door.

She hummed, a small sound of doubt and feminine pleasure, and nodded. "Guess that makes two of us then, smoke jumper."

So he wrapped an arm around her waist and swung her beneath him. Got her pressed right back against his mattress.

This time, it was arousal that pinkened her cheekbones, and when she turned her head, last night's earrings kissed the line of her jaw the way he wanted to do. The silver sparkled and moved along her skin in short, teasing strokes.

"I'm going to touch you now," he warned.

"Are you?" She tried to shift backward, the mattress halting her little retreat.

The soft cotton of his T-shirt slid farther down her shoulder when he hooked a thumb in the stretchy fabric and tugged. That white cotton coming down her tan shoulder undid him. He wanted to see the rest of her, but that would be too much, too soon. He didn't want to scare her.

He wanted to taste her.

All of her.

Wanted to lay her down here on his bed and taste every secret she was hiding beneath his T-shirt. "You're not going anywhere," he said, and it was more delighted observation than statement. "Not now."

She leaned her head back against his sheets, all tousled hair and sexpot smile, watching him with those curious eyes of hers. He wasn't stopping her from escaping. Not really. If she wanted to get out from under him, she could take one little wiggle to her left, and she'd be free and clear.

"Not yet, but I will," she disagreed, putting a hand on his arm. Her face said she wanted to ask him something, but he didn't want to talk anymore. All he wanted was to taste.

Bracing a hand by the side of her face, he threaded his fingers through the teasing mass of hair and lowered his head, wrapping an arm beneath her to gather her gently up toward his body. Strong and firm, she felt even better than she looked. Stroking a thumb over the small of her back, he stole a moment to savor the heat and the softness of her through the fabric.

His lips against hers were a simple little tease, a gentle brush of his skin on hers. He'd meant to fire the opening salvo in this sweet game they were playing, but sensation rocketed through him with that first touch of his mouth to hers. Liquid pleasure burned through him, reducing him to a single, primal urge.

The taste of her was all sweet, hot summertime. No fleeting sensation, though, because, Christ, she packed a punch, the heat and taste of her nearly knocking him out.

Mine.

He tore his mouth away from hers, rolled off the bed, and made for the door. Faye Duncan was even more trouble than he'd imagined—and that was saying something.

She made a sound behind him—outrage or protest, he couldn't tell—but he was beyond caring. He opened the door.

Sure enough, when he looked back, she was scrambling off the bed. "Stay put," he growled. "I'm jumping, and then I'll be back to finish what we started."

In case he was misreading the anticipatory look on her face, he made sure he still had her car keys tucked safely in his pocket. Then he let the door slam shut behind him and got the hell out of there.

Chapter Three

The DC-3 waited out on the runway. Their pilot, Spotted Dick, had her gassed and ready to go, the bone-jarring rumble of the engines thundering through Evan in a familiar, exciting rhythm. *Time to go. Time to jump.* The hand crew had already loaded up the plane, moving the jump gear and equipment on board with ruthless efficiency. Men's voices barked final orders and curses, and the spotter hauled himself in, ready to go.

The team would be airborne in ten.

The DC-3 could hold eighteen jumpers. Today, Donovan Brothers was fielding a team of eight. Spotted Dick, his ass parked in the pilot's seat, was running through the start-up checks. That plane was Jack's baby; he had rebuilt her, piece by piece. Evan's brother cared for that ninety-five-foot wingspan like a lover, although that might be changing now that Jack had Lily Cortez heating up his life. The betting pool the boys had going was leaning toward a September wedding and a whole string of little Jacks and Lilys following shortly thereafter.

It was still hard to reconcile that image of domesticity with Jack, the bad boy who'd caroused with the best of them.

Ten jumps already this summer and hundreds during the years he'd spent working side by side with his brothers and the jump team, but the pure adrenaline rush of facing the plane on the tarmac, of knowing he was headed up and out—that never faded, never got old. He'd do this as long as he could, until his body gave out. Domestic bliss wasn't in the cards for him.

He took the hangar at a dead run and reached for his gear, banging open the locker door. The place was already a beehive of mad activity. He was late to the party.

"Thought we were leaving your ass on the ground, soldier!" Zay hollered in greeting, and Evan flipped him the bird. Zay had fought his way across half of Asia and the Middle East, and there was no better man to jump with.

"Last one in buys the beer." Mack, another former platoon mate, winked and then charged for the plane. Bastard redefined *early bird* and was all over that worm.

"I had shit to wrap up." Which was true. "I can't always drop and run."

Beside him, Jack zipped his Nomex jacket closed, grabbed his chute, and strapped it on. "What the hell did you have to do?"

Evan ignored the jibe, concentrating for a long moment on yanking on his own Nomex and gearing up.

"That's our boy." Evan's younger brother, Rio, chortled and finished his suit-up, turning to check Jack's gear. "Silent as the grave. He gives us a heart attack because his ass isn't the first one in the hangar, and now he's holding out on the details. Was she that good, Evan?"

Shit. All of Strong probably knew he'd brought a woman home with him last night. He loved his town, but sometimes he wished like hell folks knew when to keep their mouths shut. "She needed a place to sleep." Yanking the zipper closed, he reached for his pack, fingers flying on the buckles. Outside, Mack climbed on board, high-fiving the spotter.

Jack whistled. "Chivalrous. He rescued a damsel in distress. There's a lesson in that for us, Rio."

Rio stepped away from Jack, turning so his brother could check his gear. "Lily would kick your ass," he said cheerfully. "Then she'd come after us for letting you *get* so ass-deep in trouble rescuing other women."

Jack laughed. "True enough."

"Nothing happened," Evan gritted out. "Swear to God, that's all it was. A bed for the night."

Jack nodded knowingly. "You slept on your side of the bed with this mystery woman, and she was all hands-off on her side. Right. Maybe you should think about investing in a sofa, because when Nonna hears about this, you're going to have a whole lot of explaining to do."

"Next time," Rio added mock helpfully, "take sleeping beauty over to Nonna's. Hell, bring her out to Lily and Jack's, and dump her on their couch."

"Fuck you." Evan should have done one of those things, but Faye Duncan's head had hit his chest, and his brain had turned right off. "You want to hear the interesting part?" Two more jumpers were already sprinting across the tarmac, Mack and the spotter reaching down to haul them up into the DC-3.

"He's sharing details, Jack." Rio raised an eyebrow. "He must have mistaken us for a bunch of girls."

"Don't tell me about your sex life," Jack ordered. "Or lack thereof. Leave me out of it."

"Spill," Rio ordered. "Now, Evan."

"You remember Mike Thomas, from our CFR team?" No way Jack had forgotten a fellow Marine. Mike had been right there whenever things had heated up for Crash, Fire, and Rescue. When his brother grunted an acknowledgment, Evan continued. "He up and got married when he went back to L.A."

"Wouldn't have thought he was the marrying kind." Jack sounded thoughtful.

"It didn't last. He got a divorce. Apparently . . ." Evan hesitated, because he still couldn't believe the next part. ". . . his ex-wife was headed up here, to Strong. He was worried about her, so he called yesterday. Asked me to look her up and make sure things were okay."

Rio whistled. "They get a divorce, and he wants to check up on her? Maybe the divorce was a bit premature."

Rio hadn't heard the regret in the other man's voice. "Mike said the whole thing was his fault."

"This doesn't explain why the woman is in your cabin."

No. It didn't. Hell, there was no explaining his behavior, was there? "I went to Ma's, and, sure enough, Faye was there."

"Faye being Mike's ex," Rio observed cheerfully.

"Yeah." Faye had looked up at him and fallen asleep against him. As if he was a nice guy. Safe. Someone she could count on. "She needed a place to stay, so I took her home with me."

"She pretty?"

"She's Mike's ex." She was more than pretty. She glowed with an excitement for living.

"She's Mike's *ex*," Rio emphasized. "That means she's not off-limits. Spill, Evan. If she was in Ma's, you know I'll go ask Mimi, because she knows everything that goes on in that bar of hers. If I were you, I'd be wanting to get my own version out there first." He smiled evilly.

Yeah. He was royally fucked here. There was no explaining behavior so out of character. "So she's pretty. And she was more than a little drunk. Hell, Rio. There's no motel here in Strong. You know that as well as I do. What was I supposed to do? Stick her on Mimi's office couch and walk away? Mike wanted to know she was doing

okay, and waking up on a couch in a strange bar isn't *okay*."
He knew that much about women.

"Let's revisit, because I'm missing key details here. You
put her in your bed," Jack said wryly. "And then you left
her there, and you slept on the floor? Or did you crawl
right into bed beside her?"

His brothers looked back in the direction of the cabins
tucked away on the far side of the airstrip, as if they expected to see an irate woman come flying right on out the
door.

"I'm not sleeping on my own floor, especially not after
yesterday's fire." That wasn't right either. He ran a hand
over his hair defensively. "I didn't touch her." *Except to put
her in my T-shirt.* No way he could shake his memories of
those sexy little panties. That black lace had been almost as
pretty as the gentle curve of her stomach. God, he was a
bastard, because now he wanted more memories, wanted
to see more of Faye Duncan.

"And?" Rio stared at him expectantly. Yeah, he knew
there was more to this story.

"And she's still there right now, okay?"

"You told her about Mike's call, right?" Jack had gotten
himself engaged last month, and his Lily had taught him a
few things about women, all right. No way would that
man have asked that question six months ago. He'd have
laughed, nudged Evan in the ribs, and gotten on with the
day. "You want me to send Lily over there?"

"I didn't tell Faye about Mike's call." He cleared his
throat. "The opportunity didn't come up."

"You'd better." Laughter filled Jack's voice. "Woman
might not like hearing that her ex hired her a babysitter."

Rio whistled. "She'll probably kick your ass."

"Or cry." Jack looked as if he'd take the ass-kicking any
day.

Evan should have told Faye about Mike's call. He knew

that. He also knew he didn't like the mental picture he had of Faye driving through a brush fire in that too-expensive car of hers.

He snapped the final buckle closed. Jack nodded, fingers flying as he checked out Evan's work. He had Evan's back. No one jumped with bad gear, not on this team. Not ever.

"I told you, she's a favor. Mike Thomas asked me to look her up, make sure she was doing fine."

"And is she, Evan?" Rio tossed him a gear bag. A quick check said all was in order there. Water and gloves. Fire shelter. All the necessities. "Is she fine?"

He'd stick with the facts. Like how she could have gotten hurt, badly, or even died. "She drove into Strong yesterday afternoon, right through that brush fire we got called out on. She said something that got me thinking, though. I didn't see her—and she didn't see me, but she claims she saw a first responder."

When the call had come in, he'd thrown his truck into gear and raced down the road. Ground crew had spotted the first smoke, just a lick of a fire eating up the side of the highway right outside Strong. Not too big. Not yet. There was always the possibility of the wind shifting, though, of the fire finding itself a good supply of fuel and eating its way into something much bigger. While he loved to jump, he wasn't an idiot. If he could put a fire out while it was still small, that's what he'd do.

He didn't have to put a plane up and parachute out into the middle of hell simply because that was when he really felt alive. As if he was doing something important. Sometimes the small stuff was important, too.

Jack's hands tugged on the straps and buckles. "I'll confirm with Ben that you were the first on the scene. Make sure someone else didn't jump in and not say anything. We've had a lot of those little fires lately."

"Yeah. Not like earlier this summer"—when a crazy stalker had done his best to burn up half the mountain to get at Jack's woman—"but too many fires all the same."

Rio looked over at him. "You want me to do a little investigating? Analyze the patterns?" Rio was their computer expert. There wasn't too much he couldn't make their software do.

Evan didn't need software, however, to tell him what his gut was shrieking. Even if another firefighter had been first on the scene, the man should have stuck around—not hightailed it out of there.

Jack cursed. "We don't need another arsonist out here."

"What if our burn boy is internal?" Evan didn't want to say the words out loud, but the pattern fit. Hell, the pattern was staring him in the face, giving him the fucking bird. "Lots of little fires, all called in. Plenty of action for every man based in Strong, plus enough overtime to put some cash in a man's pocket."

"Who would do that?" Rio asked. "If the arsonist is one of ours, who is he?"

Jack scrubbed a hand over his face. "Someone who doesn't give a damn that I've only got half a fire department here. Word gets out that we can't shut down an arsonist, finding funding isn't going to get any easier. I've got a photographer coming on board." Jack swore. "She's taking pictures for a magazine piece about the firehouse and my plans for it. That article is supposed to be our calling card—a little hey-look-at-me when I go out and hit up potential donors."

Sure wasn't going to look good if the article mentioned unsolved arson. Plus, the truth was, none of them wanted Strong burning up. Slow, hot anger blew through Evan, mean and strong. He had Jack's back on this. That went without saying. This fire department was Jack's baby, his dream. He'd hunt down the son of a bitch setting fires. That also went without saying.

Rio looked over at Jack. "When's that photographer due?"

Jack tossed him his gear bag. "Yesterday. Today. Whenever she gets around to coming. She's freelance, so she's not punching a clock." He looked up at Evan. "Even you can't shanghai her, Evan. She comes when she comes, and she does her thing. That's non-negotiable."

"Yeah. About that photographer . . ."

His brothers must have seen something on his face, because they stopped talking.

"Hell." Rio whistled. "He's already done something, Jack."

Jack raised an eyebrow, and Evan could feel a dull flush heating up his face. "Yeah. I'd say he has. You lock the photographer up in your cabin with Mike's ex?"

"Mike's ex *is* the photographer."

"Fuck." Jack's palm hit the closest locker. "We'd better have been joking about locking her in, Evan."

"She can leave anytime she wants." She simply wasn't getting far on foot.

Rio pointed toward the door. "Our ride is about to leave, ladies. Argue later, and get your asses out there."

"I took her car keys," Evan admitted right before they cleared the door and their boots hit the tarmac.

Jack and Rio looked at each other, and then Jack groaned. "She's going to kill you, Evan. You know that, right? You'd better hope you're not coming back from this jump, because she'll be waiting for you."

Tucking his helmet under his arm, Evan ran flat-out for the plane, his brothers whooping and hollering beside him. Last man in bought the night's beer, and it sure looked as if it was going to be Evan's night to pony up. That was fine, too, because as soon as he was on board, the plane would hit the runway and then the air. The ground and his problems would all fall away.

If only it was that simple to leave Faye Duncan behind.

Jesus. This fire business was better than porn. Yesterday, Hollis had waited until the flames really got going, eating up the side of the hill where he'd set his latest fire. He'd wanted to get a little excitement going on a slow Friday night, and the brush fire had been good stuff, although the lady in the red Corvette had given him a scare when she popped up out of nowhere. She'd forced him to put a temporary restraining order on his fire until she'd pulled out and he could fan the flames some more before he left and called it in.

Today's fire call, however, was the real deal. He had to set *his* fires in accessible spots, so he could get in and out quickly, but this new blaze was way out in the wildlands. Probably a summer lightning hit that had started a sleeper fire in some deadwood. Left alone long enough, that little spark had eventually lit up the side of the mountain. Now the jump team was headed up to check it out.

The DC-3 rumbled, making its taxi down the runway. There was a cheer from the men on the ground when she cleared the tarmac and got air beneath her. Jump team was en route, off to save the day. God, he wanted to be up there, one of the team headed out to the jump site.

Instead, he was here, parked on the fifty-five-gallon drums of fuel lined up beside the hangar. Nothing fancy here, no underground tanks or bulk fuel storage. When Spotted Dick bellowed orders, everyone lent a hand to roll those heavy motherfuckers out to the plane. Being hand crew and therefore a temporary firefighter meant he had a ringside seat for the start of the party—but no invite to what came next.

"You think we'll get called out?" The firefighter next to Hollis didn't even bother looking over when he shoved off the drum he'd perched on. Small and wiry, the guy couldn't have been a day over twenty. He was too wet behind the ears to recognize that Hollis, already on his third fire season, had the edge on him.

Dumb-ass.

Hollis kicked his way back over to the camp kitchen, trying to figure out how come he was always on the ground when what he wanted was to fly. Twenty-three, and he'd put in his time, right? He deserved a chance. He was always first on the truck, too. He pulled his weight.

It wasn't the money he was after, either, although the money was good. Real good. He liked knowing he had cash in the bank, waiting for him when the season let up some. More fires meant more hours worked. Still, he'd started out pretty small on the other crews he'd worked, careful not to set too many fires. He'd let himself have one, maybe two, each season.

Now, after three seasons fighting fire, he had himself a break. The fire camp in Strong was his ticket to the big leagues. If he worked hard enough, the Donovan brothers would have to notice him. He'd finally get his chance to join the jump crew.

Fighting fire was the first job he'd had where the work *mattered.* He got to be a goddamn hero. Not often enough, but sometimes. Even his father had had to admit that, maybe, Hollis was on to something important. Thirty years selling a laundry list of cheap-ass products no one really wanted or needed, and his dad still hit the road every week. He had quotas to make, he'd say, and that meant there wasn't time to sit home and chat it up with family. Out there, on the road, he had business to take care of, and take care of it he would.

His dad understood quotas and checks from the companies who hired him to shill and then paid out a miserly commission for each sale his dad had wrung from the folks he met and solicited on the road. His father hadn't been able to sell the program to his mother for long, because Mommy Dearest had up and left when Hollis was a baby. After that, he had been raised by an uncle. Uncle Roy had done his best, but kids weren't his strong point.

None of them ever figured Hollis would amount to much of anything.

He'd learned what a high firefighting was when he was still a kid. The old lady down the street had been inside her trailer when the place went up. Hollis had kicked in her door, thrown her over his shoulder, and gotten her out of there, exactly like it was a movie or something. The people watching him had shouted and cheered. For the first time, he'd *been* someone, someone good, someone who mattered. He wasn't Roy's screw-up nephew or the son his father couldn't be bothered to call.

You're nothing, boy. Never have been, never will be.

No. He didn't need his father's voice trumpeting in his head and he damned sure didn't want those memories. Fighting fires mattered. He had made something of himself, so the old bastard could take his dire predictions and shove them right where the sun didn't shine. Maybe Hollis hadn't finished college, and maybe he didn't sit a desk job, but he got out there every fire season with the best of them, and he made a difference. The rest of the year, after the crews shut down, he got by with part-time gigs or unemployment.

He was smart, or so the test-your-brain exams the teachers had passed out claimed, but he still couldn't seem to get the hang of bookwork. Taking tests, turning in papers—those things didn't go so well for him. But that was okay. He was out here now, where the only grade that mattered was how fast and far you dug your line.

Spotted Dick's plane was only a silhouette now, disappearing over the horizon as it winged its way toward the dark plume of smoke punching up into the sky. God, he wanted to be on that plane. One of the team.

He'd get there, too. Whatever it took, he'd make them see he was good enough. He might be a loaner from a volunteer fire department two towns over, but he could *belong* here in Strong. He knew it.

All he needed was the chance.

He hit the kitchen, and the camp cook looked up. It was so damned quiet up here that Hollis figured his stopping by had to be a highlight of the guy's day. "You don't get bored?" He lit the tip of his new cigarette from the smoldering end of his last one. "It's real quiet here."

The camp cook eyed Hollis's Marlboros, but Hollis wasn't wasting a perfectly good cigarette by stubbing that bad boy out before it was done. Fifteen bucks an hour didn't go *that* far. No way the Marlboro Man would have backed down on the issue, either. He liked the image of the Marlboro Man riding all over the range. That man was one tough son of a bitch. He'd probably have made a good smoke jumper if he'd been given the chance.

"Give me a hand here." The other man was stacking up used plastic plates as if he was running a five-star restaurant.

Hollis finished up the cigarette and stubbed it out. He wasn't shoveling plates for the remainder of the summer. No way. Sure, fifteen bucks an hour wasn't bad money for a guy like him, and the overtime helped some, but what he was jonesing for was a place on the jump team. He could pull his weight there. He knew it.

He grabbed the stack of plates. All he needed was one chance.

He'd show them how helpful he could be.

Out there. On the fire line.

Hollis's hoarse bark of laughter had the camp cook looking around, but fuck him. He gave the matchbox in his pocket a quick rub. Plenty of opportunities waited for him here in Strong.

Chapter Four

It took twenty minutes of bouncing around in the back of the plane, a clear shot down, and then four hours on the ground before the jump team had packed out. Thank God for quick jumps. The way Evan saw it, the day had been just a little same-old, same-old. Which was good. He didn't need different right now. Didn't need a shake-up. A summer lightning strike that smoldered for weeks until the dry log housing it finally gave in and combusted? That made sense.

Fires, he could do.

The woman undoubtedly steaming in his cabin back at the jump camp? Yeah. She wasn't making anywhere near as much sense. Or maybe what didn't make sense was his half-assed plan of parking her there to wait for him. He'd bet that plan hadn't gone down well.

Whatever. Just thinking about Faye Duncan made him antsy. The need to be doing something was an itch he had to scratch.

So he really didn't need Rio's 411 when the jump plane touched down to know that palming Faye Duncan's keys hadn't been his best move. He'd had a come-to-Jesus call waiting for him on his cell from Nonna, too, which meant word had definitely gotten around about his pickup at the bar last night. Christ, no matter how he looked at it now, it had been a fairly dumb move on his part.

So he'd screwed up.

Again. He'd made more than his share of mistakes in his younger days, so he recognized regret when it bit him on the ass. He left the hangar as quickly as he could, tossing his gear into the back of his Ford. Swinging himself into the cab, he hit the road.

He did *not* look left when he took the fork back to Strong. If Faye Duncan was sitting on his porch gunning for him, she'd have plenty of time to bend his ear later. Somehow, though, he didn't take her for a stay-at-home kind of woman. Not a woman who drove a red Corvette and who had gotten an entire barful of tired firefighters onto its feet with a song.

Not a woman who kissed like that.

Christ. He hated to admit that he hadn't been able to shake that kiss all day. Faye Duncan knew how to kiss a man as if he was the center of her universe. If that call hadn't come in, he'd have done something even more regrettable.

He'd have stayed in that bed.

Stayed in Faye's arms and sunk himself deep inside her. The attraction had hit him hard and fast, but he wasn't a fool. Rushing straight into sex wasn't the right thing to do. She wasn't a one-night stand, wasn't the kind of woman a man brought home from the bar—even though that was exactly what he'd done, with the best of intentions. And he sure as hell wasn't going to think about why she'd left Mike. Whatever the reasons had been, they were hers. Still, he'd put coming clean about Mike's request at the top of his to-do list.

He might not be any kind of expert on women, but even he knew that much. Secrets sank you faster than bailing without a parachute.

His phone buzzed when he pulled into Strong, and he guided the truck into an empty spot next to the Corvette. A quick glance at the screen warned him that Mike was calling again. Yeah, he probably owed the man a check-in.

"You find Faye?" the other man asked as soon as Evan barked out a hello.

"Sure did." Drunk and in a bar, but those weren't details the other man needed.

He got out of the truck and gave the Corvette a once-over while Mike clearly searched for some way to break the awkward pause. Probably Evan should have volunteered a few sentences, but the way he saw it, it wasn't his job to do the talking here. That was all on Mike.

"She seem okay to you?" Mike asked finally.

Fair enough. "Fine." He paused, the memories of her cheerful singing coming back to him. Maybe he could coax her into singing without the cocktail warm-up. "She seemed fine, like she was having a good time."

"Doing what?" There was some throat clearing on the other end of the line.

He wasn't a private eye. If Faye Duncan wanted to have a few drinks and do a little sing-along, that was her call. "She came up here to do that magazine piece, right? On firefighting." He outlined the situation for the other man. "So she was meeting some of the boys, getting to know them."

And then, of course, he'd taken her home with him. He figured he'd leave that part out, too.

"Yeah."

More silence on the other end, and then, right when Evan was ready to hang up, Mike started talking again. "Yeah. That's good. You totally positive she doesn't need anything?"

"Her car overheated, but I'm taking care of it."

"Piece-of-shit Honda she drives isn't made for mountain roads," the other man agreed. "Getting that car out of L.A. was a miracle."

"No problem there," Evan volunteered. "She traded up. Corvette."

"She doesn't have a Corvette. Hell, *I* don't have a Corvette. Is it a rental?"

"She said it wasn't. Real nice car," Evan added helpfully. "Vintage with a Rally Red paint job. Can't possibly miss it."

Mike cursed. "She doesn't have the money for that kind of car."

"Guess she did."

"This isn't like her. She doesn't up and buy Corvettes."

But she had. Maybe Mike hadn't known his wife as well as he'd thought he did. Or maybe Faye had decided to turn over a new leaf. In a sixty-thousand-dollar car. That was one more thought he'd be keeping to himself.

"Okay," Mike continued. "Well. Fuck. Keep me posted, and tell me if she needs something, okay?"

What did he say to that? He wasn't some kind of babysitter or social worker. "She'll be fine," he said finally, because he needed to end this call. Last time he'd checked, divorce meant things were over. Wherever Mike's head was at, he apparently hadn't gotten that memo. That, or he was packing a whole lot of guilt.

Either way, Evan was done playing therapist.

A handful of good-byes later, he was a free man. Tossing the cell onto the front seat, he slammed the door shut and grabbed his toolbox from the back.

Strong's main street was as sleepy and unchanged as ever. Ma's hadn't opened yet, and there was a singular lack of cars. Town looked like it had every other midafternoon this week and the week before that. He liked that predictability. Sometimes it was good when things didn't change.

Going over to Faye's red Corvette, he unlocked the driver-side door and popped the hood. The car was as sleek and pretty as its owner. Corvettes didn't care much for heat, however, and Faye had taken the car through a brush fire. He might as well take a look, see what he could do.

A car was infinitely fixable.

An hour later, he had the Corvette jacked up and the antifreeze swapped out for new. A quick check of the hoses, and Faye would be back in business. The growl of a motorcycle approaching warned him he'd finished up just in time. Sure enough, the driver killed the engine and coasted to a stop beside the Corvette.

Even underneath the car, he had a clear shot of the two women riding the bike. Faye Duncan had dug up some spare clothes somewhere, because she'd changed out of his T-shirt. The new tank top and shorts didn't cover much more, although he appreciated the view. She sat there on the back of the cycle, hugging Mimi's waist, her legs pressed against Mimi's. Yeah. He shouldn't go there, but damned if those two women paired up like that wasn't the sexiest thing he'd seen in a long time. Although waking up next to Faye was pretty damned memorable, too.

He'd wait, he decided, for Faye to say something first. There was no point in jumping headfirst into trouble here. Instead, he slid out from underneath the Corvette and got busy beneath the hood again, since the undercarriage had checked out fine. She didn't make him wait long.

She swung one leg over the side of the cycle and kept on coming, her flip-flops biting her bare heels in a sharp snap of sound. "I should kick your ass," she said.

That was perfectly clear. Still, because needling her was fun, he asked, "You should—or you're going to?" While he tested the hoses, he shot her a sidelong look. Only her

legs were visible beneath the Corvette's hood. The motorcycle helmet she clutched in her left hand tapped against
her thigh as she considered his question.

"You took my keys. That wasn't cool."

"You want help with that ass-kicking, holler." Mimi's
voice carried over the sound of the motorcycle tires
crunching gravel as she rolled the bike closer. Evan didn't
need to look to know that Mimi was watching him, a
playful smirk on her face, while she waited for him to dig
himself a hole he couldn't crawl out of. Mimi liked to look
tough. From the cowboy boots to the leather pants she
sported despite the bone-soaking heat, she screamed don't-
mess-with-me. He'd seen that look on more than one face
growing up, and he wouldn't call her on it. He liked
Mimi.

"You overheated."

"Excuse me?" She fidgeted, and the flip-flops started
their irritated back-and-forth snap against her soles again.
He grinned, knowing she couldn't see his face.

"That's a common problem with these vintage Corvettes. Come on over here and take a look." He waited
patiently for her to make up her mind and lean under the
hood with him.

Having her this close was a sweet reward for his patience. Being tucked under the hood with her was pure
heaven, the air all grease and rubber and Faye in the cozy
space.

"You're a mechanic, too?"

"When I need to be, sure."

On the other side of the hood, Mimi called a cheerful
warning and farewell. The bang of the bar door opening
and closing told him there was now one less woman he
had to worry about. Faye, though, was nervous and trying to hide it. Not sure where to set her hands, she finally

leaned over the engine, giving him a clear view down the tank top she was wearing.

"Right here." He pointed with the screwdriver at an older hose. "You run the air on your way up the mountain?"

"Yeah." She braced her hands on the edge of the engine compartment, leaning in for a closer look. Not touching him. No problem. He shifted, brushing her bare thigh with his jean-clad one. "Yeah, I did. It's summer. No one drives up from L.A. with only the windows rolled down. You trying to tell me a sixty-thousand-dollar car can't handle running the AC?"

He shrugged. "Facts are facts. Feel that hose—it's all soft, and that's no good."

She huffed disbelievingly, her hair dancing around her jaw. If he moved, he could smooth it behind her ear. "This is a vintage Corvette. In pristine condition."

"That's your problem right there. Some things you need to change."

She eyed him sidelong. "Fixing my car doesn't mean you get out of jail free."

"Nope." He kept his head down, busying himself with swapping out the offending hose. The new hose meant Faye wouldn't be making any involuntary roadside stops anytime soon. The car was a good one; it just had a few kinks. "Wouldn't expect that."

"So." Faye backed away, and he found himself unexpectedly missing that connection. She smelled good. She paced as he finished his tightening and gave the setup a last once-over. Yeah, it would hold. "Why are you doing this?" she asked.

"Fixing your car?"

"Yes." She stopped moving. Maybe he was supposed to know the answer to that one. "You're not a mechanic. I'm not paying you." She eyed him suspiciously. "So why do I come back here and find you under the hood of my car?"

"Seemed like the right thing to do." He straightened up, closing the Corvette's hood. "The car needed fixing. I know how to fix things. Simple."

"No." Her lips were slick and shiny. Peaches. She smelled like peach lip gloss as she stood there, fighting him. He wanted to lick the corner of her mouth, lick his way right inside. "It's not that simple."

"Sure it is." He tested the latch of the Corvette's hood. When he was sure it was secure, he turned and tossed her the keys. "If something's broken, you fix it."

"So now I can go?" The look on her face definitely said he'd gotten it all wrong. "This morning," she challenged, "you said I wasn't going anywhere."

"Why do you want me here, in Strong?" Her fingers closed around the keys. She could be in the driver's seat in two steps.

Too bad playing with Evan Donovan had a certain undeniable appeal.

When she'd spotted him working on her car, part of her—a very primitive, feminine part—had been intrigued. If a girl wanted to, she could have all kinds of adventures with a man like that. Sure, Evan's high-handed arrogance had the rest of her seeing red, but part of her . . . part of her wanted to pull him into her arms and give him some pointers on what else needed taking care of.

Her view of his ass in those jeans wasn't dissuading those errant thoughts, either.

Keys. She needed to use the keys.

"You should stick around," he said finally, right when she'd given up on getting an answer out of him.

"Is that an invitation?"

"Sure," he said again. "You want one, there you go."

"I don't know." She deliberately ran her gaze over him. "You kidnap women. That's not a point in your favor."

"You fell asleep on me," he countered. "I think that might count as bodily assault in some states. What was I supposed to do? Step away and let you land on the floor?"

"There is," she pointed out, since he was being difficult, "a difference between making sure someone doesn't do a face-plant on the floor and carting said someone off to your cabin and taking her to bed."

"True." He shrugged. "But what are you going to do about it now?"

Time to bring out the big guns. "I'm betting," she said, "that Nonna might do something about it for me. If I asked her."

His hands tensed on the hood. "You met my mother."

"Uh-huh." And reconciling the woman she'd met briefly with this great big taciturn bear of a man was unexpectedly difficult, although they shared the same sly, quiet humor in addition to an uncannily similar I-can-fix-this attitude.

"Adopted," he said quietly. "In case you're asking yourself right now how come Nonna and I don't look anything alike."

"You think alike," she groused. "That's got to count for something." He looked interested. How long had it been since a guy who looked like this had also looked interested in her? Last night's drunken audience didn't count, she decided. And only partially because the later part of the evening was an embarrassing blank.

"Tell me about it." He tested the hood again, the well-washed cotton of his shirt pulling tight over his back. She'd bet he looked spectacular naked—too bad he'd pretty much hauled ass out of bed this morning. Since last night was already going down in the annals of most spectacularly embarrassing evening ever, she should have gotten some benefit from it. Like a really good, really long, hot look at his bare chest. Not that five-second peek she'd had.

He was staring at her now, and she was mumbling to herself. *Crap.*

"She's a rare one. Not too many of these made," he said, nodding at the Vette and kneeling to work the jack with expert hands. A couple of quick pumps and it sure looked as if her Corvette was back in business. His eyes found hers, and that matter-of-fact glance had heat exploding in her. God, she couldn't look away, and that was one more problem she could add to her growing oh-shit list. He had beautiful eyes, dark, with unexpectedly long lashes. Those were the best kind of bedroom eyes watching her.

His gaze dropped down her body briefly—then snapped to her eyes and stayed there, like he hadn't meant to go there and was appalled that he had. While she, on the other hand, was unrepentantly imagining undressing him. Imagining exactly how she'd unbutton those jeans and push up that cotton T-shirt. She wasn't going to apologize for it, either. Evan Donovan was one fine-looking man.

"No," she answered, doing a little more looking of her own. "Chevrolet made sure these beauties were specials. Fewer than four thousand came off the line in 1965."

"She's a beauty, all right." He stepped back, all business once again. "You were a witness to that brush fire yesterday." He shrugged casually. "Fire chief—Ben Cortez—he'll still want a statement from you. We need to get that done."

When had she become half of a *we*? "I didn't see much of anything. I told you that."

He shrugged again, carefully stowing his tools in the box at his feet. "Maybe. Maybe not. Sometimes people don't realize what they saw. Plus, you've got your photos. He'll want to see those, too. Ask you some questions."

"You think I know something and don't know that I do?"

"It's possible." An unexpectedly hard look in his eyes chased away the sleepy indolence. "I want to rule it out."

"Why is this brush fire so important?"

He ran a hand over his head, clearly considering what to tell her. She sensed what he wasn't saying. This was fire-fighter business—not *her* business. That sentiment was too familiar, so she pushed him. At the very least, she'd make him *say* it.

"You gave me maybe six words this morning, Evan. In the larger scheme of things, one brush fire doesn't compare to the kind of blaze you were called out to today. Mine merited one guy and a pickup—yours earned a plane and an entire crew of smoke jumpers. And yet you're worried about that little brush fire."

His eyes moved over her face. She didn't know what he was looking for, but he was going to pony up more words. "Spill, Evan." She gestured with her fingers, and that little smile tugged at the corner of his mouth again.

God, that smile could melt a woman.

"I'm speculating," he said, his voice slow and deliberate. "I wouldn't want this to get out."

"Between you and me, Evan. That's where this stays. Just tell me why this matters so much to you. You owe me that much, right?"

"I think someone set that brush fire." Jaw tight, his gaze slid away from hers, assessing a battlefield she couldn't see. This was a dangerous man to rile up. And he was definitely riled up. Seething. He saw this fire as *personal*.

"Arson? But the only person I saw up there was a fire-fighter putting the blaze out. Are you saying it was an inside job?"

"*That* question is precisely the problem." Evan didn't sound mean, but there was a *tone* to his words. Despite the smooth rumble of his voice, that tone said he wouldn't appreciate her messing with him. Not now. "You came here. You saw whoever it was. You tell me you're not putting that into your article."

"I'm a photojournalist," she said, because she couldn't let this go. That article was a shot at something bigger than catalog work and a second chance she couldn't afford to ignore. All joking aside, living in the Corvette wasn't practical. "Of course I'm putting it into my piece."

This was magazine gold. She was on to something in Strong. Her photo documentary about the jump team's efforts to bring a new firehouse to Strong wasn't just local color anymore. This could be huge. Syndicated huge. Plus, she didn't want the arsonist to walk, either.

"Whatever you put in the article now would be guessing," he said. "We don't know the truth—not yet."

"Obviously, you believe the arsonist is a member of your firefighting team. How is that guessing?" she demanded, slapping a hand against his chest.

"I *think*," he growled. Having this big bear of a man staring down at her should have been alarming. She should have been in the car. And yet . . . his face was impassive, but those eyes were hot, hot, hot. "I don't *know*. Not yet. You don't go public with this until we both know the truth."

"That's not fair," she protested.

"I'm asking you to wait," he countered. "Wouldn't you want to smoke out an arsonist, Faye? Do you know what kind of damage fire can do? That fire you drove through was a baby. Imagine one larger, stronger, and faster. The kind no one runs from, not even in a Corvette."

"Yeah." She fidgeted with the keys, getting the driver-side door open. He couldn't force her to stay. They both knew that. "I know what can happen. My ex was a firefighter."

She'd seen firsthand the damage fire could do. Mike had come home more than once with burns. The stories had been worse, though, and she'd never known how much— or how little—he'd exaggerated. Fire was dangerous. That was the simple truth.

"Wait," he coaxed, and that deep, smoky rumble was pure trouble. That voice made her want to listen. Made her imagine things she had no business imagining. "I want you to wait a little, Faye. File the piece once I'm sure. That's all I'm asking, because there's too much at stake here. Do you know what the clearance rate is here in California? There's a really low percentage of arsons that actually result in an arrest and charge. If I can't prove arson, I don't have an arrest. It's that simple."

"And you think you can prove your case?"

"This isn't the first fire."

"You have fires every day of the week out here?"

"We've had more than our fair share. And way too many small ones. Grass fires. Fires like the one you drove through."

"And you've checked them all out?"

"I look at *all* the fires, large and small. That's my job, darlin'. Once I've got a pattern like this one, I have to look at the firehouse. That part is what I need time for. You can't turn a man into a chart and tick off what he is and isn't in a series of columns and boxes, so I *won't* flush someone's firefighting career without being sure, Faye. Because that's what could happen if I started making assumptions or accusations."

"You want time."

"Yes. All the time you can give me."

The way Evan saw it, Faye still had the bulk of her photos to shoot, but that bought him one, maybe two, days. He needed more time, because he wasn't accusing any man of arson without a hell of a lot of proof. No matter what suspicions he had, he needed more time to figure it all out. What would it take to get her to stay put?

"Stay in Strong," he said. "Tell me what it will take to convince you." Propping his hip against the driver-side door, he waited for her to process his request. She didn't look ready to open that door and fall into his arms, but she hadn't put the key into the ignition and hit the gas, either.

Her wicked smile should have warned him. "You really want to know?" she asked.

"Yeah." He leaned toward her. "Cut the crap, and tell me."

"Wow." She nodded to herself, as if he'd settled some internal debate she was having. "You're not much for conversation, are you?" When he shrugged but didn't fall for the bait, she continued. "I have two weeks, four hundred dollars, and the Corvette. Since I had this magazine gig, I started here. But when I turn in those pictures, I'll have seed money. I can *go* places. *Do* things. That's a hundred percent improvement over sitting around L.A. doing catalog work."

"Got it." He had money enough for two, but somehow he didn't think that was the offer she was angling for. "Adventure with a side of cash."

"I don't care about the money. Much." She grinned up at him. "Which is a good thing, given how much I spent on this car and what the magazine is paying me for this gig. Still, eating is always a good thing."

"No one wants you going hungry," he agreed. "And there's always an open door up at the fire camp. Plenty for one more."

She laughed, and he didn't know if that was a good thing or bad. "When I run out of cash, I'll go back to L.A.," she said. "Right now, I want to live a little."

"You want an adventure."

"Lots of them." She smiled. "Everything on my bucket list and more. That can't happen if I stay put here in Strong."

He shook his head. "There's plenty of adventure right here. You don't need to worry about being bored."

"Why not?"

"Because I'll show you around."

"The grand tour?" Faye looked up and down the street, but there wasn't that much to see. Strong was all main street and not much else. "That's going to kill a half hour, maybe an hour. You might want weeks."

"Two," he said, and damned if he didn't sound sincere.

Maybe his services as a tour guide were some kind of local secret—and maybe she was reading more into his offer than he meant. He wasn't promising two weeks of indulging her every sensual fantasy, so she needed to swallow that disappointment and move on. Even if it wasn't fair, he sounded so sexy when he was being so damned sincere.

"Two weeks," he repeated. "And I'll make sure you have an adventure every day."

"Give me some examples." She knew she sounded suspicious, but this was her new life they were haggling over. She *wasn't* settling for some cheesy pickup line.

"You ever jumped out of a plane?"

He crossed his arms, watching her. She bet he did that a lot—watched. "No," she admitted.

"Then there's your first adventure. I'll take you up."

She'd be lucky if he didn't throw her out. "And in exchange?"

"You stay here in Strong. You take your photos—I'm not standing in the way of the truth coming out—but you give me two weeks to take care of some investigative business. I get to make sure that we've really got ourselves a firefighter arsonist before you trumpet it to the world."

"You want to be sure. Very altruistic of you."

His look said that altruism had nothing to do with this. *God*. He did big and scary really well. Unfortunately for him, when you'd woken up next to him, wearing his T-shirt, and then he'd kissed you senseless, it was hard to go back to the shaking-in-your-boots part.

"You know what happens when a fireman's accused of setting his own fires? Accusations like that destroy the man and rip a team apart. When this team hears that I think one of them has been setting fires, fingers are going to point, and it's going to get ugly. Men accusing other men. Suspecting guys they've been friends with for years. Some feel betrayed. Others? They go after the accuser with their fists flying. Either way, my team gets put through the wringer. So I say nothing until I'm as damned certain as I can be that there's a real need."

"You need to know."

"We all need to know."

She put a hand on his arm simply because she wanted the contact. His skin was warm and firm. Strong hands, with a small puckered burn mark on his forearm. "Okay," she said. "I get why this matters. I really do."

"Two weeks," he interrupted. "Fourteen days of adventure. Whenever I'm not out on a call, I'll make sure you see plenty of action. Think about it, Faye."

She didn't like his assumption that she wouldn't do the right thing without a bribe. Of course, she hated the idea of ending her big find-herself-and-start-over adventure before it had even really started, but she knew how to do the right thing. Plus, it wasn't as if she wasn't used to waiting around for a firefighter to finish doing his job and make time for her.

Waiting around summed up her marriage with Mike. Two years and more nights alone than she cared to count. In comparison, fourteen days with whatever time Evan

Donovan could spare her would be a treat. Giving in too quickly, though, meant giving up her leverage—and she suspected she'd need all the leverage she could get with a man who'd walk off with her car keys to ensure her compliance.

"You win," she said. "I'll think about it."

"Good." He opened the driver-side door for her. "Do that thinking on your way out to the fire camp."

Chapter Five

The fire camp was doing a brisk business in barbecue. Firefighters lined up wielding plastic plates instead of hoses, peppering their teammates manning the grills with good-natured teasing. All those hard bodies relaxing at the handful of picnic tables or sprawled out on the logs someone had rolled around a fire pit looked equally delicious. And familiar. Faye recognized that low rumble of male voices retelling war stories, while their owners enjoyed the food and the summer evening. God, how long had it been since she'd gone with Mike to a department thing? She'd sworn them off at the end, tired of watching from the sidelines. She'd been the firefighter's wife. Not one of them.

Faye admired what they did, day in and day out, putting their necks on the line to extinguish the fires that always kept coming. Los Angeles needed men like that. So did Strong. She believed with all her heart that firefighters were heroes, and she had nothing but respect for them and what they brought to the table.

She just wanted to be more than someone who watched while others *did*.

Using their barbecue as an impromptu and covert lineup wasn't what she'd had in mind, though. Earlier, Evan had handed her off to his brother, Jack, who'd made the rounds and the introductions with her. She'd met man after man, shaking hands and trading names with the full intent of outing someone if she could.

Since Strong's fire chief, Ben Cortez, also needed a statement from her, her visit was a two-for-one. She got a good look at the fire camp and a chance to meet Evan's boys and his brothers. The camp was exactly as she'd imagined, the planes and the Harleys and the maleness of it all almost overwhelming, the whole place one big adventure.

Evan dropped onto the ground at her feet. He smelled like smoke and barbecue and something fundamentally, irresistibly male. She couldn't stop herself from looking at him. "No one looks familiar." Except that they were all firefighters. She was caught in a déjà vu that wouldn't quit.

"All right." She couldn't tell, looking at his face, if her failure made him happy or if he'd wanted to get this thing wrapped up ASAP. "You said yourself that the encounter was a quick one. You'd just driven through a brush fire. If you can't pick out the guy, that's okay."

He handed her a plate, and she took it automatically. Maybe he'd taken that whole liking-to-eat thing literally, because he'd given her enough chicken and corn to feed half a jump team.

"Sorry," she said, and meant it. This would have been so much easier if she'd walked in here, looked his team over, and pointed.

"Not a problem."

She actually thought he might mean the words. In any case, he passed her a napkin and a fistful of plastic silverware, gesturing for her to get started on the week's worth of groceries he'd heaped onto her plate.

"You know all these men?" she asked, taking her first bite. God, the food here wasn't bad at all.

Evan shrugged. "Many of them. Not all of them. Fire

season usually runs June through October, whatever dates the government agencies forecasting the weather and the possibility of fires come up with. You start with sun with a side of dry and pray like hell the autumn rains come early. Because Mother Nature here is cramming most of our work into a four month window, we hire seasonals. The local firehouses send up guys as well, whoever they can spare who wants to make a buck and be where all the action is."

"Which ones are on the jump team?" The L.A. department had been all hook-and-ladder trucks and ground crew, only because there was no way you used planes and jumpers in the city. Jumping straight into the heart of the fire the way these guys did took danger to a whole new level.

Evan's eyes crinkled around the edges. "You think we're going to look different?"

"Maybe. You, for example." She took her eyes off the plate and eyed him. "You don't look like the jump-out-of-a-plane type."

"Why not?" He popped the top on a Coke and passed her the cold can. He didn't start on his own plate until she'd downed the first forkful.

"Too big," she said around a mouthful of food. God, these men knew how to cook. How unfair was that? "I'd expect you to sink like a rock."

"I float like a feather," he promised. "Or, to put it another way, I haven't hit the ground too hard. Yet. You've met my brothers, Jack and Rio. They jump, too." He waved his own soda toward a couple of men in the barbecue line. "That's Mack and, over there, Zay. Joey." His finger moved down the line. "The next four are ours, as well."

"That's a pretty small team."

"We've got ten jumpers in Strong right now. Eight to

go up, two off, plus we've got ourselves a dedicated pilot, although half of us can fly the plane if there's a need."

"I've heard about this thing called 'equal opportunity,' " she said lightly. "Some places even hire women these days."

"Sure." He leaned back on his elbows. "I've got no problem with having a woman on the team. She needs to jump, though, and she needs to haul her own shit. Jumping's not the problem for most women. It's the ground work."

"Women can't hack it?"

He grunted. "I'm not touching that one, Faye. All I'll say is that when the fire's cresting and you're digging line for all you're worth and humping your ass over rough ground, there's an advantage to being big. Because that's where you're going with this, aren't you?"

Possibly. She looked away, focusing her attention on her plate.

"I support equal opportunity as much as anyone," he continued. "But out there, on ground zero, you have to keep up. You pull your weight, and you hold your own, or the fire eats you alive, Faye."

They chewed in silence. She couldn't tell if the lack of talking was awkward or companionable, but at least the food was good. Toward the end of the meal, when someone dragged out a cooler filled with ice and beer, the guys on the duty list came in for plenty of teasing. On-duty meant the beers were off-limits—and meant more beer for the rest of the crew, who popped the caps enthusiastically.

Rio Donovan dropped down onto the log on the other side of her, trading her a beer for the empty Coke can. She wrapped her fingers around the cold bottle that was the perfect antidote to the summer heat

Rio certainly didn't waste any time. He cut right to the chase. "You staying in town?"

Her keys burned a hole in her pocket. "Evan told you

about what I saw yesterday on my way into town?" Had Evan told his brother about the deal he'd proposed?

"Yeah." Rio watched her. He had to be, she decided, one of the most beautiful men she'd ever seen. Too bad he didn't do it for her, because he seemed like the playful type, like a big golden cat you wanted to stroke. "My brother said he asked you to stick around some while we figure this thing out."

"You don't look alike," she said, avoiding his statement.

"We don't," he agreed. "We adopted each other. We share a lot of things but not a gene pool. Too bad for Evan."

Evan raised his soda can in mock salute at the light tease in his brother's voice.

"Jack, too?" This was none of her business. But she wanted to know.

"The three of us," Rio confirmed. He took a lazy sip of his beer. "God, that's good. Too bad you're on call tonight, Evan. You're missing out here. Jack, Evan, and I met up when we were kids. We stuck together, and eventually we ended up out here in Strong with Nonna. She made things formal. Adopted us. And we all lived happily ever after."

Three brothers. All adopted. There was more story here. Plenty more. Evan didn't look particularly interested in filling in those blanks, however. He just sat there silently next to her, playing big and gruff.

She was out of conversation and about to plunge in where she had no business going when Jack Donovan showed up, handing around a stack of photos. Her photos. Sometime in the last couple of hours he'd managed to have them printed up. For a few minutes, everyone got busy trying to pick out identifying details.

"No one's admitted to being on scene before Evan." Jack turned his photo over in his hand, as if maybe there was a secret code on the back. "You saw just the one guy, right?"

They'd been over this before. More than once. She raised her bottle in silent agreement.

"Maybe five foot ten with those boots on." Rio tossed that nugget out there.

Evan nodded, like his brother was reading from his Pulitzer-prize-winning essay. "One-fifty. Possibly one-sixty. Nicely built, but on the wiry side. White guy, from what I see of him."

"Yeah. He was into covering up, wasn't he?" Despite the fire's heat and the sweat-inducing summer temps, the firefighter in her pictures was dressed head to toe. Between the jeans and the long-sleeved work shirt, the bandana and the cap, he'd bared only his forearms. Tanned and fit, he hefted the shovel easily, his head turned away from her lens.

"Hell." Jack ran a hand over his head. "There isn't that much to work with here. He could be almost anyone."

"We can rule out Evan," Rio pointed out, swapping his photo for Jack's. "This guy's not that damned big. Congrats," he said, turning to Evan. "You're the only one in the clear here. The rest of us fall within the margin of error."

"You able to match him up to anyone here?" Evan asked.

"No." She tossed her trash onto the burn pile. "Jack here marched me up and down past the food line twice, and I can safely say I'm running blind here. He really could be anyone. Between the baseball cap and the way the light was hitting him, you're lucky I'm sure he's a *he*."

"That's real helpful," Jack said dryly. "Seeing as how right now there are precisely zero women working on this fire crew."

"Happy to help." She grinned at him, taking a sip from her bottle. The beer was cold and perfect. Her sister would never believe her: here she was, parked in the middle of fire camp, with a cold one and three of the hottest men she'd ever met. None of whom were hers, but she'd leave that detail out of the story. Lazily, she set down the bottle and reached for her camera, getting off a few shots. *Fire-fighters after the fight.*

Ben Cortez, who headed up the department, ambled over to them. "Here you go," he said as he handed her her official-looking, typed-up statement to sign. "Sign in triplicate, and we're done for the night." As she flipped through the pages, dutifully initialing, he dropped onto the log across from her, leaning forward to monitor her progress, arms on his knees. He'd had a go at the pictures on her camera, as well, with equally disappointing results. The tightness at the corners of his mouth said he was tak-ing this hard. He might be a teddy bear of a man, but there was nothing benevolent about his eyes right now. He was riled up.

"She have a chance to review this?" That was Evan's voice, all calm and measured. Was he looking out for her?

"She did. Faye?" Ben prompted.

She had. Ben had gone over the need for a documented statement from her. She was an eyewitness, even if she hadn't seen crap. Now that crap was official record. "It's okay, Evan."

Hitting the bottom of Ben's clipboard, she gave the documents a final once-over and scrawled her signature at the bottom of the last page. There were no surprises in there. Ben had been efficient but thorough, going over what she'd seen and from where. He'd wanted to nail down her point of view exactly. They'd walk the scene to-morrow, he'd promised.

"Why go to all this trouble when I can't actually iden-tify anyone?"

"Because if that fire was the beginning of something

bigger," Evan growled, "I need to know. Rio needs to know. That's why your information goes into a database. We do info-sharing with local and state agencies, and Ben here does his own investigation, as well."

Rio raised his beer in mock salute, and she itched to grab her camera again. Rio was trouble, six-plus feet of pure, sweet mischief sprawled on the ground. His shoulders strained beneath a faded cotton T-shirt that sported the logo of Ma's bar. Like Evan, he was tall and well-built, but there the similarities ended. Where Evan was all hard angles and just plain big, Rio had the kind of face women liked to look at. A lot. Too bad he didn't get her toes tingling the way Evan did. Sleeping with Rio would have been simpler. A little hot summer fun and then adios when August rolled into the autumn months and fire season ended.

Instead, she settled for giving him an are-you-kidding look. "That's a lot of number crunching for what was probably just a brush fire."

Evan cracked another can of soda and passed it to her, taking her empty beer bottle. "*Probably* doesn't mean *definitely*."

"And you want to know for certain."

"It's not a question of *want*. It's a question of *need*. I told you that already." His expression was concerned. "I've got a job to do here, Faye. People to keep safe. I don't do that job by closing my eyes to the possibility that one of the guys on our team has decided to light it up on his off-hours. Small fires don't always stay small."

It was like a quest, she thought. An adventure, but also something more. Something that really *mattered*. These men were clearly a unit, their team more like family than most families were. All that laughing and teasing camouflaged close-knit bonds. They knew who they were, and they had each other's backs. Except that, possibly, one of them wasn't all that he seemed to be. One of those fire-fighters might be lying.

That kind of betrayal cut right to the core.

She knew all about firemen who lied, didn't she? She was a first-class expert on the kind of secretive asshole who got off on riding out on fire calls. Mike had taught her all about that.

She'd never taken Mike's last name, and, looking back, that had been a sign. She'd never answered to Mrs. Thomas, never even hooked his name together with hers and a hyphen. Because strong, independent women kept their own names and identities, thank you very much.

If she was honest with herself, she'd thought about Evan's offer all afternoon—and, the longer she thought, the more seductive that offer to stay on in Strong and go adventuring with him got. Maybe Evan Donovan could be her get-back-on-the-dating-horse fling. She'd never had a fling before. He could be her two-week treat to her-self. If he wanted her. She put her hand on his knee, sa-voring the immediate tension in his body.

He wanted her.

Why not? That was her new motto. And why *shouldn't* she take Evan up on his adventure-a-day offer? Sure, he was big and gruff, and making him talk was the verbal equivalent of pulling teeth. He certainly acted as if he'd rather be anywhere else when it came time to talk rather than do, which made teasing him all the more fun. Fresh out of a bad relationship and a divorce, she *didn't* want happily-ever-after. So why not enjoy him and all he had to offer? This wasn't a relationship—her trip to Strong was pure adventure, and she might just end up with the pho-tos of a lifetime.

She'd do it.

There really wasn't any reason *not* to.

Leaning in, she put her mouth to his ear. He stiffened

but didn't move away. "Get ready to pony up, big guy." She blew lightly. "I accept your adventure-a-day proposal."

Those photos were a potential problem. Hollis hadn't thought it through, not quite, when the red Corvette had zipped through his flames and pulled over. The lady had been real pretty, seated behind the wheel, and he couldn't remember the last time he'd had a female looking at him like that.

Like he was a real, live hero.

He should have hightailed it out of there, but, no, he'd been all caught up in that interest of hers. Of course, she'd been good and scared when she flew around the bend and into those flames. Her eyes had been real big and her hands tight on the wheel, like she was afraid to let go. He'd noticed, because he'd suddenly been watching *her*.

When his turn in line came, he'd loaded up his plate with barbecue. He'd lucked out when he'd been loaned to Strong's fire team for the summer. After all, he'd fixed up the lull in the action pretty good, and he was going out on calls fairly regularly now.

Despite the fact that the jump team was still off-limits to him.

He eyed the jumpers hanging out around the fire pit. Lots of things could happen. Fire season wasn't nearly over yet. He'd have an opportunity to show them what he could do—that much he was sure of. If not, he could make his own luck. That matchbox of his provided real equal opportunity.

"You know who she is?" he asked the man in front of him, because the more he learned about her now, the sooner he'd know what the chances were she'd made him.

The other firefighter shrugged and piled a load of slaw onto his plate. "Photographer for some fancy magazine—

that's what I heard. She came up here to do a piece on the firehouse restoration."

Hollis spooned beans onto his plate and thought it over. "Professional?"

A professional photographer was both better and worse than a random lady with a camera. She might actually know how to do some of those things he'd seen on TV. Maybe she'd blow up the photos, blow up his cover. On the other hand, she could also put him *on* the magazine cover. He'd done some seriously heroic shit out there, and clearly she'd liked what she'd seen. She'd taken his picture.

"Yeah." The other man grabbed a handful of paper napkins and looked around for a spot to sit. "She's getting paid. Sounded professional enough to me."

"Our shot at getting famous, huh?"

"Sure." The guy was already beating feet for an open spot at a nearby picnic table. "All she has right now is a bunch of pics of that roadside fire we snuffed yesterday. That's not much."

Fuck him. That fire had done its job, hadn't it? They'd gotten called out and spent an afternoon actually fighting fire rather than sitting on their asses at base. His paycheck would definitely notice the difference, *and* he'd gotten the eyeball from the female photographer. So that had been more than enough fire.

Picking a different direction, Hollis headed off, carting his plate. He hadn't gotten caught. He'd fucking pulled it off. True, it had been close. Kinda like getting it on right in public, where anyone might walk in on you. He'd done that once. Not with a girl, but almost as good as.

He'd unzipped and pulled his dick right out in the parking lot behind his old high school. He'd liked revisiting his old stomping grounds, not that he'd ever gotten much action out there in the backseat of his car. The girls had mostly ignored him, and he'd mostly pretended he didn't care.

Now that he was fire crew, he was finally getting some action.

That night, he'd fisted his dick and rubbed one out right there next to his car, standing in the open where anyone could see. The first stroke was awkward, but in a couple of minutes he had his groove, and his hand was going up and down like a piston, and he was harder than he'd ever been. Coming was an added bonus, a little something he got out of his giant fuck-you to all the school admins who'd told him he'd hopped the train to Loserville and didn't he want to trade in that ticket for something better.

He was a firefighter.

A damned good one.

If he kept it up right, got enough fires under his belt, he'd make that jump team. There wasn't going to be any holding him back.

As they drove away from the fire camp, Evan filled Faye in about the jump team. She knew he was giving her the pretty version, skimming over the parts that the magazine's readers wouldn't want to know. For every jump, for every fire, there were often days and even weeks of downtime. Mike had complained about the boring day-in, day-out at the firehouse, about how a man did more sitting around than he did riding out. It came with the territory, though, and it had never kept him from returning to the firehouse.

She asked questions, listening to Evan's answers, her eyes on the dark road ahead as she drove. She could hear the quiet laughter in his voice as he told her about the funny mishaps when one of the jumpers hung up in a tree and had to cut himself free. And what it looked like to clear a mountain and come face-to-face with a wall of smoke. Fire was beautiful, seen through his eyes, until you were on the ground, fighting for every inch. Even then, she supposed, there was a savage beauty to the flames, but no one he knew had time to sit around and write poetry about it. The smoke jumpers did what they had to do.

"You jump with the same team every summer?"

"Yeah." He shifted in his seat, one arm riding the edge of the open window. Summer air filled up the inside of the Corvette. "I do. You met my brothers. Together, we've got one of the best smoke-jumping outfits in the northwest. When it works well, you don't mess with that."

"And when summer's over?" She asked the question casually.

"There are always fires, Faye. But, when fire season ends and the calls taper off, we train. Rebuild planes. Plan for next year." He shrugged. "There's always something to be doing."

"No new guys for you this year?"

"Not in the last two years." The road rushing by was empty. Outside the window, the trees were taller than buildings she'd lived in in L.A. No cars and no other people—just the two of them inside the Corvette slipping through the summer night.

"It's a man's world," he said, answering her unspoken question from earlier. "I'm not saying it's right or that that's the way it'll stay, but, right now, there aren't too many women signing on to jump. We're kind of rough and tumble. Not too pretty when you look closely, but we get the job done."

"Bad boys," she said lightly, and the Corvette hit Strong's now-familiar one-and-only main street. Mimi's bar, Ma's, was already open, lights spilling out of the windows. She didn't know where they were going. There was something about the night and the ride—the *man*—that made her content to let this happen. Right now, she didn't have to be in control, even though she was the one ostensibly in the driver's seat.

"Sometimes," he agreed, that wicked smile of his tugging at his lips. "When the fires are out." He gestured for her to pull over. "Park in front of the firehouse. Home, sweet home," he added, opening his door when she'd come to a stop.

She got out, coming around the car to stand next to him. "Your brother's fixing this place up, right?" This old firehouse was why she'd come to Strong. The building was pretty but dilapidated. She could almost feel the pull of its history. It was easy to imagine the men streaming in and out of the bays, hanging out on the porch between calls. The space was deeply masculine despite the white-painted porch furniture and the black-and-yellow Lazy Susan vines. She itched to photograph it.

"Yeah. That was Jack's plan. He bought the firehouse last month, and we've been working on her in our spare time ever since. He'll give you all the details. He has a vision." He shook his head, but there was no missing the pride in his voice.

"He's going to make the place historically accurate?"

She'd been filled in by her publisher, but it never hurt to hear the local version. Sometimes wires got crossed or the locals had details she hadn't heard.

"So he says. It's going to take some cash, though."

When he headed for the porch, she followed. She had a feeling he was used to that. She'd met his brothers, and the Donovans weren't men you overlooked. The three of them were used to leading, whether it was a team of jumpers or a woman. She'd bet they didn't hear *no* anywhere near often enough. And her traitorous body sure didn't want to be the exception. She wanted to cozy right up to Evan Donovan.

He popped a key into the door, the *snick* of the lock far

too loud on the quiet porch. When she exhaled, her breath sounded rough. She was waiting for something. Was he?

He reached out, holding open the door. "So you need a place to stay."

"Other than in my car?" Which was barely big enough to hold her, even though she'd fantasized about making love on those seats, climbing onto the lap of some unknown lover. Who was now starting to look an awful lot like Evan Donovan. God, she needed to stop this. She forced herself to focus on his words rather than the heat building in her belly. "Yeah. But it's going to have to be cheap."

"Not a problem. Strong doesn't have a motel, and we're not five-star territory." His slow grin sparked an answering smile on her own face. "So, no credit, no problem. This place is livable," he explained, "but she isn't real pretty. Not yet." The laughter was back in his voice, a deep rumble of amusement she felt low in her belly. "Although when Jack's fiancée finishes up, I'm betting we'll have the prettiest firehouse this side of the Rockies. I figured you could stay here. Consider it a down payment on the adventures I owe you."

"It's not operational yet?" She could stay here, fix it up some more while she took photos for her article.

Evan shrugged. "Mostly it is. We've got a truck in the bay, and the guys are in and out, but no one's camped out in the bunkroom. Everyone except for Ben is up at the fire camp, and he's got a house of his own down the street. You'd have this place all to yourself, and no one would bother you."

The stairs he led her up ended in a bunk room that was basic but immaculately clean. Four sets of bunk beds lined the far wall, and a card table with some folding chairs filled up the rest of the space. Anyone spending the night also had access to a microwave, a coffeemaker, and a mini-fridge humming in the corner. It wasn't the Ritz, but it sure beat the Corvette.

Plus, if she was into firefighter fantasies, she had more than enough material to work with now.

"So." He watched her, and she wondered what he saw. "You want to spend the night?"

His plan wasn't great, but it was workable. Evan knew it in his gut. He'd trade her a little R & R of the exciting variety in exchange for the time he needed to eliminate the threat to his jump team and to Strong. No one hurt what belonged to him. Strong—and its people—were his. Now that included Strong's newest resident, Faye Duncan. If there was anything he could do to fix things for her, he'd do it.

And wasn't he all Mr. Altruistic? Because his desire to offer up the bunkhouse to Faye wasn't a neighborly gesture on his part. No, truth was, he wanted to keep her real close. In his cabin would have been best, but he was enough of a gentleman not to push that one. He'd brought her home last night, but that had been an emergency—and it had already been pointed out to him that he hadn't been thinking. Not clearly enough.

Faye did that to him, though. She was one of the prettiest women he'd seen, but that wasn't all. At least, he didn't think so. There was something about her. He wanted more, then still more, when he was with her.

He'd be a gentleman tonight.

Even if it killed him.

"Thanks," she said, her eyes sweeping the room.

It wasn't fancy, but he wanted her to like it. He'd spent years living in this kind of place, waiting for the next fire, the next call, or the next ride out.

She turned and headed back down the stairs. Hopefully,

she was going in search of a toothbrush, not a Motel 6.
"Point me toward your bag," he offered, "and I'll carry it
in for you. Get you settled."

"That's going to be a challenge." A rueful grin lit up her
face when she reached the car and popped the trunk—and
it became clear that the space was doubling as a closet. A
very messy closet. Clothes were heaped inside in one
enormous, jumbled pile. He had no idea how she could
find anything. Or how much time it had taken to load the
car up.

"I was in too much of a hurry to get going to stop and
pack," she admitted.

"I can see that."

Was he supposed to offer to let her talk about it? Coax
the truth out of her? Hell, he was no good in this kind of
situation. All he knew was that he was damned angry at
Mike for letting Faye come out here alone. What was she
thinking, buying a Corvette when she didn't even have
enough money for a hotel room? Still, Mike should have
known, should have concerned himself about his former
wife. How hard was it to pick up the phone and make a
reservation and fork over a credit card?

Mike had simply cut her loose. Evan couldn't imagine
anyone doing that to Faye. Goddamn it, he'd met her less
than twenty-four hours ago, and he already knew she was
special. She was the kind of woman you got your arms
around and hung on to, for as long as she'd let you.

"Okay." He eyeballed the trunk-load of clothes. "You
got hangers?"

Of course she didn't.

Twenty minutes later, he'd hit Mimi up for supplies and
hauled an impossibly large collection of clothes inside.
He'd have to make a run into the city tomorrow, and stop
at the Walmart for more plastic hangers, but he'd done
what he could for now. He eyed the bursting closet. For a

woman planning on spending one or two days in Strong, she'd packed a lot of gear. She must have one hell of a road trip planned for afterward.

From the corner of his eye, he watched her pick out a bunk and crack open a new package of sheets.

"You want a hand with that?" he asked, moving closer.

"That might be a good idea." She eyed the bare mattress cautiously, and that was permission enough to take over. There was a trick to fitting the sheets on the bunks, and showing her the way of it meant he got to stand close and drink in her laughter. The military would have busted her for her corners, and she was no Martha Stewart, but eventually she had the bed made up.

"The sky looks different out here," she said, moving toward the window while he finished up. A quick shove, and the sash shot up.

Yeah. He agreed with her there. The night sky here was pretty without the city lights to cover up the stars. Even the air smelled warm and inviting.

"No lights up here to run interference." Coming up behind her, Evan lightly dropped his hands onto her shoulders, his thumbs finding and stroking her collarbone. He had the rough fingers of a man who worked with his hands every day of the week and outdoors more often than not. Those were good hands.

She stood there, tingling with anticipation. It felt good, too, to just wait. To let go of the frenetic pace of driving up from Los Angeles and the demanding beat of life in that city. Strong was someplace simpler and slower, and Evan fit in here perfectly. She was the one who didn't quite belong, but for this one moment she wanted to try.

When he breathed lightly on her neck, goose bumps found her, and her belly came alive with nerve endings. Who knew that little connection could feel so good? For a long minute, his mouth rested against her throat. She tilted her head.

And Evan's lips found her collarbone.

A soft, damp trail of kisses moved slowly, deliberately up her neck. *Oh, God, God, God,* she hadn't known she could get so turned on by a simple kiss. Pinned between him and the windowsill, she felt heat tear right through her, even though she knew this was a game. She could move left or right, and he'd let her go. If she wanted *this,* this touch of his, she had to stay still.

And Evan made it very hard to do so.

There was no way to kiss him back in this position. There was no place to put her hands other than in front of her, so she gripped the windowsill. Right now, Evan was in the driver's seat, giving her pleasure. Taking control. His mouth covered her skin, and her own moan, husky and needy, shocked her. Evan made her *want.*

His hands slid her hair to one side, rubbing away the tension in the back of her neck and scalp in a way that was pure bliss. His mouth brushed against the nape of her neck again, and the spark low in her belly kicked up into inferno territory.

"You think someone could see us up here?" The possibility was a naughty thrill that also brought a quick adrenaline rush.

"Maybe." His voice rumbled against her ear, making her want to squirm. Did the man have *any* idea how hot he was? "Sure," he added, as thoughtful as if he was figuring out an engineering issue or where the best jump spot was that day. "Someone could see us, if that person wanted to be watching this."

When she looked around the darkness spreading out from the firehouse, she easily spotted the lights in the newer fire station that all but guaranteed company close at hand. "Would you?" Her voice sounded breathless, even to her own ears. He'd know she wanted him. Somehow, though, she thought he'd want that honesty. Evan wasn't the kind of man who played games.

He saw what he wanted. He asked. And then he took.

"Sure would," he agreed. "I like looking at you, darlin'."

His mouth brushed the sensitive lobe of her ear again, a soft presence reminding her he was right there as his tongue traced patterns on her skin.

He wasn't kissing her, not mouth to mouth, just had his lips touching her skin. And yet that simple touch was the most delicious, toe-curling, erotic thing, and she had no idea why. She stood there, fingers pressed into the old wood of the window ledge, savoring the heat of him at her back, big and solid and so reassuring. The sky wasn't the only thing different up here in Strong. She was different, too, and she liked that.

And then he stepped back, leaving her wanting more. More kisses. More Evan.

"Adventure." He stroked a finger down her nose, tapping the end before stepping back. She turned around, watching him. This was going to be good. She could feel it. This was more than just sexual arousal. There was something about this man that made her want to get underneath his skin and find out who he was. "Everything the good doctor ordered."

Chapter Six

Evan walked over to Ben's after leaving Faye tucked up in the firehouse. After holding her, kissing her like that, he was restless, and no way was he going straight back to the cabin where he'd so recently slept with Faye. If he got into that bed now, there'd be no holding back the memories of waking up next to her. Kissing her. Hell, he'd be lucky if he didn't find himself climbing right back into his truck and begging Faye to take pity on him and let him in.

She'd enjoyed that moment up there in the bunk room, too.

She hadn't moved away from him, had let him pin her between the windowsill and himself. And then she'd let him touch her. *Christ.* She felt so good. All that silky, sweet skin and the scent of her—well, he'd never look at that bunk room the same way again.

She'd liked that, and she hadn't been shy about letting him know, either.

He wasn't surprised to find his Nonna parked on Ben's porch. Something was brewing between those two. The pair practically sparked when they were together. He kind of liked the idea. Nonna deserved a man like Ben Cortez. Or Ben deserved a woman like his Nonna. Both were equally true.

It being summer, even at nine o'clock the light was still fading out, more gray than black. Crickets were singing up a storm, and a cheerful noise spilled out of Ma's whenever someone went in or out. Somewhere not too far away a pickup crunched over gravel. Familiar sounds he'd heard every summer in Strong for years. Home, for better or worse.

He could have been ten again, too, seeing that look in Nonna's eye. She wasn't happy with him, and it didn't take a genius to figure out why.

She went right on the offensive, reading him the riot act. Too bad that horse was already out of the barn, because she was all fired up, and clearly leaving a message on his cell earlier that day hadn't covered everything she had to say. "If you needed a bed, Evan, there are plenty in my house. You don't bring a girl home without asking her first, then pop her into bed with you. Not you, Evan. Rio, sure."

"Got it." He couldn't explain why he'd done it. He'd known bringing Faye Duncan back to his cabin was a mistake. Hell, even Mimi had offered up her couch. Instead, he'd reacted instinctively. "I wasn't thinking," he offered.

"No." Nonna's eyes searched his face. "I don't suppose you were, Evan. She's not a puppy you can bring home and keep. These things have consequences. You want her to stick around, you have to think it through."

He knew that, and he knew the whole town knew. And they knew that he knew they knew. It was like a goddamn television show. Problem was, he didn't care. He'd always done his own thing. The only opinions that mattered to him were Rio's and Jack's—and Nonna's.

"I put her in the old firehouse for the rest of her stay," he offered. "The bunk room's empty, and she needed a place. That okay with you?"

Ben snorted, but he clearly wasn't going to put himself

in the middle of this conversation. Evan didn't blame him one bit.

"That's not my call," Nonna said. "It's not my firehouse, not my business." Like hell, it wasn't. She was as much a part of that firehouse as any of them. Even if she didn't ride out on the truck or jump out of the plane, none of them would have been fighting fires without her. They all knew that, so he looked at her and waited. Sure enough, Nonna leaned forward, wrapping her arms around him. "I know you're all grown up. I do. I simply want everything to work out for you, Evan."

Apparently, she didn't see last night's sleepover ending well for him. Part of him wanted to ask why, but he was done talking about this. He didn't have anything to add to this conversation. Before she could bring up Faye again, he turned to Ben.

"I want to run the rosters with you." As Donovan Brothers' safety and security man, this was his baby. Jack handled the day-to-day business, and Rio crunched data, but Evan kept everyone safe. Every time.

Ben nodded, and ten minutes later Nonna had said her good-nights, and they were ass-deep in rosters and lists.

Evan got the ball rolling. "Give me the names of the first responders. Which firefighters hit the scene first?" If they did have a firefighter arsonist on the Strong team, that man was probably first on the scene or as near to it as he could manage.

Ben drew a finger down the lists, running through some kind of mental checklist. He probably wanted to go through those rosters with a fine-tooth comb every bit as badly as Evan did. There were answers hiding in here, waiting for them to connect the dots. To find their guy's pattern. He'd have one, too. Arsonists always did.

"We can rule out these." Ben drew thick lines through

a handful of names with a black Sharpie. "They check out. We know where they were when Faye's brush fire got started. Everyone else, though, is still in."

"Jump team was on the ground, too." Evan hated to say it, but facts were facts. His gut said none of the men he jumped with would do such a thing, but until he proved their whereabouts yesterday afternoon, they stayed on Ben's list. Fair was fair.

He couldn't take his eyes off all that damning black and white. Forty names and too few crossed off. It had been a slow afternoon, and most of the guys had had a freebie, leaving only a skeleton crew on call. He needed proof of their whereabouts when what he wanted to do was look them in the eye and take their word on it. He didn't like getting all up in any man's business, but now he had a problem, and he didn't have a choice.

Someone had already lied.

Someone had struck out on his own and started a fire. Or three.

And that someone was likely just getting started. After what had happened to Jack's Lily last month, they were all focused on fire patterns. When you had an inside job, you typically got a series of fires lighting up the same area. Fires that started small but got bigger. Like a roadside fire. There had been no building fires. Not yet. Their boy wasn't going to be allowed to escalate on Evan's watch, either.

"Let's see if we can narrow it down any based on height and build," he said, reaching for the stack of personnel files.

Two hours later they'd reached another dead end—and a list that still had thirty names on it. Sure, that was ten fewer guys he had to eyeball and ask if they were in the business of lying to him, so that was good. But, Christ, he didn't want to confront any of them to ask for reassurance. Being a member of Strong's team should have been enough. More than enough. How had they missed this guy? Where had all the personality tests and psych screenings and background checks gone wrong?

"That's it," he said, standing up.

"Nothing more to be done here," Ben agreed. "You want me to share this with Jack and Rio tomorrow? Or do you want to do it?"

"We'll hit them together," Evan decided. "They'll have the same questions I did. You think there's something we missed, Ben? Some clue we didn't get when we were interviewing for the jump team or the ground crew here?"

Ben straightened the stack of files, lining the edges up with military precision. "I doubt it," he said finally. "There are always too many unknowns with this kind of shit, and you and I both know those questions got to be asked. We did the background checks; these boys all came to us with references. Maybe some of them are too young, and any kink in their heads wasn't obvious. Maybe our guy hadn't had his chance to work out the stupid, and we got unlucky. You ask him when we catch him."

"First question out of my mouth," Evan promised. He was catching this guy, too. "Young and stupid doesn't excuse this. There's no room for stupid in a firefight."

"You want me to talk to the guys?"

That was a generous offer, but this wasn't Ben's mess. "Jack can do it after we brief him. We brought these guys here. We'll do it. If someone doesn't understand his limits, we'll make them clear." He'd been running options in his head since he'd pulled up a chair and started going through the rosters. There was a firefighter arson-awareness program in California, but a box of workbooks and a dozen hours in a classroom weren't going to fix this now. Inviting a psychologist to poke around wasn't the kind of fix he wanted, either. He wanted to take care of this problem himself.

"We'll schedule the heart-to-heart after we walk the fire perimeter," he decided.

Over Ben's shoulder, through the window, he had a clear view of the old firehouse. The whole two hours he'd worked on the files, the upstairs light had stayed on. Faye's light. He liked knowing that she was there, curled up in the bunk he'd helped her make up. Reading or something. Whatever it was she'd been doing, she was done now, because the light suddenly winked out, and his imagination took over. Faye would be lying down in that bed. Right on the other side of that open window.

He nodded toward the old firehouse. "I gave Faye a key when I let her in. Like I said, she needed a place to stay while we work this out, and the bunk room is empty. No reason she can't stay there."

"That's fine with me." The smile on Ben's face was unfamiliar. "Not back to your place, though?"

Evan wasn't sure what the older man was hinting at. "Not tonight. She needs to choose. Figure out for herself what she wants to do."

Ben shook his head, his hands sorting through more papers, making tidy little piles. "Don't give her too much space, boy. You don't want her too far from you."

"Personal experience talking there?" Evan didn't know what dragged the question out of him. No matter what he suspected might be brewing between the other man and Nonna, that wasn't somewhere he needed to go. Or that he even wanted to think about in detail. Ben was a good man, and Nonna deserved the best. Enough said.

"Keep her close," was all Ben answered. "You want her, you hang on to her good."

"Got it." He'd head back to the cabin, he decided. Time enough tomorrow to plot his next plan of attack. He wasn't in the market for relationship advice, but the intent look on Ben's face said the only acceptable answer right now was agreement. So he'd agree. And do his own thing tomorrow.

Right now his priority was the arsonist.

Faye Duncan was simply a sweet little bonus.

The California mountains pushed up into a summer sky that was all pretty blue and cloudless. It was the kind of day weekend visitors loved. Too many hot days, though, and the jump team would have more work on their hands. Hot weather meant thunderstorms and fires, and this month was heating up even before the brush fire two days ago.

When Evan spotted the first burn marks, he eased the truck off the road and pulled in tight to the guardrail. Ahead of him, Jack was setting up cones. Getting knocked off the road by a passing car wouldn't help their investigation any. State fire marshall had come in yesterday, so now it was local law enforcement's turn to take a look-see for the fire's origin. Donovan Brothers wasn't local, but Ben could and had requested their participation.

Any fire, no matter how small, merited a firsthand look. And a second look.

Keeping Ben's advice of last night in mind, Evan had swung by the firehouse to collect Faye in his truck. Kind of another down payment on the adventures he owed her; plus, it would be a good opportunity for her to get pictures of the boys in action. Cheap and easy. All this cost him was a few extra minutes. And since she was the only eyewitness they had, taking her back to the scene made plenty of sense.

"Showtime," he said, coming around the truck to hand her out.

She nodded, dropping her camera strap around her neck. "Tell me what you need me to do."

"Walk us through what happened," he suggested. "Show us where you pulled over, where you parked. Ben has your statement, but let's double-check it and see if there is anything else you want to add and if you can point out exactly where you saw the firefighter."

Ten minutes later, he turned her loose. This morning, they'd seen the scene from her angle. That was helpful, even though she hadn't gotten a picture of the truck's license plate. But that would have been too goddamn easy. Now, he wanted the four of them—him, Ben, Jack, and Rio—to walk the scene. Hell, he'd crawl the thing an inch at a time if it gave him the information he needed.

"Burn path is widest here." Ben pointed to a thick section of black char. "So that's where we start."

Evan nodded and fell into step with the other three.

"This could be merely a nuisance fire, another routine brush fire," Ben continued. "I'm going to start with that hypothesis, and I want to see anything that screams otherwise. If we find nothing, that's fine, too. Either way, I'm not leaving here until I know something more."

At first, walking the perimeter turned up nothing out of the ordinary. Even hours later, the familiar smell of smoke and creosote was heavy in the air. They moved up the road, following the burn.

Following the burn path was like rolling up a reel of fishing wire. Eventually, Rio pointed to the char marks on trees, the slow narrowing of the black marks. They were definitely getting closer to the origin point.

"Any chance lightning is our villain here?"

Rio looked over at him and shook his head. "Not this

time. Weather reports are all wrong for that. We haven't had a storm, wet or dry, in days. If this was a lightning strike, we have ourselves an actual act of God."

"Stranger things have happened." Jack moved ahead, taking the lead on the road's edge.

"You see strike marks anywhere here?" Ben snorted but didn't lift his eyes from the ground he was quartering.

Ben's question was rhetorical, but Evan wanted to see the answer for himself. Right now, he was on the widest end of the blackened area. If lightning had been the bad guy here, a strike on a tree could have sparked and then hopped, but the fire wouldn't have hopped too far. Instead, Evan had a black swath marching up the mountainside where the grasses were gone. Although plenty of trees still stood, none of those trees showed the kind of damage you'd get from lightning. Of course, lightning could hit whatever it damn well pleased—it didn't need a tree for a target. Still, you didn't pump that much voltage into anything, even the ground, without leaving some sign behind. The ground would be baked where the strike had landed, and there was no sign of that here.

"Not lightning," he agreed.

Rio was already nodding. "Boys yesterday put in a call to NOAA, and that's the message they got, too. The feds confirm there wasn't anything happening here, weatherwise, to set off a fire."

NOAA, the National Oceanic and Atmospheric Administration, monitored the country's weather. If lightning had hit here, those boys would have been the first to know.

"Other than that act of God." Rio's look said he didn't like Evan's suggestion. Evan wouldn't have, either, if he'd been in Rio's place. Acts of God weren't predictable. In their business, predictable was good.

This far up the road from where Faye had pulled off,

there was nothing but char. The fire had found plenty of fuel here and had hit the road fast. The bushes hanging over the guardrail and a helping hand from the wind probably explained the flames Faye had driven through.

Behind him, Faye's camera clicked softly, recording their search for posterity. He wondered what she saw, what she thought about the small, tight group of guys leisurely strolling up the side of the highway. Walking the scene was never a quick job, and they'd take it one foot at a time.

"Here." Ben stopped, pointing down. "Here's our origin." The burn pattern had been wide and broad when they'd started the walk a hundred yards down the highway. Now it narrowed. They'd found the point of their V, all right. That didn't surprise Evan any. Ben Cortez was one of the best in the business.

"It didn't get far." The fire should have, though, given the amount of fuel it'd had. The highway had been a natural firebreak, but there had been plenty of room for the fire to go uphill. That had him questioning the presence of the unknown firefighter again. If that man hadn't been on the scene, the fire would have been far worse.

A couple of smaller trees poked up from the edge of the burn zone, their bases scorched and blackened but their tops untouched. A handful of unburned, fallen branches on the ground confirmed the fire hadn't gotten that far. This was the start point, all right.

Evan crouched down, looking at the grasses. Most were gone, just a small sea of black char and ash. Dry grasses always burned fast, and there was nothing to learn. Instead, he focused on those places where the grasses were only half-burned. That grass had a story to tell, all right.

"You've got it," he agreed.

Behind him, Faye made a small noise of disbelief. "I see half-burned grass," she said. "What do you see?"

"Same thing. This grass didn't burn all the way. Fire's

going to start at the bottom and work its way up, right? Here, the fire didn't get the whole thing. When the base of these stalks burned, the rest of the stuff fell over, but it fell over out of the way. Fire was moving in the other direction, so this part didn't burn."

He stirred a finger gently through the ash and found himself a match head. He looked over at Ben. "Yesterday's boys may have missed one. You got the tweezers and a baggie?"

Ben and the Donovan Brothers were second string here. They all knew that. The primary on the case would do the coordinating with the state arson unit and the Forestry Commission, sharing information and cooperating in joint investigations. That was a hell of a lot of red tape for a what-if, so everyone would make sure they had their proof—he eyed the match head—before they let a private contractor like Donovan Brothers lend a hand in figuring this shit out.

It would have to *be* Donovan Brothers' shit. Which, unfortunately, was looking more and more likely.

"It really wasn't a big fire," Faye said behind him, sending a jolt of something right through him. He'd forgotten she was there.

"No. This kind of fire starts small. She can burn fast, though." Especially when some asshole was working the matches and the grass was this dry.

"We have the report from yesterday yet?" he called to Rio. He was betting the investigators had the match head's companions safely stowed in a state lab by now. Sometimes, though, they missed. So he'd make sure.

Rio sprawled in the pickup's cab, working his laptop. "Should be ready. Depends on how backed up our boys were."

"You got a good zoom on that?" He motioned Faye

over, stopping her when she got too close. She'd have a
more powerful lens than theirs. "Watch your feet now—
keep them over here. We need a picture of this."

"Match head," he said when she looked at him. She
lowered her face to the lens, and the soft click of the camera doing its thing filled up the space between them.

"That doesn't belong here." Her face came away from
the lens.

"No. This whole exercise is what-doesn't-belong."

Ben handed over the baggies and a pair of tweezers, and
Evan carefully picked up his find. One unburned head, all
nice and shiny red. Sealing the bag, he held it up to the
light, turning it around. Just your standard match from the
kind of box you used to get the barbecue going. Every
home in the area had a blue-and-red box of these matches.

"Label it and send it in," he said to Ben. "Let's see if
they've got the mates."

He pushed to his feet and headed back to his truck. He
didn't want to be sitting here, staring an ugly truth in its
face. He needed to *move*.

Rio called over from his truck. "They've got match
heads."

He knew that. *Fuck*. He knew that.

"God *damn* it." Evan's fist slammed down on the truck's
hood.

"Bad news?" *Stupid, stupid, stupid.* That was obvious,
wasn't it? Faye tried and failed to think of something else
to say. Evan was pacing up and down beside the truck. She
didn't think he lost control often, but right now he was
walking the edge. And he was a big man.

She watched and he pulled it together, the anger and
upset vanishing, as he forced his hands to relax by his sides.
He paused by the driver-side door and looked at her, shak-

ing his head. As if he didn't have all those emotions churning away inside him somewhere. "You could say that, darlin'."

His size and obvious strength made other people nervous. She'd seen the instinctive wariness others displayed around him, even at Ma's bar, the night he'd first walked into her life. People saw him and couldn't help realizing how much physical power he was packing. She couldn't help thinking, though, that he wouldn't use that power destructively. Not unless he was out of options.

Evan thought with his head, not with his hands or even his heart.

So, instead of running away from his bad mood, she asked, "You want to tell me about it?"

"Not particularly." He walked around the truck as if he hadn't just put a dent in the hood, and she followed him. She didn't like following, but she wanted more from him than a two-word answer.

"But you're going to."

"Yeah." Again with the too-brief succinctness. He opened the passenger-side door for her and waited until she got in before carefully shutting the door and heading around to his side. That old-fashioned courtesy was sweet. She wanted to think it meant something, but she didn't know. Instead, she kept her thoughts to herself, waiting while he drove out, lifting his hand to Rio as they passed his brother.

"I'm waiting," she said, when the truck picked up speed and they'd put some distance between themselves and the burn site.

Evan's voice was calm and smooth as he laid it out for her. If she hadn't seen him do a number on the hood of his truck, she'd have wondered if the afternoon's discovery meant much at all to him.

"Match head on the side of the road? It doesn't have to

mean anything, but you find a match head where you had a fire? You've got yourself probable cause. You pair that with an eyewitness who just happened to spot a fireman before anyone called in that fire? That means I've got a big fucking problem."

That last observation wasn't so calm. "Arson," she agreed.

"Looks like it," he said grimly. "I got the smoke, I got the fire."

"What happens now?"

"Now I try to find out the *who* before this happens again."

"You think this was more than a one-off?" She wondered if he would say it or if he'd try to convince her that everything was fine. That it was all under control here in Strong.

"Almost certainly. This kind of arsonist specializes in serials, and this isn't our first brush fire," he admitted. "We've been keeping our eye on the situation. What I didn't know before was that there was a fire-department presence at these fires. That's the piece you brought to the table."

She hadn't expected Evan's brutal brand of honesty, but it shouldn't have surprised her.

"This shouldn't be happening again," he said, and her head snapped right around from her contemplation of Strong's green-and-pretty. *Again?* "We already had one arsonist this summer. Lily Cortez, Jack's fiancée, had a crazed nut-job stalker who thought setting her stuff on fire was a courtship ritual. His last 'love note' burned up three hundred acres in the mountains."

She'd seen the arson mentioned in the handful of newspaper articles she'd read as background before coming out to Strong. She knew it had been bad. "You have no idea who this new arsonist is?"

"No." He glared at the road, as if somehow he could undo what had happened. "Only who he *isn't.*"

"Why is it your fault? I mean," she added hastily, when he shot her an incredulous look, "why are you acting like this is so personal? It's more work for you, and you have to clean up the mess. I get that. But isn't this just another job, when you get right down to it?"

Evan cursed. "Firefighting doesn't work like that, Faye. If these fires are an inside job, then it reflects badly on all of us. We're a team. Whatever this guy does, it hits all of us professionally and personally. Because we *should* have known. We should have stopped it."

"Right. Because you're a team of superheroes." Apparently, smoke jumping and urban firefighting had even more in common than she'd suspected. Those were the kinds of sentiments she'd come to expect from her ex-husband. It was all about the team. The boys. Hurt one, and you hurt them all.

"Jack has that new firehouse," Evan said calmly, ignoring her outburst. "He's looking into some grants and private sponsorships to really fix the place up. What do you think happens to the funding tap if it turns out one of our firefighters is running around starting fires?"

"That's not fair," she protested.

"That's how things work." He shrugged. "Fair doesn't come into it much. I think having a second arsonist in Strong won't paint Jack's project in the best possible light. Best case, the story about rehabbing a historic firehouse gets swallowed up by the more sensational story of a firefighter who is setting his own fires. It's better reading. Bolder headlines."

"So you don't want that story out there."

"I don't," he admitted, "but I'm not saying don't file it. That's not what I'm saying at all. If one of ours started these fires, I'll do what has to be done. He goes down— he doesn't get away with this. I just want to have the evidence first. I don't want guessing."

"Because you'd be flushing your brother's dream away."

"Exactly." The intense look on Evan's face made it plenty clear how he felt about keeping his brothers happy. She almost pitied the man who had started this fire and threatened Jack's dream when Evan caught up with him.

"There's not too much you brothers don't share." She eyed him speculatively. "You share women, too?"

"I wouldn't share you," he growled. He looked as if he didn't know where the words had come from, but they were out there now. He wasn't taking those words back, either. "You can count on that."

"I can't *not* tell this story, Evan. That's the truth."

"I know," he said, and she watched his hands tighten and then relax on the wheel. "I know you have to, darlin'. I'm not asking anyone to hide anything. I'm just thinking it's time to clean house—personally."

Chapter Seven

The hangar had a full house. Evan eyeballed the men streaming in. Both the jump team and the ground crew were present. He should have been proud. Donovan Brothers had assembled one hell of a team. These were some of the finest firefighters the state of California had to offer, and, before yesterday, he'd have been proud to go out into the field with any one of them at his back. Today, however, he was full of doubts—and that was all due to walking the scene yesterday where Faye had encountered the brush fire.

One of these guys was playing with matches in his spare time.

There were things a man simply didn't do. Lines that didn't get crossed, no matter how bad the provocation. If he was being honest with himself—and there was no point in not being straight up, since he'd taken to having these little conversations with himself—the betrayal bothered him almost as much as the fires themselves did. The guy who'd done this hadn't thought about his team. When the Donovan Brothers' crew went out there to take on the fires this asshole set, there was always the possibility that someone could get hurt. Badly.

So *unhappy* didn't begin to describe his conviction that the fires were an inside job.

The jumpers were a close-knit bunch, sprawled on their gear bags. The ground crew mingled some, but there were lines here, too, and those lines didn't get crossed much. The ground crew was made up mostly of hotshots. They outnumbered the jumpers about three to one. They were damned good men, and they got the job done, but they didn't jump, and like stuck to like.

Rio leaned in to Evan. "I'll take the left side. You take right." The two of them had agreed to hang back and let Jack handle the talking. Jack was the public face of Donovan Brothers, and if anyone could send a heads-up to their arsonist, it would be Jack. Rio and Evan's preferred approach was a little more hands-on and physical.

"Sounds like a plan," he said. When he looked down, his hands were balled into fists. Again. Forcing himself to relax, he sucked in a deep breath. Just because he wanted to beat the crap out of whoever it was didn't mean he would follow through on the urge. He'd learned firsthand on the streets, before he'd gotten to Strong and discovered Nonna's brand of salvation, that hitting didn't fix things.

Hitting just broke things more.

After a few minutes, Jack got up and did his thing. He kept it short and sweet. "Okay," he said. "Thank you all for coming in. I have a couple of things that need saying. You know Ben." He gestured toward the other man, who nodded. "Ben's with me on this one."

Behind him, Ben got up, looking grim. He was taking the *got-your-back* thing literally.

"We've had a pretty active fire season so far." That drew hoots and hollers from some of the assembled firefighters, the ones who hadn't picked up on Jack's tone yet. This wasn't a celebratory meet-and-greet, and Jack was plenty pissed off.

"Yeah. Some of these fires were an act of God—"

"We're the right hand of God," Mack hollered.

Jack shook his head. "You've got to look before you leap, Mack." More good-natured ribbing followed, and for a moment their meeting went right off the goddamn tracks. Before too long, however, Jack was steering them back to business.

"Last month, we had that big burn-up." There was a moment of respectful silence for that one. Jack had come about as close to dying there as you could and still walk away. He'd gone after the arsonist who'd kidnapped Lily Cortez and taken her up into the mountains, where he'd upped the stakes by setting a forest fire of epic proportions. "That blaze took our entire crew two days to extinguish, and we lost three hundred acres."

"But we got her out." Those words came from one of the firefighters at the back of the room.

"Yeah. But here's the thing. That fire shouldn't have happened. It was set. We all know the dangers of setting fires. Even controlled burns can be dangerous. Sometimes there's no predicting how fast the fuel will take or when the wind will shift." He turned to look at Ben. "You've set a few training fires in your day. You ever had one cross the line?"

Hooking his thumbs in his belt loops, Ben took a long look around the room. "No. But it's come close a time or two. And those were controlled burns with engines standing by. The minute things even looked like they might get out of hand, we had the hoses—and the fire—out. Thing is, there's nothing like a real fire to get your hands-on learning, but it's still a fire. It can surprise you—and then your shit's hitting the fan."

The room didn't stay quiet, but you didn't pack a room with firefighters and expect Carnegie Hall. The volume kicked up with a round of low curses followed by the buzz of men swapping their own war stories. Even if they hadn't been out there on the mountain with Jack that day, they'd all had close calls of their own.

"Training fires," Jack emphasized, "are run by the department only. You don't take it on yourself to run a training op, because that's a one-way ticket to trouble. That would be like taking on a house fire by yourself or doing a one-man jump from the plane. You can't be both pilot and jumper. No one can."

"Fucking true," Rio muttered.

"Maybe," Jack continued, his voice ruthlessly cutting through the buzz, "you get out of the plane and down to the ground, but now you're out a plane, because that baby's not flying by herself. Instead, she's crash-landing, and you've likely got two fires. Twice the trouble, and you're still just one guy."

"Time to start running," someone called out.

"All the way to the border," Mack added.

"Same thing goes for setting a small practice fire. Don't do it. Setting fires is not a fucking training exercise. Setting fires is not the way you deal with a case of the boreds."

Evan let his brother's words wash over him, while he scanned the faces of their team. It didn't seem likely that their boy was going to flash a blinking neon sign on his forehead, but watching felt like the thing to do. While he watched, he formulated a plan, running through a mental checklist.

Jack looked over the assembled team. "What I'm trying to say here is, if I catch any member of my team setting fires, for any reason, I'll have your ass. Then law enforcement gets what's left. Are we perfectly clear?"

Mack stood up. There was no missing the hostility in that legs-apart stance or the curled-up fists on those denim-covered thighs. "Yeah. I think we got it. There a reason we're having this little heart-to-heart?"

Jack wasn't backing down, though, matching Mack stare for stare. "I hope not, but we've had ourselves a veritable shit-storm of nuisance fires. Maybe that's an unhappy little coincidence. If it's not, and anyone thinks he's simply doing his part to make the summer fly by a little faster, I'm telling him right now that he's not. This stops now."

Mack jammed his hands into his pockets. "Got it. For the record, though, I don't start fires. You've jumped with us for years. Now we're potential screw-ups?"

Jack plowed ahead, because what did you tell a man you'd fought with in the desert and jumped from planes with? That all the times he'd pulled your ass from the fire didn't count? Didn't count enough? "You see something, you let me or Jack or Evan know. You've got concerns? Bring them to us. We clear enough?"

Mack flipped him a mock salute, and then a rumble of conversation broke out.

Jack approached his brothers as the guys streamed toward the exit, yakking it up. "You think that took?"

Rio's short laugh said it all. "When you leave, watch out for Mack. You've pissed him off. You do two military tours with a guy and then jump with him regularly, he won't appreciate an accusation of arson."

"He doesn't have to like it. I can't stand up there, though, and exempt the jump team from any hassle I'm going to hand the ground crew. That's going to go down even worse."

Fair enough. If Jack's motivational speech did the job, that was fine, but Evan wasn't holding his breath. Their problem firefighter clearly didn't listen to the do's and don'ts, or he wouldn't have been lighting up Strong. So, no, he didn't expect a group heart-to-heart to fix things here.

And, fix it or not, the bottom line was, Donovan

Brothers had a zero-tolerance policy on this kind of shit. You saw it, you called it out. Keeping your mouth shut was all kinds of wrong. Evan's job was to keep his team safe. If the fire setter continued down this path, someone was going to get hurt. So he needed a name, and he needed enough evidence for prosecution. The fire setter would make a move eventually, and Evan would be waiting for him.

Jack dropped onto the seat beside him. "Faye Duncan is here as a photojournalist. No matter where she spends the night, she has a job to do. We need time to investigate, and yet here she is, ready and willing to tell the world anything and everything she knows right now."

Jack didn't have to say more in the awkward pause that followed. Journalists tended to lock on to whatever story seemed most newsworthy, and even just the possibility of a serial arsonist was Christmas come early. Jack knew— they all knew—she'd want to unwrap that present.

"I have a plan," Evan offered. And he hoped that that plan sounded smarter than it felt right now.

"Let's hear it."

"Faye's willing to hold off on submitting her photos. A temporary pause," he added. "For two weeks."

Jack whistled. "How'd you convince her to wait?"

Evan met his brother's eyes and tried not to think about exactly how he'd bargained for time. He'd done what he needed to do. That was all. The firehouse meant the world to Jack. It was a dream and a challenge and maybe the first place, other than in Lily Cortez's arms, that his brother had truly belonged. So Evan wasn't letting any firefighter with the arson bug do his brother out of his dream. That simply wasn't happening on Evan's watch. Instead, he eyed the last few men trailing out of the hangar before he spoke. "She and I have an understanding."

"Is that code for something?" Rio's wicked grin said it all. "Because if it is, you let me know how I can help. Okay?"

Unfortunately, it was all too easy to imagine Rio with Faye. Hell, Rio would be a good match for her. He liked to laugh, and he lived for adventure. She could do far worse than his brother. Evan hated the idea.

"We're going to show her a fun time," he said. "Real fun. Tomorrow we have a training jump scheduled for the team—I'll pick her up and take her with us. Keep her so busy, she won't have time to be working."

The plane shuddered around Faye, and the pilot banked hard, coming around for a closer look at the mountains east of Strong. Her ass was planted on the floor because the Donovans' crew had ripped the seats out to make room for more gear, and she was currently 7,500 feet above ground.

She was crazy.

She curled her fingers into the webbing hanging from the side of the plane. The straps seemed secure enough, but who really knew? Maybe she needed to rethink her definition of adventure, because this felt dangerous as hell.

"We're running some practice jumps today," Evan had explained when she'd answered the knock on the firehouse door that morning. He'd braced one hand on the side of the door and looked down at her. "You want to come along and jump? Let me keep my end of our bargain?"

"Excuse me?"

"Jump," he'd repeated patiently. "You said you wanted adventure. I'm asking if you want to jump today."

"I don't know how." The thought of jumping, though, had that secret thrill snaking through her belly in an almost sensual jolt, part adrenaline and part anticipation. This was what she wanted, what she needed.

"No problem." He shrugged. "You can jump with me. Tandem."

She recognized opportunity when it came knocking— and right now opportunity was hammering on the door. So why not? "You promise this isn't an excuse to throw me out of the plane?"

"Promise," he drawled. "I'll be with you all the way down."

He'd offered, she'd accepted, and now, two hours later, here she was.

Having some serious second thoughts.

How could someone as large as Evan jump, anyhow, and not plummet like a rock? She'd asked him that very question as they'd walked out to the plane, and he'd told her he was right at the maximum weight for a jumper. He ran daily to stay lean and to keep his weight at the magic two hundred. The day his weight nudged over that number was the last day he jumped.

From her point of view, following his fine ass as he inched over to the doorway, Evan Donovan was six feet two inches of pure brawn. Watching those confident hands checking straps and buckles, she felt *safe*, and that was even crazier, because she was five minutes away from letting him throw her ass out of a plane. She barely knew him, and that was only partly because he didn't make getting-to-know-you easy.

"We're coming around," the pilot hollered, and the spotter waved Evan over. Clipping his safety harness to the webbing by the door, Evan leaned out for a closer look. Whatever he saw worked for him, because he took a couple of steps backward and gestured for her to join him.

Oh, God. This was crazy.

She cursed and went, sliding her feet over the vibrating floor of the plane. *Not my best idea.* It got worse, too, when she got her first look at the mountains underneath them and the small dot that was Strong. The wind roared like a freight train through the empty space where the door should have been, and that absence struck her as all wrong. The spotter was flat on his belly, inching forward for a closer look at that empty blue. Mack. She'd been introduced to him yesterday and the pilot, Spotted Dick, who was nothing more than a helmet and a pair of broad, uniformed shoulders right now. The other jumpers sitting on the floor waiting for their turn to go out the door probably should have been familiar faces, too, but right now her head couldn't get past the freak-out factor here. She was *jumping.*

"You still good?" Mack yelled over the noise.

"She's good." Evan held out a gloved hand. "Aren't you, darlin'?"

"'Cause we've got ourselves a betting pool on whether or not she clears the door." A quick smile flashed over the other man's face. "I'm hoping she makes me some money."

Evan didn't look once at Mack. Instead, he kept his eyes on her, as if he knew what she was thinking. Maybe if she waffled long enough, he'd tell her everything was going to be fine. That they'd work out an exit plan that *didn't* involve jumping into empty space four thousand feet above the ground.

Evan simply watched her, but she saw the satisfaction in his eyes. He thought she had this. "If she's got nerves, she'll work through them. Everyone thinks twice before going out that door the first time. That's what makes us smart."

He wiggled his fingers. That had to be her cue. Adventure was suddenly a whole lot more real—and higher— than she'd anticipated. Screw it. She wasn't a passenger here. She'd come up to jump, so she'd jump. Before she could chicken out, she put her hand in his, and his fingers closed around hers. She swore she saw sparks.

"How many times have you done this?"

"I've got over a thousand jumps, darlin'. I haven't lost anyone yet."

"Hung up a time or two." Mack laughed.

"And I've got my backup plan right here." Evan patted his leg, where a big-ass blade was strapped. "We land in a tree down there, we're going to do fine."

"As long as you watch out for the splinters." Mack mimed plucking splinters from his posterior.

The plane straightened out, dropping lower. Evan's hands got busy pulling her closer, until her back hit his chest. With a quick, practiced gesture, he snapped their harnesses together, and there was no going back. She was latched on to him and he to her, so where one went, the other went. The harness had her butt glued to his groin, and despite the thick flight suits they both wore, she'd swear she felt heat. Lust and nerves had something in her belly doing a hot, prickly dance of awareness.

His hands tugged her goggles down over her eyes. "This is going to be fun," he promised.

"That's what I'm counting on." That, and not dying when they landed.

All too soon, they were in the doorway, his arms braced on either side. Mack was counting down, Evan echoing his numbers. The sharp slap of the spotter's hand on Evan's arm jolted through her. Before she could scream, Evan had launched them out the door: 120 miles an hour toward the ground. For a moment, she forgot how to breathe, the air ripping past her nose and mouth before she could suck it in. *Oh, God.* Then the drogue chute snapped out behind them, exactly like he'd promised it would. The drop slowed some, but they were still rushing through the air.

She opened her mouth and finally remembered how to breathe. Air choked her, cold and rough, and she clutched the straps, equal parts fear and elation riding her hard. Except the solid, reassuring weight of the man behind her said it was okay to be elated. This wasn't going to end badly. When she looked up, the plane was moving away from the jump site in a long, lazy loop. Beneath them, the ground rushed up in dizzying circles.

There were words pouring from her mouth, she realized dimly. Some curses, some *ohmygods*, and other stuff she didn't recognize. As if her brain wanted to record the free fall and didn't know how. She was talking, talking, talking as they fell until finally Evan growled, all rough-tender, into her ear, "Faye?"

"Yeah?"

"Shut up, darlin'. Enjoy the ride."

She shut up.

Because he was right, damn him. This was one hell of a ride, and, right at that moment, she *got* why he did this. Never mind that he was usually landing boots-first in a fire of titanic proportions, or that as soon as he hit ground, he was fighting to survive. This incredible, delicious, free fall through the air was worth it.

"Jump thousand," he said seconds later, feeding her the smoke jumper's chant. The wind tore past them, swallowing up his words. The ground was so far beneath them, rushing toward them impossibly fast. Evan had her. She knew that. So she curled her fingers around the harness and held on the way he was holding on to her. Real tight.

"Look thousand," Evan commanded. Yeah. She heard him, and she looked and nearly had a heart attack. Then she couldn't stop looking. Strong and the mountains below were beautiful in a crazy way. The landscape was approaching so fast and out of whack, but those were patches of tree and field. Familiar and yet not. She'd flown any number of times in planes, but now there was literally nothing but air between her and the ground below. Everything could go wrong, and then she'd land too hard, hit too fast. Evan's name squeaked out of her tight lips.

"Reach thousand." His voice was controlled. In charge. Evan Donovan had her back, literally. "You're doing fine, darlin'," he promised. "We're halfway there, and you're doing great."

"Oh, my God." She wasn't going to win any prizes for best speech delivered two thousand feet in the air, but what else could she say?

"We're going to touch down real soon. You okay?" He put her hand on the cord even as he spoke. "You've got this. Count three and pull."

She counted, pulled hard, and, like clockwork, the main chute deployed in a hard snap up and then down. Pride filled her. She'd done it.

"You did good," he said roughly. "Just like I said. Almost there."

All of a sudden she wasn't ready for the jump to end, but they were coming down fast, the last few hundred yards a blur of speed as the wind pushed them left and then right and the ground swung around to meet them. Evan's jump had them over the center of a big empty meadow, home free and clear.

"No trees," she whispered.

"No. We're good. I'm aiming for the grass," he said, and then added, "Get your feet up, Faye."

Like they'd practiced before they'd gone up, she yanked her feet up and out, giving him a clear path. The ground was almost there, *there*. The hard shock of Evan's steel-toes touching down reverberated through her body. Evan still had his arms up, working the toggles, and he ran into the landing. He got the run under control and sank to his knees, pulling her up and back against his chest.

"Oh, my God." The yell peeled away from her lips because she couldn't stop it. Rio sauntered toward them, his
fist pumping toward the sky, an answering yell coming
from his own mouth.

Quick and hard, Evan's finger tipped her head up and
back. Her head hit his shoulder, and his mouth came
down on hers, the contact awkward and raw and delicious. Right at that moment there was only the two of
them, kneeling together in this unfamiliar meadow, while
the plane pulled away overhead and the other jumpers
hung in the sky. His mouth tasted every bit as wild as the
ride down. Rough and male, the sweet, hard pressure of
that mouth opened her up.

God, he tasted so good. She didn't want to close her
eyes—she wanted to see his face, fierce and intense, as he
kissed her and the sky filled up with jumpers landing
around them. The erotic heat of his kiss was burning her
up, his mouth moving, taking hers. She loved the sensation of being connected to him there, too, and not only by
the harness that held her to his chest.

So good.

She kissed him back, her tongue tangling with his.
Their tandem harness made the position awkward, and on
this field, she was vulnerable. Exposed for the whole world
to see, and yet she wanted the moment to go on and on.
He must have felt the same way, because he tugged off his
gloves and tangled his fingers in her hair, angling her head
back farther. *Yes.*

"You like that?" he asked when he finally stopped, and
she had no idea whether he meant his kiss or the jump.
She wanted both.

"God, yes. Let's do it again."

"We'll make a jumper of her yet." Rio dropped down
beside them. He'd seen that kiss. She didn't care. His hands
worked the buckles, releasing her from the harness and

Evan. Pulling her upright. She was riding high on the adrenaline rush of the landing, impossibly aware of herself and Evan. A handful of minutes strapped to his chest and then the landing. Those big arms tucking her firmly into the curve of his body as he took the impact of hitting the ground for both of them.

All she'd had to do was hang on and enjoy.

More. She wanted more. More adventure, more Evan. Adventuring with him was deliciously wicked—and precisely the adrenaline rush she'd been looking for. Falling through the air, wrapped up in his arms, she'd *known* she was living her life and not merely documenting the lives of other people.

He was a good choice. Evan Donovan was a big, tough bear of a man and a former Marine, she'd learned. She'd bet he was always first in, last out at a fire. Protect and defend—that was his motto. His rules would be real simple. You came home alive, you'd done just fine. This was a man who was all aim and shoot and so very, very rough around the edges—but looking at him, watching him defend Strong with everything he had, there was no way she could stop the erotic fantasies teasing her senses. This man would keep her safe every time, everywhere—and yet he was one of the boys of summer, and he damn sure wasn't happily-ever-after material.

Evan Donovan was happy-right-now material.

Chapter Eight

Evan hadn't meant to kiss Faye. Hell, kissing was *not* what a jump instructor did. It was unprofessional. It sent the wrong message to anyone watching. But nothing so wrong had ever felt so good or so right. He'd kissed her once and then twice, and all he could think was that the third time would be the charm.

Rio had brought her camera to the landing site, and she'd gleefully snatched it from him, snapping shots of the boys coming down around them. This was a job for her. He was merely the means to her end, and that was okay, too, because he needed something from her, and it wasn't sex, no matter how much his unruly erection wanted things to be otherwise.

Instead, he evaluated the rest of the team on their practice run. Most of the day's jumpers hit the meadow free and clear, but Joey had almost hung up on a stand of ponderosa on the far side of the clearing. The wind had shifted suddenly on him, and there hadn't been much the guy could do but steer hard and curse louder. He'd missed the trees but hit the pond. Evan would take soggy over splinters any day.

From the outside, the day's jumps were fun and games, but no one said work had to be all solemn and sober. It certainly wasn't a game when they went out the door and hit the air. They all knew that. He wondered, however, if Faye did.

Or if she only saw the adrenaline rush and the adventure of it all.

As Spotted Dick brought the plane around and lined her up with the runway, Faye turned away and headed back toward the hangar on the other side of the meadow. Her cheeks were pink with excitement, and her eyes sparkled with the same emotion, so he figured he'd kept his end of their deal so far. He'd given her that adventure she craved so badly. He hadn't been sure, when he'd gotten her up there and by the edge of the open doorway, if she'd actually go through with the jump. And that would have been okay, too. Plenty of guys got up there and decided that jumping was a big no-thanks for them.

And then she'd put her hand in his and let him take her out the door. He'd jumped with her, and his reward had been the feel of her against him all the way down and through the tuck and roll. Jumping with her had been sexy as hell, and the only thought in his head had been how he wanted to see her naked, all stripped down and bare. Then he'd hit the ground and come up with her laughing on his chest—demanding he take her right on up again.

Faye Duncan was game.

He had to admire that about her.

"You coming?" she yelled over at him, and damned if she wasn't waiting for him. She'd declined a spare set of steel-toes and had kept her own running shoes, but she was swimming in the canvas jumpsuit the smallest member of the team usually wore. Her goggles were shoved back on her head, and that pretty honey-brown hair of hers was all spiked up around her face. She was a delicious, windblown mess.

"We're done here, right?" She looked around the clearing, but the other guys were headed back in, and Spotted Dick was bringing the plane in. On the other side of the meadow, the wheels hit the runway, and the roar of the engine backing off filled the air. Game over.

"Yeah," he said. "We're done here. Let's go on in."

"Okay." She fell into step beside him, and he slowed up some because she was almost waddling in that suit. Her rueful grin said she knew it, too. It was good that she could laugh at herself. She wanted to live in the moment and he could understand that, too. Sometimes it wasn't a good idea to look too far behind you—or too far forward.

"So now what?" She capped her lens and shouldered the camera.

That was the question, wasn't it? He needed to decide where he was taking this thing between them and then see if she wanted to come along for that ride, too. And this was undoubtedly the right moment to tell her about Mike. She'd have something to say about her ex's request that Evan keep an eye on her. He was no expert on how women thought, but he knew that much. If he told her, though, she'd pull back on him. There wouldn't be this companionable walk to the hangar.

And he wanted this walk.

"I need to know something. You got someone waiting for you back in L.A.?" He wanted to hear what she'd say. Maybe she was done with Mike Thomas. Maybe she wasn't. Either way, he suddenly needed to know.

Because he'd kissed her. Again.

And she'd kissed him back.

Christ. This was not supposed to be happening. And yet . . . he'd gotten his mouth on hers, and he'd stopped thinking. All he could do was hang on and feel. All his plans had gone right on out the window when he'd started kissing Faye Duncan. And, of course, he had no idea if she felt the same way. She clearly didn't mind his lips on hers, but that didn't mean she wanted him back in bed with her.

She shook her head ruefully. "Evan, you tucked me into your bed for a night, and *now* you're asking me that question?"

"Do you?" he repeated.

"No." She opened her mouth, then closed it. His erection said that that half-assed answer would have to be good enough.

"I put you in that bed because you needed somewhere to sleep. If you have someone back home, he should trust you. He shouldn't be asking questions about what you do or don't do when you're away from him."

"You don't think he'd care what I did?" She tossed the words behind her as she crossed the empty floor of the hangar. A muted roar of noise from the guys packing it up leaked out of the locker room. Done training for the day, his team would strip off their gear, head back out to the cabins, and relax until the next call came in. That was their summer. That was what it took to get the job done.

"I think he'd care lots, darlin'," he growled. "That's not what I said at all. I said he should be *trusting* you. You want someone playing twenty questions with you every time you're out of his sight?"

She pulled down the zipper on her jumpsuit. Logically, he knew she had to take the suit off. Needed to return it. Still, it felt like she was undressing for him in an erotic prelude to something really, really good.

He definitely shouldn't have kissed her.

Christ, that kiss was going to haunt him longer than he could afford. The soft rub of her lips against his after she'd opened up and let him do whatever he wanted to her mouth—right before she'd kissed him back. The bulky fabric of the jumpsuit parted over her breasts. And he couldn't stop watching, following the path of those fingers. She didn't know what she did to him.

"I just got divorced, Evan. No one's waiting for me back in L.A., with or without twenty questions. Right now, what I want is some fun. I want to live a little." She shot him a grin. "Live a lot. Whichever opportunity comes up first."

He should take her back to the firehouse. His truck was right outside the hangar, and he could have her back there in under ten. He could give her the lowdown on some of the other adventurous possibilities he'd come up with, and she'd see he knew exactly how to hold up his end of their bargain.

She pulled the camera off her shoulder, then paused, flipping through the pictures she'd gotten as if she couldn't wait to see. He'd bet she was the kind of person who poked her Christmas presents. "My editor is going to love these. In two weeks," she added hastily.

He nodded. He didn't need the reminder, not right now, when his head was trying to figure out a way to take their deal to a whole new level.

"You ever take a gamble, Evan? Play some poker? Spend a weekend in Vegas?"

"I'm not much for gambling." He leaned against the wall, arms crossed over his chest. *God.* He could watch her for hours. There was plenty of mischief in her eyes right now. He wasn't sure where she was taking this conversation, but damned if he wanted it to end. So he'd feed her the next line. "I like a sure thing. Facts. Two and two adding up to four."

He heard her little hum, but then the jumpsuit pooled around her ankles, and she was stepping out of it, all long, golden legs. She bent over to pick up the jumpsuit, and he about jumped out of his skin. His hands itched to reach out and pull her back toward him. She was flat-out beautiful, his golden girl of summer.

She wasn't done playing twenty questions, however. "You ever want to have an adventure, take a chance?"

"Sure," he growled, because right now he was willing to risk everything on the chance that she'd take him into her bed. There was a little click, metal hanger meeting rod, and she stowed the borrowed suit back inside the locker where it belonged. Which left her standing there almost naked, as far as he was concerned, because those short-shorts of hers barely covered her ass. No way he could keep his gaze where it belonged when she showed him all that warm, bare skin.

"You think I'm pretty." The way she examined his face while she said that absolutely ridiculous, impossible-to-deny truth said she wasn't sure what to think about it. Then she smiled. As if her head had decided it was okay for him to look at her. "That's good," she continued.

"Facts are facts." He didn't know who had convinced her she wasn't pretty, but the urge to hit someone was waking up fast.

"You're sweet." Now she sounded delighted. "Evan Donovan, you have a soft spot."

He had several. He simply didn't advertise them. It was hard enough running security for Donovan Brothers. He took mavericks and molded them into a team, convinced them that, yes, there were a few rules meant to be followed. Maybe a man didn't care much about keeping himself safe, but his team was a whole different story. The team came first, and the team stayed safe. Those were his rules, and he made sure no one broke them. His face and his size helped convince the jumpers to eat that serving of tough love, and being nice was a liability.

"Keep it to yourself," he suggested.

"Keeping secrets?" she asked lightly.

She had no idea.

"Where does that go?" She nodded toward a utilitarian set of metal stairs.

"Loft. We rig the chutes up there."

She looked him over, and damned if he knew what was going on in that head of hers. "That works for me." She took two steps toward those stairs, and right when he started to wonder what she was doing, she turned and held out her hand to him. "Well," she said, "are you coming or not?"

That was a kicker. He stood there like an idiot and stared at her.

"Let's go on up there, and I'll kiss you some more."

She didn't wait for him to figure it out, just danced up the stairs ahead of him, all laughter and tease. He was definitely in foreign territory now. Hell. When had this happened to him? He scared the shit out of most of the world. He knew it. And yet she clearly wanted more of him, and his plans for a careful seduction flew right on out the goddamn window.

Because *she* was seducing *him.*

He scaled that stairway like it was a two-hundred-foot ponderosa and he had to get to the top because he had a fire licking his ass. Women chased Rio. They chased Jack. Him? They gave him a wide berth. He hit the loft, and there she was, waiting for him, her back to the wall, watching him come. He knew he should say something. This wasn't the right moment to keep his mouth shut, but, holy hell, what could he say to her? Other than *please?*

"Faye—" He got her name out, but, God, that name didn't do her justice.

"Shh." Leaning forward, she slipped her palm over his mouth. "There's nothing to talk about, Evan. Just shut up and enjoy the ride."

She gave him back his words, and then damned if she didn't kiss him, exactly like she'd promised.

She reached up, sliding her arms around his neck and tugging his head down to hers. Yeah. That was good. She got her mouth on his, and that was even better. She was soft where he was hard. The sexy little rubbing thing she was doing had him growling. *God.* He fisted his hands by his sides because he didn't want to spoil this or scare her off. Then her tongue darted out and licked the closed seam of his lips, and that was it. He got his hands on her waist, lifting her up against the wall and his body. He was on fire, and burning had never felt so good. Her mouth devoured him, her sweet hunger feeding his own.

She was so goddamn perfect, and he didn't want this kiss to end.

When she finally pulled back, however, he reluctantly let her go. Because, despite the space she'd put between them, the look in her eyes said she wasn't done with him. The hoarse sough of their breathing filled up the silence, and somewhere, distantly, he heard guys leaving. The jump team was wrapping up until the next call, all done, even though here he and Faye were, just getting started. She pushed him down onto the pile of packed chutes, and he went. He suspected she could have shoved him right out of the loft, and he'd have enjoyed the fall.

This was faster and harder and far naughtier than he'd expected. Or dreamed, if he was being honest with himself. His angel had a wicked streak. Damn, she was a fantasy come to life, and if she needed to be the one in control, well, he was more than willing to give her exactly what she needed. He didn't know what had happened to her before she'd come on out here to Strong, but something had. She was a woman with something to prove. And he was the lucky man who got to prove it.

Then he stopped thinking. All he could do was hang on and feel.

Her hands went to work, undoing his jumpsuit and sliding the heavy fabric out of the way. His boxers went next, and he heard his own rough growl of appreciation when she found his bare skin.

"Oh, damn, Evan," she whispered throatily, reaching out to wrap a palm around him. "You're going to be so good."

God, he hoped so. The soft touch of those fingers gripping him, tugging him toward her, had him growing harder and longer, his erection begging for more of her. She sank to her knees between his parted legs, her hand letting go of him to skim gently, teasingly, up his inner thighs.

"But I'm not going to be good at all," she promised. Her lips followed her hands, drawing his balls into her mouth and tugging gently downward. He groaned, and heat exploded through him. The pleasure was fast and hot, and he'd never expected this, never dreamed she'd want him like this. Her hands made the return trip up his thighs, massaging the sensitive area between his balls and his ass.

"Faye," he bit out, the pleasure making his hips rise toward her in silent demand. He wanted to make love to her, give her the same kind of pleasure she was giving him, but he wasn't going to be able to hold on for long. Not the way she was touching him.

She lifted her head. "I told you I was going to be bad, Evan."

"Darlin'," he groaned, "you have no idea."

With a little smile, she wrapped her hands around his shaft, her small hands fisting him as she stroked downward. Then back up again, in a torturous, agonizingly delicious return journey until her mouth met her fingers and slipped down over the head of him. Her tongue traced a damp, hot path, and he bit back a yell. He was wet, from her and from him, and the wicked look on her face promised more. Much more.

"Faye," he gritted out, the sensual exploration of her mouth making his fists clench. Instead of answering, her tongue worked around the head of his erection. Her hands cupped and massaged his balls while her tongue licked and licked. Tasting him in a wicked, heated glide as her hands gently squeezed his shaft.

When she increased the pressure, he about came out of his skin. His hands tangled in her hair, holding her still as he fucked her mouth in long, slow strokes.

And she let him.

Christ, that visual of her mouth, wet from their kisses and from him, opening up to take him, was enough to send him over the edge. Then she looked him straight in the eye, and that was another erotic broadside he hadn't expected.

"Do you like what I'm doing?" she whispered, lifting her mouth away from him. He loved that husky voice. Faye had the face of an angel, but her hands were pure wickedness. Hell, yeah, he liked this, but he had no idea *why* she was going down on him. Right now, he didn't care, either. He wanted more Faye and whatever she would give him.

"Keep this up, darlin', and you're going to find out how *much* I like you."

"Oh, good." The smile she flashed him was pure mischief. Taking a step backward, she shimmied out of her clothes. His first sight of her naked was something else again. The sun-kissed skin of those long legs sent another jolt of heat through him. She'd worn a bikini this summer and had the tan lines to prove it. Some primal part of him loved knowing he was seeing a side of her that had been all covered up. He got to see what she'd kept hidden from everyone else.

He hadn't touched anyone like this in a long, long time. That soft patch of dark hair between her thighs was pure temptation. He wanted to sift his fingers through those curls. She was so very pretty there. Yeah, he wanted to look, to touch her where she was soft and wet, but she was also deliciously impatient, and she had plans of her own.

Before he could do more than look, she'd pushed him back onto the pile of chutes and seated herself on his lap, her hands guiding his penis through her saturated folds. Right up to her clit. *Christ.* She got the tip of him against the very tip of her, head to head. A sense of connection unfolded in him. This was raw and intimate and about the two of them. His hips jerked, driving him against her as she used him, like a personal toy, stroking him against herself.

Christ, yes. She was talking, too, whispering words of praise. She made him feel beautiful, cared for. Two things, he realized, he hadn't known he needed or wanted.

Outside the hangar, a car door slammed. Two familiar feminine voices, calling greetings—right before they stepped inside. *Damn.*

"Their timing sucks," he groaned. He pulled away, grabbing for his clothes. He knew those voices. That was Nonna, and she'd brought Lily with her. He'd have to go back down those stairs and see what they wanted. When all he wanted to do was finish what Faye had started here. He was iron hard, so, yeah, there was no hiding the evidence of his arousal.

Maybe he could conduct business from up here until he cooled off some.

Shaking her head, Faye moved away from him, and, God, he loved that her legs were trembling. She'd been so close, too. She'd been right there with him, right on the edge of something hot and wild and unbelievable. She licked those swollen, wet lips, and he knew he'd see that mouth of hers in his dreams. He was sure of it.

"You're expecting visitors?"

He flashed a rueful grin. "No. I'd have been putting up caution tape and keep-out signs if I'd known what you had in mind for us."

"Maybe they'll go away?" she asked hopefully, but he knew better.

Footsteps crossed the hangar floor, and Nonna called his name again. She knew he was in here, and he got the feeling she knew *exactly* what he and Faye had been up to. Hell, it was almost like being back in high school, except Evan had never been irresponsible. Rio had been the one Nonna had busted. Repeatedly.

"Evan?" The laughing exasperation was plenty clear in Nonna's voice. Five seconds more and she'd be up the stairs and in the loft with them. "Where are you?"

"Come out, come out, wherever you are," Lily sang. She sounded damn cheerful.

"Up here," he called, and he moved to the edge of the loft. He was as decent as he was going to get for a while.

When he leaned against the edge of the loft and looked down, however, it was plenty clear that Lily hadn't connected two and two. The chagrined look on her face said she'd have given the hangar the widest possible berth if she'd known he and Faye were there.

"Sandwich delivery," Lily offered weakly, but Nonna didn't even bother with the excuse. He wasn't surprised to see them, not really. Nonna knew—hell, the entire town knew—he'd taken an interest in Faye Duncan. Nonna didn't know about the possible arsonist in the department's midst, so all she saw was the girl her son was after. He could spin it any way he wanted, but that was the reality. Faye interested him, and he'd made it clear that he intended to do something about that interest.

Maybe he should make things easier for Nonna. Take Faye home for dinner.

Of course, it wouldn't be as much fun that way. Truth was, he'd always loved to tease his Nonna. And it wasn't as if he'd produced a ring and dropped to one knee, after all. He'd had lovers before, and he certainly hadn't brought them all to Nonna's house for casserole and salad.

"We'll be right down," Faye called. She didn't want anyone else up there, either, and he liked that. Suddenly, this loft was theirs. He didn't want to share it, not even with his family. Beneath her breath, Faye muttered a short curse that was shockingly graphic, coming from that pretty mouth of hers. He still couldn't believe what she'd done to him or the gift of that dazzling sensuality.

This woman was dangerous.

Faye flew down those stairs as if her ass were on fire.

Nonna watched her, a knowing twinkle in her eye. Not wanting to face that music just yet, Evan grabbed his used canopy and started working.

His gut said he'd be going up again soon, and he preferred jumping with his own chute. Safety regs said you did your chute yourself, or a certified packer did. Since the only other people he trusted to pack his chute were his brothers, he packed for himself. The hangar smelled like rubber and nylon, all gear with a whiff of wood smoke and grease. Like a well-packed chute, that was a familiar scent, one that said all was right with his world.

Plus, he was ringside for whatever conversation Lily and

Nonna were about to lay on Faye. Double bonus right there. Faye was talking before she hit the bottom of the stairs.

"Evan is helping me with my story." The excuse clearly shot out of her mouth before she could bite back the words. She didn't need to excuse herself. They were both adults here. He was free, and so was she.

The little smile on Lily's face said she knew exactly how Evan had been "helping." When she spoke, however, her words were carefully chosen. "He's good that way. You get what you need?"

Faye's feet cleared the stairs and hit the floor, but she wasn't even trying to hold back the laughter in her voice. They knew. And, no matter how frustrating the situation was, it was also funny. "Not yet. You have a few minutes?"

"Sure." Lily put down the large bag of paper-wrapped sandwiches she was carrying. So that part had been true enough. They had brought lunch. "What can I do for you?"

"I'm doing a piece on the fire house renovation for a magazine," she explained, "and I want to include something in the captions from the people who are involved as friends and family. You all know the firefighters best. I thought you could tell me about what the firehouse means to you."

Lily looked over at Nonna. "You want to start?"

Nonna had stories, all right. Only question was, where would she choose to start? While Evan waited for her opening salvo, he folded the canopy he'd used to bring down Faye. No creases. Nice and smooth, all straight lines and ready to go. This chute would come right out the next time he pulled the cord, and he'd fly down nice and safe.

"You want me to tell you about raising three boys to be firefighters?" Nonna's laugh was a happy bark of sound. "Sure. I can do that, but you might want to take a seat. That isn't a fast-food order you put in."

"Whatever you want to share, I'd love to hear." Faye sounded like she meant it, too. Maybe it was professional curiosity, or maybe it was something else, because he didn't see a recorder or a pen and pad in her hands, but she marched right after Nonna. She was done with him and with the loft.

For now.

Because he already knew he'd be doing his level best to coax her back into his arms as soon as their unexpected company had the good sense to leave. Unfortunately, if Nonna was in a storytelling kind of a mood, he might be waiting a while. A really *long* while.

The three women headed for the door and outside. Evan wanted to follow, as if there were a damn string connecting Faye to him. She went, he went. It didn't make any sense, this need he had to be near her. He wanted to hear what she had to say about the firefighters, too—and he damn sure wasn't waiting until she'd stuck her material into a magazine.

Fortunately, his seat on the loft's floor also gave him a clear line down and out the door. He could pack chutes and eavesdrop. It wasn't nice of him, but he'd take what he could get. As soon as the women got outside, Lily and Nonna dropped their bags onto a wooden picnic table and started pulling out sandwiches. From the look of the piles, the guys merited both variety and a step up from PB&J today.

"You've lived up here in Strong for years, right?" Faye looked at Nonna, who nodded. That was a softball question. After the canopy was folded, he checked the lines, straightening them. Lines had to be good and tight. One

twist, one overlooked kink, and he'd hit the ground drag-
ging the equivalent of a bedsheet behind him.

"I've been here thirty-five years now."

"And Jack, Evan, and Rio—they've been fighting fires
for how long?"

A familiar little smile played on Nonna's face, her fingers moving over the sandwiches the way his own worked
the buckles on the chute. This was one of her favorite stories, and she loved telling it. "They joined me when they
were ten. Almost from the first day, they were fascinated
by that firehouse. They'd hang around and pelt Ben with
their questions. If the fire was small enough, he'd even let
them ride out on the truck. It was a different world then.
We weren't worried about lawsuits and liability. Ben was
real good to my boys, and they needed to see a man who
did things right."

Faye hesitated, then plunged in. He'd have told her
anything she asked, but she clearly saw an opportunity
here to ask her questions, and he kind of liked her curiosity. She wanted to know about him and his brothers.
That wasn't a bad thing. "You adopted the three of
them?"

Nonna nodded. "Eventually. As soon as I could, in fact.
They came to me as fosters, though, so at first I was afraid
someone would show up and take them away from me
again. A foster parent has to be able to let go, and I knew
almost at once that I wasn't ever going to be able to do
that." She stepped back and eyed the mountain of sandwiches critically. "Those boys get right under your skin
and into your heart."

"And you didn't mind their riding out on the fire truck?
Or that they grew up to be firefighters themselves?"

"There's no *mind* about it. Those boys scared me half to
death every time they walked out the door. They were
doing the right thing, though, and boys need to grow up.

I knew Ben would look out for them, best he could, and they needed to go."

"And now?" Faye asked. "Now they're all grown up and they're going places where they're not safe, and they're spending most of their time away from you."

"Not so far away," Nonna said. "I'm right here, aren't I?

"Yes." Faye didn't sound convinced. She waved a hand toward the hangar. "You don't feel out of place up here?"

"Because this hangar is brimful of men and testosterone?" Nonna laughed. "Honey, those men need to know someone is looking out for them. I don't want to jump, and I'm not digging line with them. Sometimes sandwiches are enough, and sometimes they're not, but I'm always here. They know that."

Faye looked over at Lily. Evan's brother's fiancée hadn't jumped in yet. Evan figured that if anyone had a good handle on what it was like, living day in and day out with a jumper, Lily Cortez was that woman. His brother was a lucky man, having her by his side. Jack had told him once that Lily hadn't been sure about living with and loving a jumper, but she seemed to have embraced her fate with both hands. The two of them were talking about a late-summer wedding date.

"You and Jack are engaged," Faye said, and Lily nodded. "We are."

"And you don't mind when he goes out on a call? When he leaves you behind to go out there and jump?"

"It's not my favorite thing," Lily admitted. "But it's what he does. He's good at it, Faye. Really, really good. I know he'll stay as safe as he can, and someone needs to do it. He thinks it has to be him."

Yes. The Donovan Brothers were the best, Evan silently acknowledged. He straightened the lines and folded the chute's tail up with military precision. His chute would open up, nice and symmetrical, next time he jumped.

"Still," Faye pressed, "it can't be easy, loving a smoke jumper." He could almost hear the list of downsides running through her head.

He tucked the last fold and gave the whole package a once-over while Lily hesitated but finally handed Faye an answer. "I don't like thinking about him coming home hurt, or not at all, no. That's not an easy thing."

"So Jack still jumps every chance he gets?" Faye sounded as if maybe she'd been hoping the engagement would convince his brother to ease up on his jump schedule some. He could have told her that Jack would never quit while they needed him. He'd jump, and he'd fight fires until the day he was too old and too broken to do it anymore. That's what any Donovan would do.

"They don't stop, ever." Nonna's quiet murmur was almost swallowed up by the crinkle of paper. "Question is, honey, are you asking because you're doing a story for a magazine—or because you're wondering what it would be like to be with a man like that?"

"Busted." Faye laughed, and that husky sound made him want to go right down those stairs and take her back into his arms. He'd kiss her again, and they'd pick up where they'd left off. It would be good, too.

Nonna's soft hum of amusement said his mother approved. "You and Evan do seem to have hit it off."

"He's a good man."

"Are you seeing him?" Lily was more forthright. Maybe Jack had already given her an earful, or maybe she was tired of the whole beating-around-the-bush thing. She was asking straight out. Too bad he didn't know the answer himself.

"No." Faye's quick shake of her head said it all. "I think you're both misunderstanding this," she said apologetically.

Well, hell. He looked down at the nice, neat package he had all ready to slip inside the D-Bag. Suddenly he was a whole lot less interested in getting the chute inside the deployment bag.

"We aren't dating," Faye continued. "Evan offered to show me around, give me a feel for smoke jumping and Strong."

His Faye was a sweet little liar. That was okay, though, because he didn't want all their private details paraded past Nonna and Lily. And *fuck*. How had he come to have *private* feelings about Faye Duncan?

"I'm just passing through Strong," Faye explained. "I'm out of here as soon as I've finished my piece. So it doesn't really matter, does it? I only have a handful of days."

Lily's sigh spoke of personal experience. "The Donovan men aren't easy. That's a real tight timeline you've got there, Faye. Evan's going to have you rethinking things soon."

"Pure challenge, the Donovan boys," Nonna agreed. "That hasn't changed in almost twenty years. They'll give you a run for your money, but it's all worth it in the end."

"He's a bad boy." He could *hear* the little smile playing on Faye's lips. "That's fine with me. In fact, that's perfect. I'm not looking for happily-ever-after. Not right now. Maybe not ever."

That was plenty clear.

He got the repacked chute beneath his knees to force out any air and then neatly slid the lot inside the container. When the next call came in, he'd be good to go.

With a divorce just behind her, no way she'd hop straight back onto that horse. His Faye was still broken, wasn't one hundred percent. That made him mad, even though it shouldn't have. He didn't need her heart—he didn't want it, he told himself, because that was the kind of thing Jack or Rio would have been good at—but he wanted to fix what had gone wrong for her. If she wanted him just for a while, she could have him.

"I'm heading back," she announced. "Can I hitch a ride with you two?"

He hung the newly packed chute on the wall with the others. "There's no need for that, darlin'," he called, taking the stairs fast and striding out of the hangar toward her. Behind Faye, Lily smothered a smile. "Faye and I have unfinished business here."

Chapter Nine

Evan was a silent presence, waiting behind her while Nonna and Lily called their good-byes. He lifted a hand in farewell as the other women got into their car. Faye, however, simply turned and stared. God, he was worth staring at. He was all tall and broad-shouldered beneath his white cotton T-shirt. The flight suit he'd worn for their jump was still unzipped and shoved down to his waist, and the bulky material made his muscled thighs seem bigger. Harder. He ate up the ground as he came toward her now, and she wanted to look and then look some more.

"Unfinished business?" She grinned up at him. That sounded like pure promise on his part—a promise she was totally on board with.

"Absolutely." One large hand shot out, catching her around the waist. He pulled her up against his side, and then he was moving fast, taking her back deep inside the hangar. The contrast between the sultry, mind-melting heat of the outside air with this deliciously cool, shadowy place hit her. She eyed the stairs to the loft, but he wasn't taking her there. Not yet. For the moment, she was happy to put herself in his hands and see where he could take them both.

Right now the touch of those hands on her waist burned through the thin cotton of her tank top, and seeing his darkly tanned fingers on the pale fabric made her feel intensely feminine in the masculine space of the hangar. That was good, too, a delicious treat she could allow herself. In the distance, car doors slammed. Nonna and Lily were leaving and, with them, her ride. She'd need Evan to take her back to town, after all.

She watched his face and didn't know if that ride was a sure thing or not.

That was one hell of a possessive look he had. He stared at her as if she was his and he wasn't letting go until he was good and ready to do so. Which could be trouble. This was a temporary thing. She had a road to hit and a life to live. She wasn't staying in Strong.

And yet, oh, God, when he walked her backward with delicious intent, all her plans flew right out the window. This was Evan Donovan, big, solid, dependable Evan, who was going all primitive on her. There was no forgetting how he'd felt at her back as he'd launched them both from the plane. He'd held on to her all the way down, keeping her safe. This man was the same man—and yet not. As if he'd let go of that tight, disciplined control just a little.

She liked it.

She liked *him*.

Her back hit a wall. Distantly, she was aware that he'd moved them into an empty space where the jumpers' chutes hung, waiting for action. Each breath she took smelled like leather and nylon and something indescribably smoky and male.

And then his hand slapped against the wall next to her head. "You teased me, Faye."

His deep growl shot straight to her belly. Oh, yeah. She

remembered that pleasure. And she sure had teased him, because, God, it had been fun. "Are you complaining?" she challenged. She got her hands on his T-shirt, curling her fingers into the soft fabric. The man beneath the shirt was anything but soft.

"Maybe I'm not," he admitted. His other hand tightened on her waist, then started a wicked slide upward. "But I am wanting to finish what we started."

"We're alone now," she pointed out.

"Not for long," he growled. "You know how busy a jump hangar gets when there's a fire? There could be a call any minute. We've got watches on two spots already. There could be smoke soon."

"You always expect trouble?"

"It's summer, Faye." His thighs pushed against hers, parting hers and pinning her there. Making her want more. "There are always more fires and always more calls. There's never enough time."

She was going to do this. Why not? It had been too long, and Evan was the kind of adventure she didn't want to resist.

"So we'll need to be quick."

Bad boy.

Faye's earlier words still rang in Evan's ears. A pink flush of arousal stained her cheeks, and her lips parted as she rocked his world. He recognized the greedy look in her eyes as she watched him, waiting for him to make up his mind. As if there was any doubt about his decision. He wanted her badly. He was simply afraid that he would hurt her.

"Faye," he rasped. "We should slow down."

She shook her head, her fingers tightening in his T-shirt. "That's not what I want."

"*I* don't want to hurt you," he said pointedly. *Christ.* He was so big, and she was so very, very small.

"You won't," she said confidently, and her fingers smoothed the fabric of his shirt against his chest, finding his nipple. She stroked, and he groaned. The sound hung in the air between them, raw and needy. "You wouldn't hurt me, Evan."

He was glad she was so sure, but he still didn't know why she'd want to do this. Her ex was a fireman. Why would she pick a smoke jumper for a quick summer fling? *Adventure,* his brain supplied. *Sex?* Maybe.

"This isn't the kind of thing I usually do," he warned, because she needed some kind of heads-up here. He wasn't Rio, and he didn't seduce countless women. He wanted to make Faye Duncan an exception, though. *Her* he wanted.

"You don't play sexy games in the hangar?" Her mouth curled up at the corners, pure naughtiness. Her hands moved over his chest and over his shoulders, as if she enjoyed the simple feel of him. That soft, slow glide of her skin over his clothed body was setting him on fire, though. He wanted more. He wanted whatever she would give him.

"No," he said, his voice hoarse. "You might have the wrong brother here."

"I'm pretty sure I have the one I want." That naughty grin peeked up at him again, her hands meeting behind his neck to tug him toward her. "You're more than enough bad boy for me, Evan, so shut up and kiss me."

If Faye wanted bad boy, he'd give her bad boy. If she wanted him to make love to her in the Donovans' flight hangar, he'd do that, too. She was so damned sexy, a sensual flirt who didn't mind getting caught. The other jumpers could walk in, and she wouldn't care. She'd let them see exactly what Evan made her feel. There was nothing sexier than that.

"Whatever you want, you can have, darlin'." This close, she couldn't miss the thick ridge of his erection. He wanted her, too. This hard-on was all for her, all because of her. She looked up at him, her face dazed and flushed, and the hunger he saw there was blazing deep inside him, as well.

He lowered his head, spun the moment out. He wanted this kiss, wanted it to last, and yet the need burning him up from the inside out said this was going to be hot and fast and over almost before it began. So he closed the little distance still between them real slow, his mouth coming down on hers in a sweet, sensual tease. Just brushing her lips with his own. Letting her know he was right there with her.

Once, twice, his lips rubbed softly over hers. And she was soft. That mouth of hers was pure perfection, the bottom lip full and giving. He licked and tasted, learning this small piece of her. Nipped playfully and swept inside when she opened up. He kissed her and kissed her, until his own breathing was a rough sigh of sound in his ears, and he no longer knew who was kissing whom.

"I love kissing you." His voice sounded rough and raw, but he guessed she didn't mind, because she shivered and pressed closer.

"You do?" She tipped her head back, shifting closer. Her breasts pressed right up against him now.

"Yeah." His voice was hoarse. "You taste so damned perfect, Faye."

Evan picked her up effortlessly, spreading her legs around his waist. In his arms, Faye felt light and sexy and feminine. The rough fabric of his jumpsuit rubbed against her thighs, reminding her of exactly how open she was right now. Reinforcing the erotic feel of her soaked folds parting beneath too many layers of clothing. He leaned back, looking down at her. There was no hiding here, not in the daylight and not when he looked at her like that. That was okay. This was what she'd wanted.

Evan Donovan knew *exactly* who he had in his arms.

"Hold on," he growled, and then he took her up the stairs. God, there was nothing sexier than the raw power of him, that big hand cupping her ass and the other pressed against the small of her back. He had his fingers tucked against the bottom of her pussy. Almost naughty but not quite. Her hips pressed against him, the muscles of her thighs tightening around him, and each step ratcheted up the arousal another notch, leaving her deliciously tense with anticipation. She was stretched around him. Waiting for more.

"You liked that."

"I did." God, her arousal was a slow, sweet pound. She wanted him, wanted him groaning out her name as he explored her body with those large fingers of his. As he pushed inside her where she was slick and wet with need. He'd give her whatever she needed. Whatever she wanted. The promise of that pleasure had her heating up more, his name a greedy whimper on her lips.

He set her down for a minute. Long enough to push the jumpsuit down his legs. His erection was as big and blunt as the rest of him. She was a lucky, lucky woman.

She touched him, and he jerked. "Someone's eager," she whispered, and then she reached out both hands. She was feeling a little eager herself. Eager and greedy for him.

Wrapping her fingers around his shaft, she moved her hands up and down, letting her fingers slip away when she found the tip. Gently she twisted her palm over the head where he was soft and silky hard. Her fingers relaxed and covered him, gliding down again. Her other hand closed around him, repeating the upward stroke until the center of her palm was pressed against the heat of him. Right now, he was all *hers*.

"I'm getting you naked," he warned. He wasn't going to hear any objections from her. She wanted them both naked. Preferably about twenty minutes ago. He must have agreed, because his hands made short work of stripping off her tank top. She hadn't bothered with a bra, so her breasts sprang free when he got the shirt off.

His fingers unsnapped her little denim shorts. The cut-offs were too short and too small, dating from before she'd married. The thought flashed through her mind that she was probably too old for that kind of peekaboo denim, but she'd wanted to feel young again, like when she'd been in her teens and waiting for a boyfriend to pick her up.

"If we had more time," he said roughly, "I'd be kissing these." His hands swept up, cupping her breasts. His callused palms weighed her, brushing against the sensitive tips.

"But we don't." She wet her lips with her tongue.

"No," he agreed. His fingers stroked down the curve of her hip, tugging gently. Her panties were a little scrap of white nylon and lace she'd chosen because they made her feel feminine. Sexy.

The hot look in Evan's eyes said he liked those panties, too. A whole lot.

His big fingers found her core through the lacy fabric, teasing the edges of where she was wet and needy for him. He'd said they had to be quick. This wasn't quick at all.

Three fingers glided over her, pressing in. One big finger found her clit and stroked. Moving up and then down. The hot, full burst of sensation through the lacy fabric was perfect. Not too much, until his thumb slipped beneath the edge, finding her wetness. *Oh, God.* She sank down, desperate for more. That wicked thumb teased and stroked, parting her just an inch and then retreating. Returning. The hangar around them was an inferno of need, the heat driving her higher.

"I'm taking them off now." He growled the warning, and she tensed in anticipation.

"Please," she whispered.

He was as good as his word. His fingers found the delicate ribbons holding the sides of her panties together. One hard snap of his wrist and the little scrap of fabric disappeared. She needed him now. Needed to feel him deep inside her. Needed him touching her more. Her entire body was on fire, alive to his touch and his presence as she'd never been before.

"Hurry up," she demanded, and he braced her with one arm, leaning away for a moment to reach for his wallet. "Please," she added, because she was willing to beg for this.

"Whatever you want, darlin'," he promised, his hoarse, dark words already making good that guarantee. He tore open a foil packet and rolled on a condom one-handed. "Let me take care of this. Let me keep you safe."

She wrapped both legs around him, spreading her thighs wide around his waist. The bunched-up fabric of his jumpsuit hit her heels, and that added to the naughty thrill. He lifted her, and the muscles of his back surged beneath her legs. He was big and raw, powerful and male—and all hers. She moaned, acknowledging that sweet truth. Right now, Evan belonged to her.

"You going to be quiet?" he asked in a rough whisper. "You want anyone else to hear you coming for me, Faye?"

She moaned. His hands smoothed over her skin, petting her, stroking that place where she wanted him most, and the sensation was almost agonizingly pleasurable. She needed him desperately, with an unfamiliar, wonderful ache. Her back hit the wall again, and she pushed her hips up. "You come find out, Evan."

His hand cupped her ass, supporting her, and the tip of him found her.

Nothing had ever felt better.

He held her up, cupping her bottom securely. She looked up at him, and he could feel the need rippling through her. She trusted him to hold her. To give her what she needed right now. The hunger was eating him up, and he was done holding back. He wanted to be inside her right now, and she was as ready as he was.

Tucking his erection at her wet opening, he pushed slowly inside her. She was killing him. Inside, she was all hot and creamy. Little moans and half words spilled from her lips, and her hands found his shoulders again and urged him closer. He gave her what she wanted, just took his own sweet time about it. The heat was reaching for him, too, building into a white-hot storm of need.

He didn't want to hurt her. He wanted to drive deep inside her, sheathe himself in one swift thrust, but instead he moved inside her one hard inch at a time. And she took him. That pretty pussy of hers opened up, fisting him in hot, wet velvet.

Harder. Deeper. Faster.

"Tease," she growled, nipping his shoulder with her teeth. His body answered, surging into her. He could feel the answering heat building inside her as she lifted herself up, pulling on his shoulders and then sinking back down onto him.

"Christ." Fighting to hold back, he moved with her, driving himself into her as she rode him. Ecstasy grabbed hold of him, and he pumped, in and out, losing himself in her heat. In Faye.

"More," she demanded. "Give me more, Evan."

His name on her lips sent him over the edge. He wasn't some mindless smoke-jumper fantasy for her. He was Evan. He kissed her, fucking her mouth with his tongue the same way he was thrusting into her body. He pushed inside her, tangling a hand in her hair, and she welcomed him, still talking. His Faye was never quiet.

Then she froze in his arms, pulling her mouth away from his, and he let her go. She buried her face against his neck, his name a relentless whisper against his skin. Holding her now in his arms, touching her as she came over the edge to join him, was the rawest, sweetest of secrets. Even if the entire jump team showed up, this would still be about the two of them. And then, thank God, she was coming and coming in sweet, hot contractions. She'd found what she needed, and his hands locked her in place so she could ride him, ride out that pleasure storm. This, *this* was what he'd wanted for her.

"Darlin'," he whispered. "Faye."

Sex with Evan was something else. Something amazing. She'd known he'd be a fantastic lover, and he had been. The emotions, however, were unexpected. She'd thought it would just be sex. A pick-me-up adventure to prove to herself that she was still sexy and desirable. Mike had chosen someone else, but this man, Evan, had chosen *her*.

She'd thought that's all it would be. Now she wasn't sure. Maybe that was because her legs were still shaking from the most intense orgasm of her life. Maybe it was the way he'd focused on her face, fisting his hand in her hair and coaxing her over the edge. As if it wasn't simply sex for him, either.

Evan had known her for precisely two days. He couldn't have feelings for her, and neither should she for him. So what if this wasn't the kind of thing she normally did? This was adventure. So why was she uncertain now? She didn't know if she should pull on her clothes and pound down the stairs or curl up on the floor and nap until she was certain the melted-bones feeling had left her and she could walk.

She'd had hot, wall-banging sex with a smoke jumper.

The sensation of him sliding free and gently lowering her legs back to the ground sent an echo of pleasure through her pussy. Her breath hitched with heated recollection and arousal. God, he was so good. So good.

He got an arm around her waist as if he wasn't ready to let go, either. She couldn't believe she'd done *that*. With Evan Donovan. And, God, she'd do it again. When she'd caught her breath.

He turned away for a moment, disposing of the used condom and adjusting the jumpsuit. She hadn't even got him all the way out of his clothes.

"Thank you." The words shot out of her. She'd never been able to keep quiet, always had to fill up the silence, because silence was awkward.

He stared at her; then that slow smile of his tugged at the corner of his mouth. "Those weren't the words I was thinking of."

He prowled toward her, and, for a moment, he wasn't the big, laid-back, protective man she'd met at Ma's. He was different. Determined. Possessive.

"What *were* you thinking of?" That smile of his had her curious. And nervous.

He brushed a thumb over her mouth, lowered his head, and his lips followed that thumb in a heated, luscious kiss. "I don't know," he whispered against her skin, "but 'thank you' is for when you hold open a door or pass a beer. I don't think 'thank you' is enough here."

He pulled back gently, and this time she didn't hold on to him. He opened his mouth, as if maybe he'd found the words he was searching for, but his pager buzzed. She knew that sound too well.

It was like all those nights with Mike. Nights when, whether or not they'd had sex or he'd held her, he'd gone out that door because, call or no call, the firehouse always came first. He'd made no bones about that. She'd wanted to be first but had accepted that she wouldn't be. Still, Evan was in no rush to answer the page or even pick up the vibrating device, and for that she was strangely grateful. He stood there, watching her, as if he was as off balance as she was.

She wanted him to pull her into his arms and hold her. Wanted to feel those strong arms close around her. She didn't want him to go, and she definitely didn't want to send him off on a fire call.

Outside, a pickup truck approached fast, tires chewing up the gravel. That was reality making a house call.

"Fire call?" She was proud of the fact that her voice sounded so matter-of-fact. "You go on now. Go fight fire, save the world."

This was damn awkward. Did he pull his jumpsuit back up and hightail it out of there? The page buzzed angrily, and this time Evan looked down. Yeah. Incoming.

Her words hung in the air between them. He had to say something. But he wasn't some kind of superhero. He didn't have a cape, and he wasn't riding to the rescue. He was just doing his job.

"I have to go." He took a step toward the exit, and that last foot of space suddenly looked about the size of Siberia. Miles of icy white waiting to freeze a man to death. That one page had sucked all the joy out of the evening and replaced it with a whole lot of pissed.

"Yeah." She didn't look sure, though, and he knew he was screwing this up. That really wasn't a news flash, but he still felt bad. How had something so smoking hot gone so cold, so fast?

"You want the keys to the cabin?" he asked, because, without him, she had no way to get back to town now. "Or you can take my truck." He'd never let anyone else drive the beast, but he owed her. And she needed the wheels.

Her eyes widened, and he wanted to tell her she could stay put right there in the loft, too, and he'd be back as soon as he could, but why would she wait?

Instead, he tossed her both sets of keys and beat a hasty retreat.

Evan hit the lockers because he needed to get his ass into the air. Rio and Jack had beat him into the locker room again. When he came slamming in, taking out his frustration on the door, they both looked up as if they'd been waiting to razz him—and then shut the hell up when they got a good look at his face.

Yeah. He figured he wasn't much of a Welcome Wagon.

Instead, he got busy fast, pulling on his jumpsuit and grabbing gear.

"We got an ETA?" he asked, when the silence got a little too long.

"Sure thing," Rio drawled. "Glad you could make it. In the nick of time."

"Five minutes," Jack interrupted, clearly more interested in keeping the peace—and a full jump team—than in razzing his brother. "Spotted Dick's gassed up and ready to go. All we have to do is get out there, and we're cleared for takeoff."

"Good." He snagged his gloves and gestured toward the door. "Ladies."

Shaking his head, Jack moved out. "Jesus, Evan. You check your good mood at the door?"

"Must be the company he's keeping," Rio observed to no one in particular. "How's Faye doing, Evan?"

"She's fine. You want to have a heart-to-heart right now?" He wasn't feeling all come-to-Jesus himself, so they could back off. Covering the fifty yards to the plane's open door suddenly seemed like it would take a fucking eternity.

"Not particularly," Rio said, way too cheerful for Evan's taste.

"Look, she's up here all alone, and Mike asked you to look in on her." Jack shot him a look. "I know you. That's all. You like to look after the lost and lonely. Make things all better."

"You kept us," Rio volunteered.

"That's different." Evan wasn't going to make the plane without hearing how they felt—that much was clear. But when had the three of them gotten into the business of discussing feelings?

"How?" Jack threw up a hand to hold Evan off. "No, hear me out here, Evan. She doesn't have a place of her own, she's alone, and—"

"She's damn hot," Rio inserted.

"So you start thinking about keeping her. That's okay, but—"

"You don't even have a cat, so a woman might be a bit of a learning curve," Rio pointed out. "Although I hear you can learn lots from books these days. Let me know if I should be swinging by the library for you."

"Looking after Faye is a favor to an old friend," Evan emphasized.

"That all?" Rio stared back at him, skepticism written all over his puss. "You sure about that?"

"One hundred percent."

Maybe ninety, because, climbing into the plane, Evan had plenty of time to admit the truth to his own sorry ass. He was in over his head. The flight deck and the jump were both familiar territory. These were his world, and he knew where he fit here and what was expected from him. Faye, on the other hand, was rapidly turning out to be un-charted, dangerous territory. She made him *feel,* and he wasn't at all sure he wanted that—yet he couldn't keep himself from thinking about her, from dreaming about the welcome she might give him after tonight's jump.

It was just sex, he reminded himself. Really, really great sex.

She didn't want more than that, and he didn't have it to give.

He had no idea what to do with a woman like her, any-how.

Sure, Jack had decided to take the plunge with Lily Cortez, and the two of them were busily planning their happily-ever-after together. Their engagement was work-ing out well for the two of them, and Evan was happy for Jack. Whatever it was Jack had found with Lily, it didn't take a rocket scientist—hell, it didn't take a second *glance*—to see that what they had together was all kinds of special. Lily lit up when Jack hit the room, with his brother doing his own version of neon, too. They were good together.

This thing he was feeling for Faye Duncan wasn't the same, though.

Not that his team had gotten that memo.

"Heard Evan here had a date," Mack roared, climbing in. Joey looked interested in confirming deets, as well. *Hell.* That was the thing about Strong: people talked, and it was all neighborly good fun—until they got up into your personal business. There was no way to shut them down, because they were good people with good intentions. And shitty radar.

"Does this look like date night?"

Joey flicked him a mock salute and let it go, so one hurdle surmounted. Instead of making eye contact and joining the conversational roar filling up the plane's belly, Evan concentrated on shifting his gear bag and getting comfortable. Whatever hot spot had been called in, Spotted Dick would get them there, and then it would be ass out the door, feet first, tearing toward the ground, because getting there fast counted, no matter what it took. Today they had a ride, but he'd done more than his share of ten-mile hike-ins with a hundred-pound pack strapped to his back. If there was no way to chute in, you walked. It was that damn simple.

You got there.

You got the job done.

That was what holding the line was all about.

Faye Duncan was simply a different kind of a job. A real pretty, sweet kind of a job, but a job. And, no matter how much he enjoyed his work, he couldn't afford to forget that.

And yet a primal part of him was *glad* he'd marked her. Worse, he'd wanted to leave part of himself inside her. He couldn't do that, though. It wouldn't be fair or safe for her. But he'd still wanted to do it. To know she would carry the scent of him inside and out, on her skin and deeper.

That was fucked up, not to mention just plain wrong.

There was no right way to have both Faye *and* the jump team. She'd already made it damn clear that wasn't what she wanted. He got that. She'd only recently come out of an empty marriage with her L.A. firefighter husband. With Mike. She wasn't in any hurry to get back on the marriage train or even the love train, and it wasn't as if these were things he'd ever thought much about himself.

He'd never seen himself as husband material. The odds of his screwing up a marriage were high, and he wouldn't do that to a woman. Or to any kids she'd have. He'd keep his screwed-up to himself. He had a job to do—and no room for Faye Duncan.

Spotted Dick gunned the motor, and they barreled toward the end of the runway and liftoff.

Chapter Ten

As the plane came around, smooth and easy in Spotted Dick's capable hands, Evan knew the fire was going to be a bad one. The first clue was the massive column of dark smoke punching up into the sky far too close for comfort. But smoke jumping wasn't comfortable. He knew that, too. His brothers and the team were in danger every time they went out there.

"Door's waiting, ladies." The spotter had to yell to be heard over the roar of the slipstream tearing past the open door, but a grin lit up his face. The same grin Evan saw painted all over the other faces in the cabin. Hell, they were all adrenaline junkies. They should start weekly meetings or something. *Hello, my name is . . . and I'm a smoke jumper.*

He angled closer to the door and got his first full-on view of what they were facing today. The jump down was straight into the fucking inferno from hell. They'd had three hundred yards of drift when the spotter tossed the streamers, but the winds had picked up below two thousand feet, which was going to make a tight jump trickier. He'd jumped worse, though, so he nodded his understanding to the spotter and lined up behind his jump partner.

Jack was first up to go out the door. Evan and he

bumped fists, and then Jack wedged himself in the exit, the spotter bawling last-minute instructions and warnings as he pointed out the jump spot. It was a damn small target on a narrow ridge, more of a bare patch in the forest with fire eating up the bottom of the slope and creeping toward the ridge itself. It was going to be one hell of a night.

Spotted Dick leveled out the plane.

Here we go.

Jack was fighting to stay balanced in the door, the slipstream sucking him toward the opening. The spotter's hand rose and fell. Evan couldn't hear the spotter's slap hit Jack's shoulder over the roar of the air, but Jack was out of the plane. Evan dropped down into the empty doorway, ass on the edge and feet hanging out. It was as toasty as a beach because of the fire—and it was going to be hotter than hell down there on the ground.

When it came, the spotter's slap hit his shoulder hard, and he threw himself forward, all muscle memory. The world spun crazily around him, the plane fell away overhead, and his brain kicked in, starting the countdown to pull the chute. *Jump thousand.* Head down and boots up, spinning ass over teakettle at eighty miles an hour toward the fire and the mountain slope. Landing on his head wasn't part of the plan, so he straightened himself. Now he and Jack were flying like damn geese in a formation.

Look thousand. Being heavier, he'd made up Jack's three-second lead. When he looked over at his brother, he knew the crazy-ass grin painting Jack's face was on his, too.

Reach thousand, and he got his Nomex glove onto the ripcord, ready to go. *Pull thousand.* He yanked, the chute deployed, and he flew up hard. Then it was all in the steering as he rode the wind and the air right down to a ringside seat in the biggest fucking wildland fire Strong had seen this month.

He looked again for the jump spot, reorienting himself as the wind pulled him right and then pushed him left. *Shit.* This wasn't going to be an easy ride in. Jack was coming in fast on his left, steering and cursing like a bitch. There. There it was. He spotted the meadow—and the wall of mean, son-of-a-bitch pine trees ringing it on all four sides. At least he wouldn't overshoot and fry his ass. No, all he had to worry about was imitating a pincushion. He dropped and dropped, steering like a madman and whooping and hollering for all he was worth, because this was one hell of a ride.

The ground came up fast, and the impact jolted through his steel-toes. Running, he pulled in the chute behind him. The other jumpers would be right behind him, and he needed to get clear ASAP.

The landing zone was strangely pristine. The clearing hadn't burned or even caught yet. All pretty green, the grassy patch looked strangely normal, given the wall of black smoke punching up on their right. When he looked up, he had an excellent view of Jack—caught a good fifty yards up a ponderosa.

The freight-train roar of the fire chewing up the hillside toward them was deafening and plenty of warning that, despite the hot air, this was no day at the beach. They needed to *move.* Jack already had his knife out, sawing through the line. If he could curse and cut at the same time, he'd be okay.

"You'd better stick that landing," Evan roared to the others dropping into the clearing. The second and third jump pairs were down already and rolling up their chutes. The last pair cleared the treetops, coming down fast and hard for the center. He got the hell out of the way and let them have it.

Above them, Spotted Dick held the plane steady while Mack unloaded the cargo. That gear was essential, especially the five-gallon cubies of water. No worries, though. With surgical precision, Spotted Dick and Mack put the cargo down dead center in the jump spot. Thank God. Climbing ponderosa to retrieve gear was a bitch. Behind him, there was a crash, followed by a graphic curse, and then Jack came along, sporting a long tear in the arm of his jumpsuit.

Evan wanted a look at that arm, but Jack was moving on, and that probably meant he was fine. Still, he'd give his brother shit, just to find out if Jack was feeling spunky enough to push back. "I'm not giving you a ten for that landing."

His brother flashed him the finger and grabbed a Pulaski from the drop, sliding the ax into his utility belt.

"Yeah. Five-point-five," Joey hollered. "You'd better go back to the ribbons routine, Jack."

Five minutes later, with the gear unpacked and every man armed for the coming fight, they huddled up. Today, Evan was the team leader, but smoke jumping was more democracy than aristocracy. No one was shy about sharing his opinion.

After they'd hammered out a plan of attack, he leaned in to Jack. "That arm of yours okay?"

"Souvenir," was all Jack said, and then they were moving, because that fire was roaring up the hill like a son of a bitch.

Thirty-six hours later, they'd lost the ridge and fallen back to the next one. Waterloo, Armageddon—take your pick, Evan mused. Hell, he might as well choose both, because right now, he definitely wasn't on the winning side. The team had spent one long night of digging and sweating and digging some more until the act of lifting a Pulaski was pure torture. And yet stopping wasn't an option, because the black column of smoke punching up over the ridge was even darker and wider than when they'd jumped. He could see it again, now that dawn was coming, lighting up the sky. That morning pink looked way less rosy from the middle of a forest fire.

The lack of any water nearby made the job harder. The tankers were roaring overhead, dropping their loads, but all that water hadn't made a dent yet. Still, somehow, they'd get this done. Evan just had to figure out how.

The radio barked again, and he was all over it. Out here, down on the ground, that scratchy connection was vital. Without intel, fire could overrun you before you knew it.

"Johnson, Donovan, you hit the head yet?" Johnson's voice bellowed out of the radio, loud and clear as the dispatcher identified himself. Four years out of the military and the man still sounded like the drill sergeant he'd been.

"Donovan, Johnson. Fuck, no. The fire's perimeter is at least a half mile out from us, moving fast, and we're not having any luck with the burn out. If the wind picks up any more, we're not going to hold it."

"Copy," Johnson said.

"You got any good news for us?"

"We've got one more tanker headed your way, but then they've got to turn around and head back to base to reload. You're going to be on your own for the next hour after that. Can you get me a closer look, let me know what you think?"

"Will do. You got updates on the other teams on the ground?"

"Sure do. Jump oh-two is holding their line about two miles southwest of you. Jump oh-three is pulling out now. They've got fire eating up their flank, and they can't hold it. Wind's looking good, though, so if you hold your line, maybe we'll all go home tonight. Roger that?"

"Copy that. Donovan, clear." Signing off, he rammed the radio back into its holster on his belt and took another look around the clearing. One line holding. One lost. Those weren't good odds, and Donovan Brothers were in the hot seat here, taking the worst of it. Smaller waves of flame were running up the ridge, where the jumpers would beat them back. Not to mention fifteen feet of flame on their left flank, waiting for them to blink.

Yeah, the night had just gotten longer.

The promised tanker came in, dropping loads of retardant in a long, pink stream, but the fire ate through it, circling back around as if it had a life of its own.

"We're losing ground here." Rio's hard-eyed assessment earned him nods of agreement from the nearest team members. His younger brother's soot-blackened face wasn't so pretty now. Eyeing the fire, Rio was a mean-faced son of a bitch with one purpose. Hold the line. Unfortunately, that was looking like a suicide mission. Spot fires were breaking out, and the air was almost superheated.

"We're going to hike out a half mile, and then we'll dig a new line. Connect that line up with the second jump team. Third team got overrun, so they're hiking out, and we can join forces with them. Hit this thing harder."

He didn't know where their inner reserves would come from, but somehow they'd push on. Thirty-six hours of hell while they dug line as if their lives depended on it, because Johnson's radio reports said their lives *did*. If that fire started to run, they were down to a handful of safe spots. They had unburned forest north and west of them, which meant hauling ass to the south or east, where the fire had already burned over and there was no more fuel. Embers were falling around him, making it harder to keep a visual on the line. He needed to be able to close the distance between himself and that line if the fire started to burn over. He had to see what was coming.

"We've got to go." Joey jogged toward him. "We're losing control fast."

Joey had been the one patrolling the burn out, watching for movement. If he said it was time to go, it was definitely time to fall back. Joey was the kind of fighter who figured he could stand nose-to-nose with a speeding truck, and—maybe—he'd step two inches left when he felt the bumper kiss his chest.

The fire had cooled some overnight, but now that the sun was coming up again, she'd heat back up. Over the roar of the saws chewing through trees, Evan checked the perimeter. And, yeah, it was bad. The fire was making a run for it, right for the trees they were working on. Worse, there weren't any good spots here to pitch the fire shelters and wait out the burnover until they could hike out safely.

"Move, move, move." He barked the order to clear out, his feet already in motion. This spot wasn't defendable anymore, and his team needed to fall back and regroup. He wasn't losing anyone. Cursing, they started jogging back, covering ground fast. They looked rough, all dirty hard hats, steel-toes, and soot. It wasn't a damn beauty pageant, though, so they'd do.

He did a quick head count—and came up short. Seven. *Fuck.* Grabbing Rio, he swung his brother around. "Where's Jack?"

Rio's face got worried, his boots backtracking. "He was setting fusees. Downslope." Right. Jack would have been the one to burn out the virgin expanse between their fireline and the advancing fire. Eat up that fuel before the fire got to it.

"We need to get out of here. Now." His instincts yelled they'd already lost control of the situation. The air shimmered around them, an intense wave of heat that was like being on the wrong side of a desert oasis. There was no refuge here. Anyone still on the spot in another two minutes was a dead man. The air was going to superheat and cook his lungs from the inside out.

"Jack can go into the burn out," Rio countered. "Where he's been working, there's nothing unburned. If he gets in there, the fire is going to go around him."

That shimmer in the air, the way the light rippled and bent when he looked at it, said otherwise. It was too hot, too much, too fast. A burn out wasn't going to be enough protection today. The flames might not make it in to Jack, but the heat would sear him alive.

"Go," he ordered. When Rio hesitated, he added, "That's an order from today's crew chief. Take the rest of the team out. Now. I'm going to be right on your ass."

Rio cursed, but he went. Another day, another fire, it would have been Rio giving orders and taking the lead, but today it was Evan's turn to be crew chief, and that made it his job to go back for Jack. It was Rio's job to leave when he was ordered to do so.

And, job or no job, they both knew Evan wouldn't leave Jack behind, and he *needed* Rio to front the retreat. So when they each played their part, no one was surprised.

Running fast, Evan headed back toward the inferno, moving swiftly downslope. Sure enough, a hundred yards in, he had a clear line on Jack. His brother was still fifty yards away, setting a final, futile fusee, when the fire exploded upward, roaring upslope. *Fuck.*

He bellowed out a warning, pausing on the top of the slope. He could go down and would, but it was better for Jack to come on up alone. Evan's size meant he wasn't built for speed. Jack was leaner, faster. He could take that slope in half Evan's time.

Jack must have finally spotted the danger—that or Evan's bellow had carried over the roar of the fire—because Jack dropped the last fusee and started to run. For one moment, Evan thought fate and God had gifted them with a happily-ever-after, because, despite his gear, Jack sure could sprint with the best of them when he had a fire licking at his ass, but then he stumbled. He went down, grabbing his ankle, then popped right back up on hands and knees.

Evan was already moving, headed down the hillside. The loose soil gave way, and he dug in for purchase. In the back of his head, he counted like a madman, knowing he had seconds to do what he had to do. Sliding to a stop, he grabbed Jack's hand, crouched, and lifted. His muscles screamed against the strain, because Jack wasn't light and there was no time to do this right and barely any time to do it at *all*.

"Hold on," he bit out. "You see a wall of flame coming, you do the praying for both of us, okay?"

Then he was pushing up the hill. Left foot. Right. His boots ate up the unburned ground while embers sizzled around him. He'd do this. He knew where the escape route was. Centering Jack's weight over his shoulder, he kept running. Forcing his legs up and down. Heat blasted the side of his face and cooked his left arm. The air all but vibrated now with tension, embers raining down all around them. *There.* On the other side of that slope. The mental counter in his head shrieked, *Danger, Will Robinson,* but he needed two, maybe three more seconds to hit the top and go over.

Behind them, the fire hopped the line and charged up the hill. He made a last effort, knowing soundless obscenities and prayers were dropping from his lips. Jack pushed up on his back, as if he wanted to pop off and lighten the load, so Evan held on tighter. There was no room for any goddamn heroes in the Donovan family—they all went home. *There.*

The top of the hill was a fucking beacon of hope. *Almost there.* Jack cursed, but Evan concentrated on sucking in air, because there was a freaking elephant parked on his chest, and his knees were buckling from the weight. His team reached out for him and Jack, pulling them over to safety.

Joey slapped him on the back, knocking off embers.

"Best twenty-yard dash ever," Rio roared. "We've got ourselves a new record-holder. You do that again, Jack, and I'll kill you myself."

Other hands reached out, pulling him and Jack onto the ground. *Drop and roll and smother.* Spent, he lay there, just breathing and breathing some more, watching the Nomex steaming on Jack's right arm. Yeah. Jack was done for the day. Hell, they all needed a break. This one had been too close.

"Fuck me." Jack blinked up at him. "You weigh half a ton, Evan. Next time, I get to be on top."

When the DC-3 touched down, Faye knew there was trouble. Frozen behind her camera lens, she watched the ground crew run out onto the runway with medical kits. That urgency was her first clue something bad had happened out there. The second clue was when she started counting heads. Eight up yesterday, so there should be eight guys walking off this plane.

Unless something really bad had happened.

Inhale. Exhale. Evan was fine. He had to be.

And yet Ben Cortez was tearing across the tarmac, roaring for an ambulance. "Now, goddamn it." Her stomach took a five-story plunge, and she wanted to run out right behind him, demanding he produce Evan.

Six men staggered off the plane, clearly exhausted but walking, and she realized she was holding her breath. She couldn't identify the smoky, dark shapes until she focused

the telephoto lens with shaking hands. Mack. Joey and
Rio. Three others. Who else had gone up? Where was
Evan? She gave up the pretense and started running for the
plane. She wasn't Switzerland, and she wasn't staying out
of this.

As she got closer, Evan dropped down out of the plane,
reaching up to brace someone else. Jack. Helmet off, face
blackened, Jack put a foot down cautiously, his mouth
twisted in a grimace. Evan was right there waiting, slinging an arm around Jack's waist to take the other man's
weight. Jack's jumpsuit was down around his waist, his
arm bandaged.

Evan seemed fine.

Jack, on the other hand? Not so much. She couldn't
squelch the burst of relief, though, even as guilt reared its
head. Her man was okay. Lily Cortez's wasn't. Still, Jack
was upright, and that had to be a good sign, although instinct warned her you'd pretty much have to cut the leg
off a Donovan to keep him down.

It was no surprise when Lily came running across the
tarmac. Faye stopped her sprint and hung back. She was
the temporary visitor here, and that was Lily's man, her future husband. That made Lily first in line—and Faye dead
last.

Nonna was right behind Lily, throwing her arms around
the Donovan brothers and hauling them into her chest as
if she needed to hang on and reassure herself that all
of them were standing there on the tarmac. No one left
behind. No one missing. This was Nonna's family, and
their closeness was something Faye suddenly yearned for
fiercely.

Instead, she was right back on the sidelines, waiting.

Two minutes later, Evan spotted her and jogged over to
her. She tried to ignore how her heart did a little jump,
watching him come her way, the slow and steady pump

of his legs promising he really was okay. That he simply couldn't wait to be there with her, so walking was out of the picture.

When he reached her, he didn't stop. No, those big arms came right around her, picking her up, camera and all, and swinging her in a big, wide circle.

"Hey," he said quietly, setting her back on her feet. He didn't let go, though. Just pulled her into his side really close. He was covered in dirt and ash and probably a dozen other things she didn't want to identify too closely. He stank of smoke and sweat and the sharp, new-rubber smell of fire retardant. There was nowhere else she'd rather be.

"Rough day at the office?" She gave him a quick visual inspection, but the only obvious damage was a couple of red patches on his forearms.

"You could say that." He squeezed her again, so she figured that said it all.

"He okay?" She asked her question quietly, her eyes on Jack, pretending she hadn't given Evan the once-over.

Evan's face got still, as if he wished he had the answer to that question. "Not entirely. Probably good enough, although he needs to go to the hospital and get that arm of his checked out. Lungs, too. He popped an ankle good, too. He's not doing jumping jacks on it for at least a week."

"What happened?" She let him turn them both back toward the hangar, her feet falling into step with his while she waited for him to answer her question. A pickup truck passed them, headed out to the DC-3. Jack's ride, because apparently he wouldn't go on a stretcher with sirens flashing.

Evan ran a hand over his head. "One minute, we're holding the line. The next, we're hauling ass for a safe spot. Jack tripped."

"He made it, though." She looked back. The pickup had stopped, and Lily was alternating between yelling at Jack and kissing him, while Ben Cortez gestured vociferously at the truck, as if he was considering bodily stuffing Jack in there himself. Between the two of them, they'd take care of Jack. He was in good hands.

"He's going to be okay," Evan said. "He'll take a couple of days off, maybe a week. His Nomex did its job, and he's got more scrapes and steam burn than anything, other than the ankle."

God. Her brain was feeding her images she didn't need or want. "How about you?" He stepped inside the hangar, and she didn't wait politely outside for him. No, she went right in with him and sat on the bottom of the steps leading up to the loft while he stripped off his gear and she devoured him with her eyes.

"I did okay, Faye."

"Prove it." She needed to see that jumpsuit come off. If he were keeping secrets, he wouldn't be for long.

"I need a shower," he growled. "Something to eat. And sleep. Sleep would be real good right now."

She sat there. What else did he need? What did he *want*? He prowled closer, as if there was *something,* all right, and despite the guys all around them, it was as if they were alone in their own little space. That, or maybe Evan's jump team had more manners than she'd given them credit for.

He leaned over her, caging her in his arms. "You want to know what else I need right now, Faye?" His smoke-blackened face was fierce and triumphant.

"You tell me," she murmured, "and I'll make sure you get it."

"That sounds good." He was close enough now that his mouth was only inches from hers. The good manners were fading now; some of the jumpers called good-natured jibes, watching the two of them getting up-close and personal on the stairs. "I want that shower. You want to know why?"

She looked at him, but, God, his thumb was caressing the corner of her mouth, and she didn't have anything more to say.

"Because," he continued, his voice rough and low, "I'm taking you to bed, Faye, unless you say no. I want to hole up and make love to you and forget all about this damned fire for a night. I don't even want to talk about it."

"No talking, just kisses. Got it," she said breathlessly.

He backed her into the stairs, letting her feel the hard metal railing at her back. "So you up for kissing me all better tonight, Faye?"

He didn't wait for her answer. Instead, he kissed her, hard and raw and primitive. His mouth devoured her, his fingers threading through her hair. She was pinned in place. There was no shame, no worry about any audience. Only him and her. She gave back as good as she got. She wanted this connection. His mouth on hers and hers on his. He was alive, and he was there, and, in that moment, this homecoming was all that mattered.

Scooping her up into his arms, he turned away from the stairs and strode toward his cabin with her.

Ben watched Rio's pickup pull out, with Jack in the passenger seat and Lily riding shotgun between the two brothers. Rio would get Jack down to the local hospital stat to get him checked out. An ambulance would have been better as far as Ben was concerned, but Jack was every bit as stubborn as Nonna. *Mary Ellen. She asked me to call her by her name.* He liked having access to the part of her that wasn't all maternal.

Goddamn it, but that fire was a big one. Could have been worse, too. Ben knew it in his gut. If the wind had shifted sooner or faster or there had been fewer tanker runs—any one of a hundred variables—they would have lost thousands of acres instead of nine hundred. Another six to eight hours, though, and they'd be officially declaring the fire under control.

He pulled off his work gloves, slapping them against his denim-covered legs. The pants were already filthy, so no loss there. Still, it didn't make much of an improvement in his appearance. His wrists were black from the ash that had crept inside the gloves. And, beneath that frosting job, his hands ached, reminding him he wasn't twenty anymore. Or thirty, forty, or fifty. Still, his hands were good enough to swing an ax even though tomorrow was definitely shaping up to be a Ben-Gay day. In another ten years, he'd be buying stock in that damn company.

"You ready to go home?" He knew without looking that Nonna was right there behind him, watching her boys head off in every direction but home yet again. Jack had a date with an M.D. and some pain meds, and Evan was clearly headed back to his cabin with their pretty little witness.

"You think he's going to be okay?" she asked, avoiding his question.

"Jack?" He watched the puckered furrow between her eyes get deeper. He hated it when she worried.

"Jack. Evan." She exhaled. "Rio sure looks like he's only the driver, so if he's up to anything else, you tell me now, Ben Cortez."

"Rio's fine." As far as Ben knew. The boy's good looks weren't always a blessing. Trouble found Rio without Rio going looking. Ben didn't need to tell Mary Ellen what she already knew, however.

"Good." She turned away. "Evan's going to have to figure this thing out with Faye, but it looks like he's making a start."

It looked to Ben as if Evan was planning on having sex

tonight—and there was nothing wrong with that plan—but Ben wasn't stupid. He wasn't going to spell that one out for Mary Ellen. Instead, he gave his right hand another once-over—still not as clean as it could be, but Mary Ellen was a good sport—and held it out.

"We should go home." No more questions.

He'd called her as soon as he'd gotten word the DC-3 was on its way back. She'd needed to meet the plane, especially since Spotted Dick's latest update was that Jack had taken a hit out there. Exhaustion crumpled her face now, suggesting she hadn't slept while those boys of hers had been gone.

He'd coax her to nap. Then he'd take her down to the hospital to see Jack, because he was betting the doctors there hung on to the man for a night or two.

Fate tossed a wrinkle into that plan.

The firefighter striding up to him moved really quickly, as if he had something urgent to say. The man was too damn clean, however, to have been out in the field, so Ben figured that, whatever it was, it could wait.

"Hey," the firefighter hailed, stepping squarely into Ben's path. "Hollis Anderson. I'm part of the hotshot crew."

"Nice to meet you." Ben nodded, ignoring the hand thrust out at him. Right now, he didn't care whether or not the man was part of the elite crew battling the wildland fires from the ground. He didn't want to make nice with anyone, and his right hand had better things to do. Like holding on to Mary Ellen. He made to step forward, but the other guy didn't budge. "There something you need from me?" The question wasn't particularly polite, but he definitely wasn't in the mood to exchange pleasantries.

"The jump team has an opening, and that spot on the plane is going to be mine." There was an expression on

Hollis's face that said he wasn't leaving until he had an answer. *Fuck*. Last thing Ben needed right now was a guy looking to prove himself.

"Not my call," he snapped. "I'm local. Jump team is all Donovan Brothers."

Hollis's knowing smile said he knew the truth of that one. "Ma'am." He nodded politely toward Mary Ellen. "The Donovans are out here on your call, Mr. Cortez. You speak up for a guy, and they're gonna listen. I'm on probation with my firehouse until they approve my permanent assignment and I came up here for fire season. We're fifty miles south of you. I've proved my chops there. You just ask them."

"Congratulations." Ben tried to step by again, but Hollis Anderson went right along with him. *Hell*.

The man was definitely determined. "You need someone to fill in, Mr. Cor—"

"Not now." Ben cut him off.

"When you're considering names, I want to be one of them." Hollis looked the part. He was young and well-built. A white guy in his early twenties with a by-the-book military buzz cut and a still-new firehouse T-shirt. He could have been one of a dozen guys, except he was here, getting up into Ben's face.

"This is not the time to be asking for a job interview," Ben bit out. "You got that, boy? Jack's fine."

"He's not jumping," Hollis insisted. "Not with an arm like that and a busted ankle. And, even if it turns out he can jump, he's not digging line."

Ben fought the urge to yell. That was the exhaustion pricking him, he knew, but even so, he didn't need or want to play this game just now. "That man is like a son to me. He's not a number on a jump team. I don't know how they jump in your neck of the woods, but that's how we do it in *mine*."

Hollis Anderson swallowed nervously, as if maybe he was finally realizing that this approach wasn't working out for him. And yet he still didn't shut the fuck up, just kept right on yammering about all the reasons he should get what he wanted. "I've done the coursework. I've got a couple of practice jumps in. Give me a chance."

"This isn't a fucking classroom. You want to learn, that's good. Out there, in the middle of a wildland fire? That shouldn't be your first choice." Kid not only possessed bad timing, but he was stupid. He'd be dumb enough to die out there, chasing the blaze he thought he wanted to fight.

Fingers flexing by his sides, Ben turned away. Yeah, he was pissed. Wanted to hit something. Instead, he practiced maturity, sucking in air and breathing out until the urge to pummel something—someone—subsided.

Mary Ellen's hand slid into his. "This," she said quietly, laughter lurking beneath the surface of her words, "is where I'd be telling my boys to walk away."

"Go," he said shortly to Hollis. "You want a new job, check the job boards. Jack's going to be fine."

Hollis opened his mouth. Closed it. "Sir," he said. His right foot slid backward.

Mary Ellen's hand pulled Ben along, and he went. If Hollis Anderson wanted to stand there and keep jawing with himself, he could do that, too. Ben was officially off the clock.

Evan turned the key and kicked open his cabin door, making straight for the bed.

"Strip," Faye ordered. "Show me you're okay."

Yeah. He was so on board with that. His hands made short work of his clothes, unlacing the steel-toes and stripping off his T-shirt, pushing the jumpsuit and jeans down and off. He wanted inside her right away, because he needed to reassure them both that everything was okay. He wasn't dead. That was a plus.

Her eyes devoured him, and he knew he wasn't a pretty picture. Not after a day and a half in the field. He was more eau de smoke right now than he was Polo. "I should shower."

"Later," she said. "Right now, stay here."

He could do that. That was no problem at all. He loved the way she stared up at him, doing an inventory of his face. Her eyes got that soft expression, and her hands were reaching for him. She smelled good, too, unlike him. All female and flowery soap. He didn't know the names of flowers—she could have been sporting peonies or roses, for all he knew—but, damn, she smelled good. Like a sun-warm garden where she happened to be waiting for him. And that waxing-poetic crap was the kicker.

She scooted over on the bed, making room for him, and her hands got busy on the buttons of the little sundress she was sporting. The dress was some kind of pink plaid thing with a whole row of white buttons marching past her breasts and down her belly. Real pretty. Buttons parted as her fingers flew—she was feeling greedy, too—and the top half of the dress came apart in her hands, giving him a good look at her breasts hiding in the lacy cups of her bra.

He was done looking—he wanted to be doing. He lowered himself onto the bed and pulled her beneath him. She came willingly, laughing as she rolled into the hollow created by his weight.

She wasn't going anywhere now. She was all his.

"Welcome home," she said, watching his face.

"This is good." His brain wasn't sending clear instructions to his tongue anymore. The feel of her was short-circuiting what was left of his thinking. He thought just enough to worry about crushing her—she was a tiny thing compared to him—bracing himself over her on his forearms, his legs pinning hers to the mattress. One hand tangled in her hair, while the other took over the rest of the buttons. He flicked open her bra with his thumb, and she spilled out into his hands. The sight of her framed by all that pretty pink and lace was something else.

God. He was a lucky son of a bitch.

"Are you okay?" Her hands ran inspections on his body now, and he heated up all over again as her fingers petted his shoulders and back. Tracing a ticklish path down his ribs to his front.

"If you can talk, darlin', then I'm not doing this right." Shut down his emotions and get the job done—that was how he worked. Now, when he touched her, he was *feeling* things that had nothing to do with sex. Which was plain crazy.

Lowering his head, he took her mouth. He kissed her as if he'd been out there fighting fires for a year. His mouth was hungry and knowing, his tongue parting her lips and stroking deep inside her to tease and taste. She pushed right back, rubbing against his tongue. The feel of her laid out beneath him, skin to skin, framed in the undone dress, was undoing him. She was something else.

She was *his.*

To prove that point, he moved on down. Her nipples were hard, welcoming little points, and her fingers tightened in his hair when he kissed them. He sucked and tongued them, showing her with his mouth how much he wanted to please her. All she had to do was let him give her this, and he would be a happy man.

Her hands pulled him closer, her hips rocking his erection in the best possible way, as if she couldn't get close enough, either. "I worried about you," she admitted. "Damn it, Evan. You made me worry."

"I'll make it up to you," he promised, his voice rough

with need and unfamiliar emotion. "I can take care of myself, darlin'. I always have, always will. You don't need to worry about me."

She tugged his head up and planted a fierce, hard kiss on his mouth. Her teeth nipped his lower lip—a bright sting of pain and then sweet, sweet pleasure, her mouth sucking gently where she'd hurt. "I want to take care of you, Evan."

Well, hell. That was—unfamiliar. Not unwelcome, just not something other women, other lovers, had wanted to give him. Taking care of her was his job. That was what he did, who he was. She rubbed against his dick again, though, and he forgot how to think, inhaling sharply at the pure pleasure of her.

He kissed her again.

She liked that. Christ, he did, too. His dick was painfully hard, straining against her thigh. That part of him wanted inside her in the worst possible way. That little brush of her soft skin against him made him want to pounce. Instead, he moved down more, feeling the muscles in her belly quiver in anticipation. Yeah, she knew right where he was going.

"You like these?" he growled, fingering the tiny straps of her panties.

"My favorite," she gasped.

"Then lift up, darlin'."

She lifted obediently, her lace-covered mound teasingly close to his mouth, and he slid the panties off.

Faye's panties disappeared down her legs. Evan's hand tugged, and the little scrap of white flew through the air, dropping onto the floor beside the bed.

The mattress was soft, and it felt so decadent to lie there and let him take care of everything. To do nothing but enjoy him and the pleasure he gave her. His shoulders parted her thighs, spreading her open. Those big, warm hands cupped her hips and ass, keeping her right where he wanted her.

"I bet you taste real sweet." He grinned and lowered his head.

His thumbs opened her up where she was already aching for his touch, and she whimpered. He was going to make her go slow.

"Please," she groaned.

"Oh, I intend to, darlin'," he said, and his mouth found her in a kiss that was so, so good. His tongue drew circles where she was wet and needing, licking long, lazy strokes up her folds, as if she was the sweetest thing he'd ever tasted.

Then he found her clit and painted the same wicked path there, too. Over and over, as if he had all the time in the world and there was nothing he wanted to do more. Just taste her and love her. More and more until her hips were rolling gently, putting her clit right where she wanted his kiss.

A lazy energy woke up in her, and she could have spent the whole night like that, lost in the sweet pleasure of his kiss, but his mouth closed over her, sucking, and the pleasure was building, and the "slow" disappeared, replace by hot urgency. *Now.* She wanted him in her and on her now.

"May I?" he whispered against her, and she felt his words there, where he was touching her, kissing her, easing her toward some other point and place. He left her long enough to slide a condom on, and then he was right back there, pushing into her.

"Please." She pulled him toward her, and he obliged, her legs falling open around him as he lowered himself on top of her, giving her as much of his weight as she could take. When he entered her, her body welcomed his. This was what she'd wanted, the long, sweet moment she'd been striving for. Homecoming. Welcome. An end reached. The orgasm found her, bursting through in a bright ripple of pleasure.

He moved, pushing deep inside her, and she lay there beneath him, watching his face work in the darkness. He was reaching for something, too, something special, and she saw when he found it, when his hips picked up speed and he drove himself into her again and again. He stiffened and groaned, planting himself deeper, and she held on to him.

Right now, he was hers. Just hers.

For one long moment, he pinned her to the mattress, his weight pushing her down, his legs spreading hers almost painfully wide. Then he slid carefully out of her.

She wanted to say something, but she didn't know what. He pulled her into his arms, but there was all that silence that needed filling up, and she ached inside where he'd been.

She opened her mouth, closed it. Tried again. "Evan—"

"Go to sleep, Faye." He sounded tired. He'd been out there in the field, working nonstop through the night. That was all those words meant. Behind her, the sheets rustled as he left.

Getting out of bed.

"Where are you going?" she blurted before she could stop herself.

"I'm going to shower," he said, and that tiredness was back in his voice.

She didn't want him to go. What if the shower was merely an excuse to get up and leave? Logically, she knew she was in his bed, in his cabin. Where would he *go*? He had to come back to her.

God, she needed him to want to make that return journey. She closed her eyes, pretending the sleep train had come for her and that she didn't feel every dip and sway of the mattress as he stood up and headed for the shower.

Evan was more like her former husband than she'd wanted to admit. He was another big, silent, strong man whose kisses were hotter than hell—and who was always headed out the door and into danger. He didn't want to talk. That was a bad recipe, because eventually kisses weren't enough. Mike had met someone else. Someone who'd done a better job than she had of filling up those empty spaces in his heart and his head.

She couldn't do this. Not again. Rolling over, she hugged his pillow to her stomach. The water kicked on in the bathroom. She wasn't looking for marriage and babies, not right now, but she needed something more than really, really hot sex.

And Evan Donovan had walked away.

Her boys were home. All four of them. Ben was as stubborn as the other three, and wrestling him into his pickup and getting him back to his place had been a bit touch-and-go. For a moment there, Nonna had thought he was going to go after the hotshot who'd been arguing for his chance at making the jump team.

That was Ben. Fiercely determined, fiercely loyal. It had been a long day of firefighting, and he was filthy and reeked of smoke. He needed a shower and sleep. And she was so very, very glad to see him. He'd spent the last thirty-six hours out there, directing a hotshot crew. She knew the ABC basics, but that hadn't kept her from worrying.

"I need to clean up," he said, when they pulled up in front of his place in Strong. Even that short drive had been too long. She wanted to scrape that top layer of dirt off, see for herself that he was okay all the way through. She knew her men. Any injury they could hide, they would.

"Sure do." Her feet didn't stop moving, though. Just kept following him up the steps of his porch and into his house. He had, she realized, a clear view of her own front door. She should go there. He'd clean up and be out soon enough. And yet she didn't want to let him out of her sight—and it wasn't simply because she was dying to do an injury check.

"Come on in," he said, opening the front door and stepping inside. He hadn't locked it. Maybe he never did. Not that it would have mattered. She'd known for years where he kept the spare key.

He kept on moving, through the living room and down the hall, pausing long enough to open a cupboard and snag an armful of towels. When he hit the bathroom, good manners said she should stop. She wasn't his wife or his girlfriend or any other female entitled to wait around while he undressed. She belonged outside. Nevertheless, her feet took her closer. Some primal part of her still wanted him where she could see him and to judge for herself that he wasn't hurt.

He didn't seem to mind, either. He simply shot her a glance she couldn't interpret and turned on the water in the shower with a deft flick of his wrist. All that hot water soon had steam filling up the small space. Apparently, he still wanted heat even after his night in the forest.

"You might want to look away." His hands tugged the T-shirt over his head. "Or not. Lady's choice."

"You take that shower, and *you'll* look better." She could feel the little smile tugging at her mouth, but she pulled a bottle of shampoo from his bathroom cupboard, placed it on the side of the tub, and then went down the hall to fetch him clean clothes. Ben's bedroom was as neat and masculine as the man himself. Big California-king bed with a silky brown coverlet. Two large pillows, but no decorative throws. There wasn't too much in the picture department, either. Just the silver-framed wedding photo of him and the wife he'd lost to cancer ten years ago.

When she made the return trip, he'd stripped off, dropping the dirty clothes on the floor, and disappeared inside the shower. She picked them up, folding them carefully before flipping the lid down on the toilet seat— what *was* it about men?—and parking herself on the fuzzy seat cover.

"I've got your clean stuff here." She figured she should announce herself, in case he hadn't noticed the blast of cooler air when she'd opened and closed the bathroom door.

"You sticking around, after all?"

Maybe he'd thought she'd left. She touched the dirty clothes gently. One go-around with Tide wasn't going to be enough. He didn't sound disappointed that she'd come back, so she'd stay a little bit longer. She didn't want to go home. Not yet.

"Sure am," she said, then asked what she'd been dying to know. "Tell me about it. Tell me all about the fire."

She'd always loved Ben's openness. He wouldn't fill her in publicly, where there were others who could hear, but once she got him alone, he'd tell her about the fire calls he'd gone out on. What he knew, she knew. Tonight, he gave her the lowdown on the fire, sharing all the details he had. She didn't like to think about her family out there facing down such an inferno, but it was harder when she didn't know the facts. This way, she only feared the stuff that needed fearing.

Sure enough, he gave her all the details. It took two rinse cycles, too, as he got busy with the soap. The fire was big and hungry, but, so far, more or less contained. They'd lost two lines—her boys were going to be pissed about that, because they prided themselves on holding their line no matter what the fire dished up—but the third one was holding, and the tankers were making new drops right now. In the next eight hours, he hoped things would be finally under control. Right now, though, the Strong contingent was taking its mandatory break, so if she was lucky, that fire would be out before her boys had to head back into the field.

"That one was Mother Nature all over." His hand reached around the shower curtain, feeling for the shampoo bottle, and she hooked him up. "Probably a lightning strike that simmered for a while."

"How many acres?"

There was a pause on the other side of the curtain and then the sound of a washcloth getting busy. "We won't know for certain for a few more days. Nine hundred so far. We've still got multiple teams working the firelines up there, and it's looking good. Real good. Unless the wind shifts on us tonight or we have sleeper fires, we might have this under control."

"Good." She wanted to say something else, but some things were hard to put into words. "The hotshot who stopped you on the way home tonight—"

"That was obnoxious, wasn't it?" She could hear him moving around in the shower behind that curtain as he answered her. What would he do if she reached out and nudged the curtain a little to one side?

"Maybe he's ambitious," she offered.

"And stupid," Ben snorted. "You don't pitch yourself for a job five minutes after you learn someone's been injured."

"So he's not Mr. Sensitive," she agreed. "That's not a crime. Still, what kind of person does that, Ben?"

"He's hungry, all right. And his timing certainly sucks." He killed the water. "I'm coming out."

She had the towel waiting for him when he slid the curtain back. Sure, she kept her eyes on his face—mostly—because she was being a lady tonight. Just until she'd made up her mind about where she wanted this thing with Ben to go. Maybe he hadn't noticed her peeking. Much. He didn't say anything, though, so it had to be okay.

She went out into the living room, and Ben followed, pulling on the clean clothes she'd left folded up on the toilet seat.

"Actually, I've been watching Anderson for a while," he said grimly, picking up their conversation where they'd left off. "He's been ready to go out on far too many calls. And he's always hanging around the jump team. He's punched overtime every week."

"He can't be the only one." She was all too familiar with boys who had the fire bug and who wanted desperately to be firefighters. "Maybe he thinks this is how you get what you want, how you make the team. If he shows a little initiative, then—*boom*—he's in."

"Sure," Ben said, as he sank onto the couch. "But I'm watching all the firefighters in Strong, looking for a possible arsonist. I got ten names left on that list of mine, and I'm keeping my eye on every single one of them. He shot to the top of the short list tonight. God, sitting down feels good. I'm too old for this all-nighter crap. Come over here and join me." He closed his eyes and held out a hand.

She debated the pros and cons of his offer far too briefly before she went to him. That was where she wanted to be, anyhow, and he'd asked. Just a little friendly comfort. "Maybe," he continued, "the boy likes fire. God knows, I do. Jack and Evan and Rio—they're the same way. Maybe that's Hollis, too, but if so, he picked a damn poor time to make his case."

The couch swallowed her up, and his arms closed around her. *Mmm.* She laid her head on his chest, listening to the steady *thump-thump* of his heart while he held her.

Better. This was definitely better.

Chapter Eleven

Hollis slammed out of the hangar and made for the row of pickups and beat-to-shit Hondas hanging out on the far side of the bay doors. Fuck Ben Cortez. Hollis had asked real nice, too, and he'd still been shot down cold. He'd shown initiative, and Ben had acted as if Hollis were kicking puppies or spitting in the communal guacamole. He wanted that empty spot on the jump team, and no matter what Ben said, any idiot could see that Jack Donovan was going to be taking some R & R. The Donovan brothers had limits, too, even if the entire town acted like they were fucking superheroes. Jack had a busted up foot and arm. He was going onto the medical list. That was a fact.

What *wasn't* a fact was who'd take Jack's place.

Hollis needed them to look at *him*. To *see* him. He could do this job. He tossed his gear bag into the back of his truck and, two minutes later, had the gears slamming into place as he peeled out of camp. He wasn't in the mood right now to hang out with the boys and discuss to-day's fire. He took the dirt road away from the hangar too fast, gravel spitting up and chewing at his paint job. He could see the DC-3 parked out there on the runway, as if the plane was also waiting for him to say the right words, do the right thing.

He'd earned his spot, and he was getting it.

He didn't have to be stupid about this, though.

It felt good to open the truck up when he hit the highway. It wasn't the same as flying, not even close, but it was definitely as close as he'd get today.

Goddamn Ben Cortez and his *not nows*. The way Hollis saw it, he'd been sung that same-old, same-old tune for too many weeks and months now. His local department had fed him the same line. *Wait. Put more time in.* And, oh, yeah, *we'll call you.*

He was done waiting. No one was going to hand him an opportunity, so he'd make it. He'd show them—over and over—if he had to. He could put out the same fires they did. He could do it fast, and he'd never been afraid of hard work.

He wanted his chance, that was all.

It was too damn bad, when you thought about it, really, that he had to go set stuff on fire to get some attention. Maybe the fire camp's higher-ups should have been more awake. That was how he saw it, anyhow. The first fires had been all about fun. He'd made himself a chance to get out of the fire camp and into the field.

These last fires? Not so much. These were serious practice. Kind of like having a business card. He liked that mental picture. A little flick-flick and his boys had themselves another fire, and he had himself another shot. With Jack Donovan down for the count, even if it was a temporary seat on the sidelines, Hollis had a real chance at going up. If enough fires lit up these mountains, the jump team wouldn't be so laid back about filling up the holes in that roster.

Thirty minutes later, he pulled the truck over. This time, he'd hike in a mile or so. If he set this one right, he'd be back in the truck and halfway to base camp before the smoke cleared the treetops.

He got out, did a quick look around, because he didn't need any more photographers popping out of the wood-work, thank you very much, and grabbed his bag of sup-plies. He had plenty of matches and newsprint with a side of gasoline.

Time to get to work here.

The ringtone sang its wake-up call, and Evan flipped open his cell and snapped out a hi-how-are-ya. He recog-nized the number. It was about time Mike Thomas called. If Evan hadn't been out in the field for most of yesterday and the day before, he would have had the other man on speed dial.

Last time, Mike had been way too fucking cheerful. This time the man sounded cautious. Which was good. Evan wasn't happy about how this particular favor was playing out.

He angled himself out onto the cabin's front porch. "About time you called." He'd cut right to the chase. "I thought I was going to have to head down to L.A. for some answers."

There was a pause on the other end, and then Mike jumped right in. He had plenty to say, all right—but not anything Evan wanted to hear. "Yeah. So, sorry," Mike finished up some long-ass story about being on call, and wasn't that a bitch of a fire that ate up a block of office buildings, and had Evan seen the coverage on the news? "You found Faye, right? So what's the problem there?"

"The problem," Evan gritted out, "is that she still doesn't know you asked me to look in on her, okay?"

"She needs to know that?" Mike's bewilderment might help explain why his marriage had ended. "You did me a favor, and I asked you to keep it on the down low because I didn't want to upset her. Any more than she already was," he added hastily when Evan muttered a curse.

"She needs to know," he said firmly.

"Why?" The noise from the other end said he might not have Mike's undivided attention. Evan could hear men's voices and truck doors slamming. It sounded as if Mike had placed his call in the middle of the firehouse bay.

"She just does." He could imagine Nonna's face if this came out. She'd be disappointed. Hell, he wasn't happy with himself. He hadn't been straight with Faye at all.

"I don't think it matters," Mike objected.

Which is why you're divorced, asshole.

"So you don't mind if I tell her." *There.* That was clear. Keeping this kind of secret from Faye was wrong. But, sure, he was torn: he'd agreed to help Mike for the right reasons. He hadn't known then how he'd feel about Faye.

"Well . . ." Mike hesitated, clearly reaching. "I still think this would all be much easier if you don't. I only wanted to know that she was going to be okay."

"You want to know that, you ask her. She'll tell you."

"Okay." Another pause, as if Mike wasn't ready to let him go yet. "But you think she's doing okay?"

Evan didn't want to talk to Mike Thomas about Faye. Hell, Mike was the last person he wanted to go heart-to-heart with. What could he say? He could hardly explain how badly he wanted Mike's ex-wife. That wouldn't go over well. And sharing his opinions on Mike's marital and communication skills? Equally bad idea.

Mike wasn't done complaining, though. No, he kept right on trucking. "She said I wasn't there for her. Said she was all alone, and she was tired of it. She knew what the firehouse was like. It shouldn't have been a surprise."

Faye definitely knew far too much about how a firehouse worked. Maybe she'd see smoke jumping differently, but Evan didn't think so. She'd sounded pretty down on the whole lot of them when she'd been trading chitchat with Nonna and Lily back there in the hangar the other day.

"She said," Mike continued, "that there was no way we could still be friends. So I figured it was easier to get you to check up on her. Make sure that things really were okay."

"She's okay," he repeated. He sounded like a damn broken record, and he had no idea if it was the truth, anyhow. Was Faye okay? Was she secretly missing Mike, fantasizing about going back to him?

Somewhere in the background a siren started up, wailing insistently. "Truck's going out," Mike said, and then the noise nearly swallowed his voice. "Tell her. Don't tell her. It's your call."

The old firehouse was a man-fest, firefighters swarming the porch and the truck bay, and Faye watched them climbing ladders and wielding paintbrushes. The guys laughed, tossing jokes back and forth, trading cans of paint and hammers and nails. They were working together, and it was clear that, sooner or later, the firehouse would be everything it had been before and more. The building was going to look spectacular.

Perfect for the magazine's cover.

She took a step back, bringing the camera up so she could snap off another shot.

Since it was midafternoon, there was no escaping the summer heat. Shirts had come off, and garden hoses had come out. Rio had stripped off his top first, and the rest of the jump team had gotten on board with the plan. That meant a whole lot of hard, muscled bodies on display. The smoke jumpers were clearly comfortable in their own skin.

Joey hit Mack with a hose, and the other man brought him down with a playful nelson right before Rio turned his own hose on them. Someone dragged Mimi in, and then there were hoses pointing everywhere and way too much water running down the street.

The whole town—what there was of it—had turned

out for the fun. A bunch of folks had brought barbecue grills, and Mimi had opened up the bar, passing out sodas and bottled water. Some of the guys slung arms around women, taking a break and chugging down water. There was a casual intimacy that was hard to miss, along with a few heated glances shared between couples. Donovan Brothers might be a temporary addition to Strong while the summer fire season raged, but there was clearly a make-hay-while-you-can thing happening here. No one was going lonely.

Except her.

She stood there, watching. Jack folded Lily into his arms, tucked her head underneath his chin, and pulled her back against his chest. The two of them were facing the world together, watching and laughing and holding on to each other. They looked good together. No, more than that, they looked *right,* like two pieces of a puzzle that you knew matched up. No question about it. No rough edges, just an easy, seamless fit.

She took a quick step backward, the camera in her hands suddenly blurring. She wasn't going to cry about this.

Jack and Lily looked so happy.

Months and months ago, before it had become painfully clear that she and Mike weren't going to fix the cracks in their relationship, she'd liked to look at their wedding pictures. They'd had a quickie ceremony on the Vegas Strip in a pretty little wedding chapel. Outside the door, were acres of slot machines and people, but inside the chapel, at first there had been just the two of them and the flowers. The place had gone all out on the flowers. Huge white lilies that had smelled divine. The florist had done something clever to keep the scent and lose the pollen, because when she'd brushed her fingers across a stamen, the pollen hadn't stained her skin. The flowers were all prettiness, no mess.

Then the officiant had come in, two hotel-provided witnesses in tow, and she and Mike had said their vows to each other, and they'd gone back out into the noise and the din to start that new life together they'd promised each other.

Jack's fingers smoothed the hair away from the side of Lily's face. She said something, and Faye didn't have to hear those words to understand the slow smile heating up his face. The white-hot sexual tension between the two of them had Faye betting those two would slip off together before the day got much older.

Jack really *saw* Lily when he looked at her, and he clearly loved what he saw.

Had Mike ever looked at her like that? The wedding picture she'd kept in a silver frame her sister had sent—with their names and date engraved on the curlicue edges—said maybe he had. He'd loved her enough to marry her, but he hadn't loved her enough to pick her over the boys at the firehouse. Or that other woman. Yeah, that was the real kicker. It wasn't just that he'd left her alone—he'd been trying out replacements.

He'd married her, and they'd honeymooned in Vegas, and then they'd come back to L.A., and he'd made it perfectly clear that he had a job that was important. She hadn't argued. She'd agreed: fighting fires was essential, and someone had to do it, even if she wasn't sure why he had to do it practically every single night. Why the beeper had to come into their bedroom and pluck him away at least four nights out of seven because he'd agreed to cover for other firefighters. When she'd complained, he'd offered to sleep the night shifts at the firehouse.

Yeah. As if that was what she was angling for—for her new husband to be gone more than he was present. She'd wanted him at *home*. In bed and close enough to touch, even if they were only sleeping. It didn't have to be all about sex.

She'd been patient and supportive. She'd rolled out of bed to see him off and made him coffee to go and heated up dinners when he came back at all hours of the night. Then she'd grown tired of never sleeping through the night and of lying there worrying about what could happen to him even though it never did, and she'd stopped fighting when he suggested that he sleep at the firehouse.

So he wouldn't disturb her.

He'd been so fucking considerate. She'd wanted to fight, to yell, and he'd stood there calmly, saying that he could see she was tired and wouldn't it be easier on her if he only came back on his days off? Right then, their marriage had become a weekend thing, a hobby he indulged in when he had a few spare hours. He'd claimed he didn't even have time for counseling to see if they could get over his landing in bed with another woman. He'd put every spare minute into fighting fires and a shot at driving the truck and making lieutenant.

The day Mike had made lieutenant, he'd gone out celebrating with the guys from the station house. He'd sent her a goddamned text, and she'd sent him divorce papers. She was surprised he'd even noticed.

Her fingers tightened on the camera. *Click*. Rio aiming a hose at Evan. *Click*. All that water glistening on rock-hard abs. It was a full-blown erotic fantasy, and she wanted to cry. What was wrong with her? She got the camera up again, the lens between her and the firehouse. That was better. *Breathe in. Then out.*

Why did she have to fall apart like this? She had a ringside seat, watching Strong's jump team go all DIY on their firehouse, and that was no reason to feel so alone. She didn't want to cry. Goddamn it, she was done crying.

She'd left all the tears—and, yes, the loneliness—behind her in L.A. That was the whole point of having a really fast, really amazing car, right? She'd driven too fast up the freeway, but she'd been free, free, free, flying over the pavement with the music blasting. She wasn't really going *Thelma and Louise,* but she'd always loved that last scene and how that car had hung there in the air, flying for one long, glorious, fuck-you of a moment.

No good . . . the tears weren't stopping.

As she backed up, beating a strategic retreat, she kept the camera up and her finger flying on the equipment. So what if the pics were complete and utter crap? Right now she wanted that cover between her face and the rest of the world. When she reached the relative safety of the Corvette, she opened the door and dropped down onto the ground beside it. Yeah, it was childish—and she didn't give a damn. Not right now. It was far easier to pretend to be fiddling with the camera. She'd take the alibi. She was a mess. No way she could rejoin all those happy, laughing, let's-build-us-a-firehouse people.

Angrily, she rummaged on the floor of the car for a package of tissues. Her dirt seat wasn't the most comfortable place to be, but she'd take hiding behind a car door over public exposure any day.

Voices close to her car put the K.O. on that plan. Damn it. She swiped at her nose with the tissue.

"You ready to go?" That was Jack's deep voice. Lily's laughter answered him. Yeah, this wasn't going to be awkward at all.

"Depends. What are you offering?"

Lily's voice was all sexy promise. Jack rumbled something in response. Faye couldn't catch the words, and she didn't want to. Her face flushed with an uncomfortable prickle of emotion. *Please, God, don't let them see me. . . .*

"You sure you can deliver on that promise, firefighter?"

"Uh-huh." Denim brushed against denim. "You come right here, baby. Exactly like that."

There was that low laughter again and then the sounds of two people kissing. Playfully, hands sliding over clothes, mouths fused together. A little silence that meant the world and a soft exhale as they broke apart.

Jack had backed Lily against the door of his truck, and now he leaned into her. And wasn't this a new low? Not content with hiding behind her car door, Faye was peeking around the edge of it. She let her head fall back, and it hit the seat as she groaned. A simultaneous male groan outside said Jack was feeling just fine today.

Jack Donovan was all firefighter, yet he kissed Lily Cortez as if she was the center of his universe. That was what Faye had wanted. Before.

Who was she kidding? She wanted Evan to kiss her like that, all tender and hungry. Like he was sure they were going home together to do something more about that hunger. She wanted Evan to kiss *her* as if she was the most important girl in the world.

Faye Duncan, she warned herself. *Don't go expecting a happily-ever-after.*

Chapter Twelve

Two days later, with her editor's voice yelling out of her cell, Faye wanted to throw the phone at the nearest wall. Hitting something hard would be good. Problem was, that kind of close encounter of the immovable sort wouldn't be good for her cell—and she didn't have the cash to burn on indulging her feelings. Which, right now, fell right into the categories of *pissed off* and *running scared*.

The magazine's editor wanted his piece. Yesterday. He'd take tomorrow, and he might even go three days, but he wasn't giving her the rest of the week and change that she'd promised Evan.

This wasn't how she'd imagined her magazine debut, either. No, that had been more along the lines of "Here's a breaking news story—with a side of fantastic photography." She could still do that. If she reneged on her bargain with Evan.

And that was the heart of the problem, wasn't it?

"I need that piece, Faye," her editor said, and now he sounded more frantic than angry. "I need to finish the issue. This can't wait. Shoot it, send it—or I'll use something else."

"Could you push it to the next issue?"

"Faye—no. I'm booked. It's now, or it's never. How

hard can this be? You said you were ready for this. You wanted to shoot this story. This was your chance."

"You'll have it," she promised.

"When?" He wasn't ending the call until he had a date. They both knew that. It was his job.

"Soon," she promised.

"Two days," he countered. "That's it. That's all the time I have to give you. This isn't me going all hard-ass on you, Faye. I have deadlines, too, and you've left me with a big fucking hole to fill."

"I haven't. I won't," she said quickly, and then she hung up before he could move on the next step in his collection effort. Sure, the magazine couldn't force her to turn in her photos—but she also couldn't force them to pay her. Or employ her again. She had a sneaking suspicion, too, that editors talked—and she was headed straight for the shit-list if she didn't deliver.

And she didn't blame the editor.

He had a job to do, and she'd made promises. So the real question was, why wasn't she planted in a chair, working up her photos? She'd already taken enough shots for two pictorials. All she had to do was finish editing them—and *choose*. Which ones. Which story she wanted to tell the public. She'd started with that first set of images, driving into Strong.

Grabbing her laptop, she paged through the earliest set of pics. Those photos were some of the best she'd ever shot. Even though she hadn't known the full story at the time, the strength and determination of the unknown firefighter seemed to jump right out of the image. He was fighting. Taking a stand. Giving it all he had. The punch line, though, was that he was almost certainly the bad guy in this story—and so far he'd gotten away with it. He was a pretend hero in a town full of the real deal.

If she included those pictures, gave them the caption they merited, Strong's firefighters would pay the price. They deserved funding for their new firehouse and they'd certainly earned their dreams.

Her cell rang again, and she turned it off, tossing it onto the bunk bed. Denial wasn't a permanent solution, but right now it worked for her. She had to deliver pictures— and she had them. Good ones, but she'd promised Evan two weeks. True, her track record with promises wasn't the best. She and Mike had promised each other eternity and had settled for two years. She'd promised Evan two weeks, and now it looked as if he'd be lucky to get one.

She could wait this out, give Evan the time she'd promised him, but she'd be left holding the bag. No magazine job. No pay. She didn't need to check the contents of her purse to know that wasn't a good thing if she wanted to continue eating.

Or she could finish the job. Hand everything over to her editor and let him make the call about what he ran. Pretend to herself that he wouldn't be over-the-moon happy to run pictures of an unknown firefighter-arsonist so the magazine's readers could run a lineup themselves, comparing the faces of Strong's bravest with the unknown guy setting fires.

She had four hours until Evan showed up for tonight's date. Real country line-dancing on a genuine sawdust floor, he'd promised, although that wicked grin of his when he'd waved the flyer for Ma's Friday-night extravaganza said he had a lot more planned than line-dancing.

Four hours to decide. Time was ticking down, and she had to pick her photos. Pick a side. Pick how her Strong adventure was going to end.

Evan parked his truck outside the firehouse, and Faye tried not to think about the promise of that act. That parking job said he would come back with her tonight. After her phone call earlier that day with her editor, she needed the hope that today could still end well. Their walk to Ma's took them past Nonna and Ben slapping red paint onto a pair of old Adirondack chairs. She liked the color, a real take-no-prisoners red. Like her car.

"See you later," Evan called to the pair, but his feet didn't stop moving. Maybe he wanted to be at Ma's, or maybe he liked the walk. The disappearance of the sun beneath the horizon had brought one of those deliciously cool summer nights, and the crickets were already singing up a storm.

Evan had skipped the dress-up and was wearing his usual faded Levis and a white cotton T-shirt tucked in, paired with another pair of steel-toed boots. Did the man own anything but shoes made for shit-kicking? Sure, she'd seen him relaxed and casual, but that was in bed and naked. She mentally tried to imagine Evan in flip-flops, the happy little slap of plastic against his bare heels. Yeah. That was hard to picture.

"You ready to do this?" He looked over at her and gave her that little smile of his. From the cheerful noise and light spilling out the half-open door, Ma's was a hot spot tonight.

"Yeah. Absolutely."

He'd volunteered to take her out for a night on the town and show her how firefighters lived it up when they weren't jumping. She had a feeling this wasn't pure altruism on his part, though. Maybe this was Evan code for *date*. Either way, she figured she'd get more background for her piece and more time with him. He was a tough nut to crack, but he had to talk sometime, right?

Evan got them inside, past the enthusiastic line-dancers filling up the barroom floor, and then past the jukebox. She thought he smiled when they drew near it. Yeah.

There it was. The happy spot where they'd met and she'd fallen asleep on him. That had *so* not been one of her finer moments.

Evan cut straight across the floor. She stared shamelessly at his fine ass, enjoying the way the denim cupped him.

He snagged them a table and then spent the next hour rounding up firefighters to come over and talk with her. Two Diet Cokes later—no rum punches tonight, she'd decided—she knew plenty about Strong and what kind of mischief a jumper could get up to there.

Mack and Zay and Joey, three rough and tough, not-quite-civilized men, crowded around the table swapping stories and making sure she had everything she needed. All of them shared the same precision buzz cut, shadowed eyes, and steely determination to do what it took.

"You were all in the military together?"

"Yes, ma'am." Joey's earnest face watched her as if he couldn't wait to hear what she asked next. As if he was focused only on her. Those eyes were going to do a number on some woman someday. Curious. Eager. As if there was nothing more he wanted to do than talk her up. That kind of attention was heady.

"Two tours of sun and sand," Mack drawled. "At the military beach."

"Middle East," she guessed, and he shrugged and nodded. Somewhere, he'd acquired an armful of tattoos. Before or after his tour of duty, he'd gone and gotten some ink, and he hadn't stinted.

He didn't seem to mind her attention. "It's not a state secret."

"Anymore." Zay tipped his longneck back.

"And serving in the Marine Corps together gave you the idea to go into the firefighting business?" she asked.

Mack smiled real slow. "Well, now, see, we were already in the firefighting business there, honey. We simply moved our operations back to a more palatable base of operations."

Joey whistled. "Fancy words, man."

Mack flipped a good-natured finger in Joey's direction. "We all baked in that desert. Hotter than hell during the day, and then you froze your ass off at night. The wildlife wasn't friendly, and the locals were even less so. At least here I can have a beer without watching my back."

"So by 'firefighting,' you mean gunfights?"

"That, too." Evan slid another Diet Coke in front of her, dropping down onto the booth beside her. "We were CFR crew."

"We sat our asses in the crash truck and watched the planes come in. If any of those boys missed, we were the Welcome Wagon—you get me? Most of the time, you're baking from the afterburner, waiting for the windows of the truck to stop rattling, because all of those boys hit hard."

"And then, sometimes, they'd miss or run into trouble up above, and we'd have work to do."

"Yeah. Military Jaws of Life—that was us. If a pilot came in hard and went off the taxi, we went out there pronto and got him out."

"How would you do that?" She couldn't imagine these guys hanging out at the end of an airstrip, waiting for something to go wrong.

Zay shot her a devilish grin. "Well, first you beat down the flames, because those flyboys don't do things the easy way. Then you pop the cockpit and fish him out, toss him down to the paramedics. It's an exciting way to pass a day, and the flight line's not a bad place to be. Planes come in, planes go up. Here, though, you've got a bigger area to cover."

"Yeah. When you pull duty, your ass isn't parked in a truck waiting for trouble to come to you," Joey teased.

"You've seen a plane go down?"

"Yeah." The hard look in Mack's eyes said he'd seen more than his fair share. "You see the plane coming in, see how she's going to land, and it's like watching a highlights reel all slo-mo. You've got the truck going, and you're pedal to the metal all the way, but there's nothing you can do to stop the crash. That's already happening. You're going out there to pick up the pieces and make sure no one else gets burned."

"Imagine it." Zay leaned forward, planting his forearms on the table. "You look up, and there's this fighter jet coming down all wrong. You know it. The pilot has to know it. First there's all this noise, a real roar as the plane heads for base, and then there's nothing. You've got silence because the engines just died, and silence is bad. That pilot stuck up there in the cockpit, well, he probably knows what's up, and he's fighting to minimize the impact, because he won't leave all that machine to free-will it across the tarmac. When you look around, you see the buildings and people there. If he hits, he hits, but the other people need to walk away, because dying isn't their job, and flying the plane is his."

Mack picked up the story, as if he couldn't see the tears prickling the back of Faye's eyes. "Worst one came in nose down. The engines cut out maybe three hundred feet up. The pilot stuck her nose into the ground to avoid further casualties, and she did cartwheels for two hundred yards."

"But he put her down," Joey said.

"And we fished what was left of him out of the cockpit after we got the fire out," Mack countered.

"So you'd rather be here."

"Sure would." Joey turned his beer bottle in his hand. "Serving was good. That was important shit, but this is home. We're keeping things safe where we come from. I like that more than waiting at the end of the flight line for trouble to fly into me."

"Better to go looking for trouble," Evan added. "There's plenty of bad shit out there you don't want knocking on your front door."

"Amen to that," Zay agreed. "Far too many wildland fires burning stuff up these days. We had that one last year that we couldn't contain. There we were, called in as backup, but it was too late, and she ran free. After eating up two thousand acres, that fire came knocking on the door of the nearest town and took out whole neighborhoods of houses."

"Good men there," Zay said quietly. "That's a hell of a way to go, and those boys made every second count."

"So that's why you're here in Strong?"

Three pairs of eyes swiveled to Evan, like her answer was sitting right there.

"To fight fires? Sure." He leaned back in the booth and resumed being silent.

"That's not what I meant, and we both know it. Why Strong and not some other town? Donovan Brothers is a well-known outfit. Last summer, you ran jobs at multiple sites, including national parks. There was more action there, more jumps. Strong doesn't have the budget of even one of those places. And yet here you are."

"Upper-management thing," Mack said cheerfully. "Joey, come dance with me. I'm out of here."

Evan's boys left double-time. Before the song finished up, Mack and Joey were switching off the male "lead" in the dancing as they twirled each other down the line.

Evan stared out at the line dance as if it was the final quarter of the Super Bowl and the score was tied. Boots slapped the floor as pairs of dancers sashayed down the line. Mack twirled Joey again, and the rest of the jump

team whooped it up with good-natured teasing and a chorus of clinking beer bottles, but no one, she noticed, had
gone too far. These men knew their limits. They'd all be
good to go up tonight or tomorrow. Whenever the call
came in.

"I need you to talk to me, Evan." She flipped off the
recorder and got her hand on Evan's knee under the table.
Even that small personal connection threatened to drown
out any words.

"You ask. I answer." He picked up his beer bottle, then
set it down again. "Go ahead."

"Okay. No." Frustrated, she reached for her paper napkin, shredding the thing into pieces. Her fingers rolled the
scraps into long cigarillos, piling one on top of the other.
He wasn't going to talk. He was large and grouchy. Too
damn big and unconcerned, sprawled there in the booth.
She should have walked away and interviewed the other
firefighters, but she wanted to hear *his* story.

"What is it, Faye?" He leaned forward, topping off her
soda.

"You're giving me all the *whats* except for one. What
this place means to you. Why you want to be here so
badly. Why you came back to Strong when you could
have set up shop almost anywhere."

"You going to print every word I say?" he said finally.

She started arranging the cigarillos into a little fence.
"Probably not. I'm writing a handful of captions to go
with a set of photos, Evan. Not an encyclopedia."

"You think I should do a lot of talking?"

"You could do more." She knocked down the fence
with a little flick of her finger. "I asked you why you
picked Strong. Why are you and your guys working on
this firehouse in this town?"

"Yeah. I heard that." He eyed her carefully and brought
the beer bottle to his lips. She shouldn't be watching the

muscles of his throat work or staring at that big hand wrapped around the bottle.

"You said it was what Jack wanted," she said.

"That's true."

"But what do you want?"

The bottle hit the table. "What he wants."

She'd gotten a short version of that story already. It was a pretty story, but she knew the reality had to be ugly. Three young boys alone on the streets definitely wasn't a happy beginning, even if the ending had ultimately turned out okay. More than okay. She couldn't miss the fierce devotion these three men had for one another and their adoptive mother.

"That's not enough, Evan. I want to know the why of it."

He picked up her hand and turned it over, running her fingers through his. "So is this for your readers or for you?"

"Me."

He shrugged. "Thing is, I don't know if I have the why of it. Some things just are, Faye. Sometimes there aren't a whole bunch of words waiting to be said."

"Try." She shoved the mutilated napkin away. "Just once."

He gently swept away the napkin. "You want to dance?"

The jukebox was working through a slow song, a cowboy promising heaven to the woman in his arms. Evan held out a hand, and she went with him. She'd picked out a white tank top and another flirty little skirt made from some kind of floaty, silky material, all light purple with tiny white dots. Damned if he knew what it was called, but he sure liked the way the fabric spilled around his legs when they danced.

He wanted to pick her up again and carry her right out that door. He'd done it once before, and something warned him he'd never stop wanting to do that. He didn't deserve a woman like this one, though, and she had no idea who or what she was asking for. Worse, without knowing it, she was asking him to give her all the reasons she should be picking out another dance partner.

"Ask your questions," he said gruffly, putting a hand on her back. The thin cotton tank top made it all too easy to feel the gentle outline of her ribs where his fingers curved around. He'd always liked this dancing. The touching. The way her fingers curled into his shoulders. He wasn't much of a dancer, but this wasn't much about dancing, either. Yeah, this kind of dancing he was good with. Faye's questions? Not so much. But she wanted words, so he'd give them to her. He simply didn't know where to start, so she'd have to do the starting for both of them.

She looked at him, and those brown eyes of hers looked doubtful. She didn't think he'd go through with this.

She lobbed a real softball at him. "Why is it all about Jack and Rio?"

"You already got the CliffsNotes version, right? You heard the bit about how the three of us were fosters, but we decided we were tight. That we were a family."

"I heard that." Her fingers rested lightly on his T-shirt. Move her fingers an inch and she'd be touching bare skin. "You were ten when you came to Strong and Nonna took you in."

"I ran away from the house I was in for the first time when I was, maybe, seven. I spent the next few years living on and off the streets, fighting the system, fighting to live anywhere but where I was. Jack and Rio were the same. We three boys probably had 'trouble' stamped on our faces. We were completely out of control and completely sure we knew what was best. Since we were only kids, I doubt we had even half of it right."

His boys filled up the barroom floor, doing a little dancing themselves. They made space for him and Faye, though, the line opening up and closing around them. Only Jack was sidelined, although the way Lily was looking at him, his evening would still end happily.

"Did your families know what had happened to you?"

"Our family is right here."

She gave him a look that said evasions were off tonight's menu. "Your birth parents," she said.

"Don't count. They didn't want me. I certainly didn't want them." He didn't remember much of that first place, and he certainly wasn't calling it home. It had never been that. He had flashes of ugly memories he didn't like and didn't want. A pantry tucked under the stairs where he hid when things got real bad. A shed in the yard with barely enough room for a small body between the top shelf and the roof. He'd been big for his age, and he hadn't fit well, but he'd spent hours lying still there. Waiting for something to be over.

"Rio and Jack and I met up." He shrugged. "And it took. After a few months, we were family. We figured that if all those child-welfare workers wanted to reunify a family, they could damn well reunify *ours.*"

"I'll bet that was a hard sell." Her mouth curved in a grin, and an answering smile spread across his own face. Carefully, he scooted her out of Mack's way. Dancing wasn't Mack's strong point. He and his newest partner were working out an attempt at a tango that had nothing to do with country music and everything to do with too much beer.

"Almost impossible. County would split us up and farm us out. In a matter of days, we'd have run away, and we'd be back together again. Eventually they got tired of it all and found Nonna, who was crazy enough to take us together."

"Nonna loves you." The look on Faye's face wasn't what he expected. Envy? That thought made him uncomfortable. A little sad. Even if it was true. *Especially* if it was true.

"Yeah." He admitted it out loud. "Nonna's better than I deserve. We were damn lucky to end up here with her. We all knew it."

Nonna had been a safe haven he hadn't known he needed—or wanted. Sometimes, a person needed a pair of warm arms, and Nonna had always made sure he had that. So he'd make damned sure Strong was safe for her.

"You belong here," she said quietly, and he had to drop his head right next to her pretty mouth to hear her. "You all do. That's a special thing, Evan."

"Yeah," he said again, because he'd about used up his words for tonight. He definitely wasn't winning any poetry prizes here. So maybe he had spent too many years looking, needing a place to fit in. Strong had been that place and maybe that explained why coming back had been so easy, like slipping into a familiar pair of shoes.

He hadn't recognized the feeling because he'd never come home before.

Yet that's what he'd been doing. All those trips back to Strong when he had leave, and then again during the year when Donovan Brothers could spare him. Jack hadn't been back, but Evan had. He'd come back every holiday and two weeks in the fall, when the fires wound down and his time freed up.

He'd driven past his childhood house in Sacramento only once. It had been run-down, with knee-high weeds in the front yard, no grass. Someone had put up a chain-link fence, and even from the street he could see signs of dogs. There hadn't been dogs when he'd been there, but then, his parents hadn't been able to take care of him, either. Tax records said they still held the title to the house, but he hadn't gone any further than that. No way he was knocking on that door. Not now. After him, there had been one more kid. He hadn't been ready to find out what had happened there. Every instinct he had was hollering for him to keep on driving, so he had.

"It's good to have a place like this." Her fingers bunched the fabric of his T-shirt, then smoothed out the little wrinkles she'd made.

Maybe she'd get tired of talking soon. None of his current thoughts painted him in a good light. Maybe they could discuss the weather instead of where he'd come from. Too bad she lobbed the conversational ball right back at him.

"I like Strong," she added.

"Maybe you'll stay," he said, the idea taking root. Making Strong *his* permanent home, too. It suddenly seemed right. This was a good place. A real solid place, with doors that stayed open. "You ever think about staying here for more than two weeks?"

Fuck. Where had that come from? The words had flown out of his mouth, and they were all wrong. She stiffened right up in his arms until the foot of space between them could have been Siberia. He didn't know why he'd said that—or what he'd wanted her to say.

"I just came here on an assignment, Evan," she said lightly. "I certainly can't stay forever."

"Why not?" He exhaled roughly. "Why can't you stay here, if that's what you decide you want?"

The music slowed, the cowboy crooning out the final refrain as the song wound down.

"I just can't." Her eyes slid away from his.

"Okay," he said, because he needed to back off fast before she ran. If he kept this up, she'd be planting herself in the Corvette before the night was over. "You should think about it some, though, Faye. Maybe Strong's the right place for you, too."

"I don't think it can be." Was that a wistful look he saw

in those brown eyes? He and his brothers had been determined they wouldn't stay put. Even now, Jack had itchy feet and needed to move. Evan had gone with him when Jack tore out of Strong ten years ago. They were family first and foremost, and Jack had needed him. It was that simple. Jack was square now, though. He had Lily, and he'd made his peace with Strong. Nonna looked like she might be thinking of taking on Ben—and Rio was busy being Rio.

So maybe, if Faye needed him now, he'd take care of her.

He liked that idea a whole lot.

Damned if he didn't. It was too soon to jump on this, though, so he settled for pulling her closer. That would have to be enough until he had the future figured out. Until he came up with a plan. "We'll have ourselves one more dance, Faye, and then I'll take you home."

Chapter Thirteen

Walking Faye back to the firehouse, Evan was fresh out of conversation. He'd given all he had, so now she got silence. Fortunately, she didn't seem to mind much. She walked along beside him and kept real quiet herself. Could be she was drinking it all in, because the night was a pretty one, full of stars up there in the inky black. Or perhaps she'd gotten enough of an earful back at Ma's and didn't feel the need to fill up the silence anymore. That was fine with him. Sometimes no words were okay.

The firehouse was lit up, waiting for her. The big side porch was bathed in light, with more wattage than a stadium. If he stood there with Faye for too long, he might as well go take care of his business on Nonna's porch. No way Nonna hadn't been watching for the two of them to come walking back from Ma's, even if right now she was making a big show of that paint job she and Ben were doing on her chairs. No, his Nonna was as curious as anyone else living in Strong, and her cheerful wave and call would be just the tip of the social iceberg unless he got inside stat. Faye must have recognized that, too, because she returned Nonna's wave before she ran up the steps as if her ass was on fire, then paused, fumbling for the key in her bag.

"May I come in?" He curled his fingers around her wrist, rubbing the soft skin there.

"Nightcap? I think I've got half a pot of coffee left. From this morning." She wasn't looking in her bag now. No, she was looking right at him. Asking all sorts of silent questions with her eyes.

"Coffee's great." He took the bag from her, found the key, and got the door open. Any minute now, Faye was going to start talking again. He wanted to be alone and inside before that happened.

"Or not," he added, handing the bag back to her. The feminine scrap of pink and beads defied the laws of physics. Faye had crammed enough stuff in there to stock a small store. It was no wonder she couldn't find the key. "I'm not after coffee."

"What are you after, Evan?" She moved in front of him, and he followed her, content to watch her ass moving beneath the filmy material of that skirt.

"You, of course." His comment must have surprised her, because her breathing gave a little hitch. He liked that. She was aware of him every bit as much as he was aware of her. Watching her dance, all alive, laughing and teasing, had been almost as good as holding her. He didn't know what made her different from other women, but she was, and he loved that about her.

Love?

No. He *wanted* her. That was all, wasn't it? He'd asked to come in. He'd made that first move. When they hit the bunkroom, though, they both paused. She'd done a little redecorating since he'd been up there last, and it looked good. Almost homey. She'd put stuff on the bed. Pillows and a crazy-colored quilt. In short order she'd made the empty bunkroom hers, just like she'd moved right into his heart and made that run-down place her own.

Hell.

He stepped toward her. He would put the question out there. See what she had to say. "May I stay?"

She eyed the bed doubtfully, and, yeah, he had some doubts of his own. The firehouse's bunks weren't made for two. Hell, they barely held one with his kind of build. He'd been a lot younger and smaller the last time he'd slept there. Scooping her up and putting her into his truck was a better plan. He could have them both out at his cabin in under five minutes. He wanted her there, too. He could picture her in his bed, her honeyed hair spread out on his pillow.

"You think we'll both fit?"

"Only one way to find out, unless you want to try that coffee instead." He figured he won either way. Worst-case scenario, she could sleep on top of him.

She took a step toward him, sliding her hands up his arms, over his shoulders. "Can I tell you a secret, Evan?"

"Whatever you want, darlin'."

She put her mouth right next to his ear, and damned if her tongue didn't trace a sensual path around the sensitive lobe. "I make really, really bad coffee."

Their laughter broke the awkwardness, and then he killed the lights. Nonna was going to know damn well what he was up to, but he wasn't a boy anymore. He and Faye, well, they were both adults, and no one was getting hurt.

Getting into that bunk meant more playful laughter and a tight squeeze. He got his boots off first, because even he knew you didn't lie down with a woman with your boots on. Not unless you were asked to. Rio had tried explaining some complicated Captain Jack fantasy to him once, but Rio played in a league of his own, and he loved his games. Evan? He liked things simple. And there was nothing better or more crystal-clear-simple than Faye in the shadows of the bunkroom. That was pure beauty.

She giggled again when he got an arm caught underneath her and eased them both down onto the mattress.

She was ticklish, and now he knew one more thing about her. That could be fun next time he got her clothes off. Right now, though, he just wanted to lie there next to her and enjoy.

Her laughter was good, a husky, no-holds-barred snort that had her hand flying up to cover her mouth, as if she wanted to take back the sound, when all he wanted was to tell her how much he loved that laugh of hers. That sound was one hundred percent happiness and all Faye. No one else laughed like she did, and that was one more thing to love. As if he needed more reasons for feeling something that wasn't reasonable to begin with. It was one hell of an emotional bombshell he'd dropped on himself. Just a few days and he was in love with her. Talk about rushing in. He wasn't sharing that little revelation with her, though. Not yet.

"You really love being here," she said in the darkness.

That hit his panic button, his stomach dropping as if he'd gone out of the DC-3 and then remembered his parachute was still back in the jump bay. He sucked in a breath and sorted his head out. She meant Strong. She wasn't talking about her bed or his heart. Which was good. He wasn't ready to talk about what he might feel for her. Not out loud. He needed to figure out what to say and how to say it. Strong, on the other hand, was kind of an open secret after their dance-floor conversation. Yeah, he loved this town, and he'd made that clear enough.

"I do." He shifted his arm underneath her, and she rolled straight into him.

"You want to play sleepover, I plan on getting comfortable," she warned. Her fingers got busy on the buttons of her skirt, undoing things with teasing clicks and moving fabric. The bed dipped, and her shimmying had him gritting his teeth and thinking *he* was anything but comfortable, because his dick was all wake-up-and-play, harder than hard, and then that skirt of hers disappeared over his shoulder. That left her with the tank top and a pair of tiny panties that weren't doing his good intentions any favors, either.

"So why'd you leave?" She was back to talking, but her voice was finally sleepy. She kind of sank into him, her feet rubbing against his legs until she got herself comfortable. She was entitled. It was her damn bed, and he was only here because she'd let him in. He inhaled, and her hair smelled like fruity shampoo and Faye. A sweet, clean scent that had him sniffing like some kind of pervert.

"Jack needed to get out, and I wanted to make sure he had someone to watch his back, because sometimes life sends a shit-storm into a good man's way. Sometimes it doesn't." He pressed his face against her hair.

"And you knew he'd be okay with you there." Jack and Faye were alike in some ways, only Jack had been running from Lily and a happily-ever-after in Strong, and Faye was just running, trying to find out what she really wanted.

"Tell me about Mike." He'd opened up on the dance floor, so that made this her turn.

"Are you asking because I made you talk to me on the dance floor?" There was suspicion in her voice, along with a strong note of sleepiness. She'd be out like a light if he didn't keep her talking. Palming the back of her neck, he rubbed gently.

"I want to hear what you've got to say." He did, too. Even more, he wanted her to tell him. He had a feeling she hadn't shared much with anyone about her failed marriage. Instead, she'd hopped into her car—her very new, very expensive, fuck-you of a car—and driven up here. To a place she'd never been before. Yeah. He could do that math.

"Everyone thought we'd get back together. I thought that, too, for a while. I spent weeks waking up each morning, wondering if Mike would call that day and our second chance would start."

"He didn't call."

"I didn't call him, either. There were two of us in that marriage. The funny thing was, I was waiting for him, and yet I was relieved when he didn't come. I was glad it was over. I didn't have to try so hard to make the marriage work anymore. I was done. All those years of trying, and I was glad to be done with it all." She paused. "We weren't fighting. It wasn't that."

He rubbed her back gently. "What happened?"

"I found him with another woman." She stated the ugly truth matter-of-factly, and he wondered precisely how she'd reacted when she'd found her husband wrapped around someone else. "Just friends, he said, who went a little too far one night. A gal from the station. It wouldn't happen again."

"I see," he said. He wanted to kill Mike. "But that's his story. What did *you* do? How did *you* feel?"

She was silent for a moment, but he knew she wasn't asleep or dodging. She was looking for words. "Nothing, and that was the problem. Somehow, nothing happened, and I couldn't bring myself to care. We sort of drifted apart, and there was nothing left. We lived in the same house, shared a checking account and utility bills, but that was it. He spent more and more time down at the firehouse and yet he couldn't even tell me about what happened there. The firefighters had this code of silence thing. Whatever happened down there, the good days, the bad, the inside jokes and everything that had gone right or wrong on a particular job . . . that wasn't my business. It was his and theirs. It was all about his boys. The rides out on the truck and what the fire had done. Then we stopped talking at all because there was so much not to talk about. One morning, I woke up and looked around and asked myself if this was what I wanted for the next ten, twenty years, thirty. And I didn't."

"You filed for divorce."

"When he made lieutenant and couldn't even be bothered to call to tell me." Her voice was fierce. "Then, for no reason, I waited for him to realize that we'd made a mistake. I waited for him to come back home anyway and tell me he wanted to try."

He didn't like that mental picture of her waiting. He wanted to tell her that it didn't matter, that she was worth ten of Mike Thomas, but that truth wasn't going to make up for how she'd felt. He respected her for being honest. Right or wrong, her breakup had hurt her. "He didn't come back."

"No." She laughed and smoothed out the edge of the sheet. This set had one of those decorative bands of curlicue embroidery to tell you which end was up. Real feminine sheets for a firehouse of big, tough men, so he was betting the cotton was a Walmart special. "So you know what I did then, Evan? I cashed out my 401K, and I bought that Corvette. Sure, part of it was a fuck-you to Mike. He'd always lusted after a Corvette. But I had, too. And I decided I was done with waiting for life to happen to me. I may end up living in that car when I'm seventy and looking to retire—so it's good it's a damn nice car."

"Do you love him?"

"Of course I did."

"No." His hand stroked over her back. "*Do* you love him, Faye?"

"Some part of me always will." Her sigh was a tired little puff of air. He wished he knew what to say to her. But he didn't, so he held on to her and waited for her to finish saying what she needed to get out. "And that's okay. It is. Because I *have* moved on. Our divorce was no one's fault and both our faults. Fundamentally, though, we weren't right for each other. We were—are—better off apart."

His rumble of amusement filled up the silence. "And you got the car."

"Yeah." She laughed and rolled over, ending up face to chest with him in the darkness. "Yeah, I got the car."

There sure wasn't much room in the bed. Barely enough for the two of them to lie there, side by side, facing each other. It was late, and she was tired. She needed to sleep, and this was crazy, like they were two teenagers sneaking into bed together.

The night outside wasn't any too quiet, either, although she liked those sounds. Crickets sang up a storm, and guys called to each other faintly, truck doors slamming and motors gunning to life until there was nothing but crickets again. She was alone in the dark with Evan. Being wrapped up in his arms and more than half naked should have been sexy as hell, and yet she also felt *comfortable*. For the first time in months, she didn't feel alone. Getting him to talk to her had been like pulling teeth, true, but he'd done it. He'd opened up, and she'd opened up, and now there was all that emotional sharing hanging in the air between them and a new kind of silence that all the crickets in the world couldn't fill up.

Right now, there wasn't anything more to say, and yet he was still there. He was under the sheets with her, and he wasn't leaving. Not tonight. Those were his boys leaving Ma's, heading back to the fire camp in their trucks, and he'd made his choice. For tonight at least, he was with her, and yet she was almost too damn tired to do anything but listen to the crickets and wonder how insects could be so damn loud.

He slid a leg over hers. She could feel him watching her through the shadows, as if he was searching her face for some kind of clue. She didn't know what he was looking for. His leg was a heavy, warm weight, anchoring her to the mattress as she drifted toward sleep.

His hand was still at her neck, rubbing away the tension before dropping to her shoulders. She relaxed into him, into the warmth and lazy, sleepy desire. They didn't have to have sex, but they could. If they chose. Or, if she wanted to, she could slip into sleep easily from here. The desire for Evan was there, but this time it was no raging fire. Tonight the heat and the need was all slow burn.

"I figure we're both done talking." That deep, gravelly voice did something to her, something that made her insides go liquid with heat. "So let me hold you for a bit, Faye."

"Stay with me?" She hated the plea in her voice, but she'd already given him so many secrets tonight, the little sting of shame seemed small in comparison. He knew more about her now than Mike ever did.

Wasn't that strange? This man she'd met just a few days ago knew her better, knew her more intimately, than the man she'd been married to for three years and had dated for twelve months before that.

"Absolutely," he promised. "You want me to stay, I stay. Although next time we should take this to my cabin."

"You think so?" Her head was all muzzy cobwebs that had her sinking into the bunk's too old, second-rate mattress. A few coils pressed into her side, because this wasn't memory-foam territory, but she didn't care. If she wanted, she could let her eyes drift shut, and she'd float off into sleep in Evan's arms.

"Yeah." A kiss brushed the side of her forehead. She could hear the grin in his voice. "My bed's bigger. You go to sleep now if that's what you want. I'm going to hold you."

For long minutes, that was what he did, too. Held her,

surrounding her with strength and heat. The night was all lush stillness except for the crickets, cooler air pushing in through the open window. It was just the two of them, squeezed into a too-small bunk.

She wasn't alone. He was right there with her.

His mouth rested against her temple, where she could feel the soft in-and-out of his breath. The rough stubble of his jaw was a blunt reminder of how different they were. That, and the heavy leg pinning hers to the bed like the best kind of anchor, his coarse hair against her skin.

His fingers brushed briefly against her cheek as he slid her hair away from the sensitive skin at her nape, gently massaging what he'd uncovered.

"Good night, darlin'," he whispered. It *had* been a good night. She wanted to sink into the bed, let the exhaustion take her, and yet she wasn't ready for the night to be over yet.

She turned over, stretched and pressed herself against him, enjoying the feel of him.

"Darlin'." His husky groan said he liked that move. He wasn't sleepy, either. He wanted to do more than hold her. Lots more.

"We don't have to go to sleep right away," she said. The thick ridge of his erection pressed against her, trapped beneath his boxers, and all she had to do was reach between them and let him out. So simple and easy. Tempted, she moved against him. Slow and sweet with no rush now to be anywhere else.

"We don't have to do anything." His voice rumbled in her ear. "You're tired. You should sleep."

"I should have you, Evan. That's what I'm thinking." She slid against him again, and, yeah, she was definitely teasing him now. She was tired, but she wasn't dead, and she wanted him.

His hands touched her gently. Stroking carefully like she

was something precious, something soft that felt real good beneath his fingers. At first, he only petted her shoulders and her forearms. Eased the cotton up to find her belly. There was nothing naughty about his touch, just a deeply sensual appreciation of having every inch of her tucked up against him.

She mattered to him.

His fingers found the bare underside of her breast and followed the curve. He was melting her from the inside out. Those big hands loved her and held her and made everything all right in the dark.

"This okay?" he asked hoarsely.

"Yeah." She hummed softly, a little note of pleasure. "Too good, Evan. You're too good."

"I'm not good enough," he said fiercely. "I don't deserve you. I know that. But you let me give you this tonight, okay? I'll make this good for you."

When her whispered *yes* and *please* filled up the space between them, he went back to touching her, his hand moving down her belly. Slowly, as if he had all the time in the world. All night long.

As soon as her breathing picked up and got that hitch that said maybe she wasn't sinking into sleep anymore but something else, he explored further. Moved his hand, and the muscles of her stomach tightened in anticipation as he went down.

He covered her pussy and rubbed, slow and undemanding. "I love feeling you."

Still no rush, still just the warm anticipation spiking through her. He touched her there, over her panties, soft and slow. His thumb gently pressed down and found her in a long, slow stroke. Up. And then down again. Heated bliss.

Long minutes later, foil crinkled as he rolled on a condom and then slid her panties down her legs, tucking himself against her back and slid into her slowly. A little push and she gave around him, took him in. She was tired, but this was so good. Somehow, he'd connected the two of them, and now he was wrapped around her in one sensual bear hug.

The words were on the tip of her tongue—*I love you*—but he wasn't ready to hear them, and she wasn't quite ready to say them. Words were for tomorrow, and tonight was for doing, so she pushed back against him, taking him one slow inch at a time.

He moved in and out of her in slow, steady strokes, and she held him to her, clutching the arm wrapped around her waist as he coaxed her into melting around him. She relaxed, drifting away into his touch and not expecting anything, and then the orgasm was right there, a delicious surprise.

Her heart pounded against his, and she wasn't sure whose heart beat harder. Beating together. "Come with me, darlin'," he whispered, and she did, the sweet, sharp clench of her pussy pulling him over the edge with her and down into sleep.

Chapter Fourteen

The cheerful strains of the CD Mary Ellen had popped into the player were still going strong. Ben liked Sousa marches fine, but two hours of the stuff was a recipe for Tylenol. Maybe it was time he introduced her to iTunes. Evan and Faye had wandered past a good hour earlier. The pair had hit the porch at the firehouse and disappeared inside quickly. If he'd been them, he wouldn't have wanted an audience, either. Now the lights were all out over there, and he figured things were heating up between those two. He wanted Evan to be happy, and maybe Faye Duncan was exactly the woman that boy needed.

Him, on the other hand, well, he'd been working the paintbrush for the last hour, and there wasn't much thrill to be had from that kind of work. Nonna—*Mary Ellen*—had clearly read every home-renovation handbook the hardware store stocked on those racks by the checkout, because she'd dictated a course of sanding followed by priming before even a drop of paint hit her chairs. Hell. They were forty-year-old Adirondacks, and she ought to be worrying about wood rot or termites, not a perfect finish.

Or going crazy from the shrill, marching-band shit she liked to listen to.

Nevertheless, he'd sanded and primed like a madman

because he wanted her happy. That was crazy right there, but so was the truth. He had paint on his cheek and probably in his hair. His favorite jeans looked like a paint sample, and his wrist hurt because he was too damned old for this much up-and-down.

And yet, thinking things over, he wouldn't change a minute of this night. Mary Ellen had her hair up in its usual loop, a neat little twist and tuck that made him want to reach over and let the whole thing down. One quick flick and she'd come undone. She wore it up unless she was headed to bed, and that was the problem, wasn't it? He wanted to be headed to bed with her. He wanted to thread his fingers through her hair, trace where the brown met silver. He wanted to kiss her.

No, this wasn't working out for him.

His Mary Ellen had dug into his heart good and deep over the years, but she was keeping the friendship line firmly between them. He understood why. He'd been thinking this over for years, and she'd only had a few weeks. He didn't know if he was ready himself to put a label on what he was feeling, but he had his suspicions. This had *love* written all over it, and he wasn't going to kid himself anymore. It was time to take the offensive. Time to hop that line and show her exactly how sweetly fire could burn.

The band switched gears—loudly—and that was a cue he wasn't ignoring. Apparently, the CD was serving up the full menu of Sousa tonight, and they'd hit one of the guy's few waltzes. The woodwinds got into it, pumping out a cheerful, light tune rather than a hell-bent march. All good. He tossed his paintbrush aside.

"The bristles will stiffen up," she protested, carefully setting down her own brush on a neat little square of newspaper. "I need to wash that, Ben."

"The brush will keep," he growled. "This won't. Dance with me, Mary Ellen."

She rocked back on her heels, looking at him as if he was pure crazy. Maybe he was, but he was pure crazy for her. He held out a hand. That part of him was paint-free—mostly—and it had to be a sign.

"You want to dance, we can go down to Ma's," she suggested. She bit her lower lip, and he loved that little feminine gesture. His girl was nervous. Maybe, just maybe, she'd finally decided to take a good, hard look at him.

"I want to dance here." He wiggled his fingers. *Take the bait.*

"All right," she said finally. "But if you bump me into those chairs and smear that wet paint, Ben Cortez, you're the one starting over."

"Deal."

She put her fingers into his, and he tugged gently upward until she came right into his arms. They'd danced together before, and sometimes during those dances he'd wondered. Wondered what it would be like to hold her as a lover rather than as a friend, but he hadn't pushed. He'd done his dancing, and then he'd let go and walked away.

Not tonight.

He pulled her toward him, palm to palm, his fingers threading through hers. They fell into the familiar rhythm, him guiding her forward and back again, her right in step with him. Sweet and easy, they did a slow two-step on her porch, and Sousa had never sounded so good. Each step they took smelled of fresh paint and newsprint, the sheets she'd spread beneath the chairs crackling under their feet.

"The chairs look good," she said, filling up the awkward silence. The clarinets in the band segued into something unhurried, deeper, and he slowed his steps to match.

Maybe awkward wasn't a bad thing.

Maybe, she'd been *too* comfortable with him before.

He twirled her around in a leisurely circle, maneuvering her closer. His hand closed around her waist, and he could feel the heat and softness of her through the cotton shirt she wore. His other hand slid down her arm, and he counted off the steps, grasping her wrist when they moved apart to promenade down the porch.

She looked up at him, and there was that laughter he loved so much in her eyes. His Mary Ellen had pretty, pretty eyes. Those eyes had kept watch over him for years. They reached the end of the porch, started back, and then finally that laughter of hers bubbled up and out.

"You're crazy, Ben." The music picked up speed. He'd better pick things up here, too, or he'd end up trying to dance to a march. He might not have dated in years, but he could imagine how that would end. Epic fail. "We're two old coots. The boys see this, you'll never hear the end of it."

He had her closer now, their legs brushing as they danced. Would she admit to the sexual attraction between them? Maybe she wanted to keep the friendship and the sure thing. Or maybe he could convince her to explore something new.

"I'm not too old, Mary Ellen." The sudden stillness in her body said she knew where he was taking this. "All that crap about age being a state of mind? There's something to that."

"Ben . . ." He heard the warning note in her voice loud and clear.

"I want to see you. Date," he clarified. Maybe more. He was done treading water. He wanted this woman.

"Ben . . ." she said again. He didn't know if she didn't know what to say—which would be a real bad sign—or if she was trying to remind herself of who he was. Well, he was done overthinking things. His feet stopped moving, and he slid a hand up along her shoulder. He cupped her neck, then feathered his fingers over the back of her neck, where she was so sensitive.

"You don't need to give me an answer tonight, Mary Ellen. I'm just giving you some food for thought, okay?" He wouldn't push—*much*—he told himself. And yet his fingers stole upward, finding the clasp on her barrette. The hook was easier to slip free than he'd thought it would be. The metal popped open, spilling her hair into his hand. The long strands smelled fruity from her shampoo and, beneath that, something indefinably *her*.

"What if it doesn't work?"

"Then it doesn't work. But I want to give it a shot. I want *us* to have a shot." He moved her back, taking the last steps in this dance of theirs.

"Why now?"

"And not before?" Hell if he knew. For whatever reason, the two of them had lived parallel lives. That was part of the past, though. He wasn't interested in reliving his youth—he was interested in now. He wanted the woman she was today—not who she'd been before. "I don't know." He was no psychologist. All he had to offer her was the truth. "This just feels right. It's what I want. Question is, honey, what do you want?"

The music picked up speed like a train shooting right off the track, racing to a raucous crescendo, and he twirled her in a fast, hard circle, her hair whipping around them in a soft cloud. Their feet hit the porch together, beating out a rhythm he could hear even over the shrill complaint of the woodwinds and the newspaper shuffling underfoot. Mary Ellen looked at him when they reached the edge, and it was stop or fall off.

"You want to change it all?" She puffed out her cheeks

in frustration. "You have so many friends that you can chance this, Ben? This is crazy."

"I don't want to lose you, Mary Ellen."

"Then don't do this," she snapped.

"I have to."

"*You* have to."

He tightened his grip on her fingers before she could pop right out of his grip. She was going to make this difficult. Fire had hopped the line all right, though. He'd doubled back and surprised her.

So maybe Mary Ellen had put her sex drive on hold while she'd raised her boys and earned a living for the four of them. That hadn't been a bad thing—it had been her choice, and she'd never regretted it. Sure, she was older now. They all were, and that was the price you paid for living. You got older until the day you died, so she'd always made a point of enjoying the living part. Even now, twenty years after she'd opened the door and met the three boys standing on her front porch, she didn't feel different inside. This aging business wasn't so much a slowing down as it was like a drive in the car, where you suddenly realize that what's outside the window is beautiful, and you want more of it. She'd spent a lifetime getting somewhere, and that somewhere was a good place. Now she wanted to treat herself. Take a look around. Why not have a new dream?

Why not have Ben?

He was a handsome man and always had been. From the little creases around his eyes to the sureness of his hands, his body and his face were a map of where he'd been and what he'd done. Sure, he wasn't perfect, but she liked what she saw. So why *not* give this thing between them a chance?

"You want there to be an *us*?" she asked him. He hadn't moved. Simply stood there like her rock, waiting for her to decide. Her call. He'd put the words out there, and now he was standing by them even as he hung on to her.

"I do," he said, and he stepped closer still. His jeans brushed against hers. One more breath and they'd be chest to chest. He'd be kissing her, unless she took that step backward.

An *us*. Two people pairing up, pairing off. But what would they do together? He'd run a firehouse for years; she'd run a successful veterinary business and raised her boys. Sure, they'd always been part of each other's lives, but not front and center, not living and striving side by side. That could change.

Still, she was old enough to know, she told herself, that sex was about far more than a penis and a vagina. Sex wasn't just a little in-and-out. Sex had to be adventure and romance, where you set out on a journey with the man holding you and you holding him. She wouldn't settle for less.

She looked him in the eye. "I want there to be an *us*. I want *us* to do something together. Something more than two people in a bedroom," she warned. "Although maybe that, too."

"Okay," he said. "That sounds good to me, Mary Ellen."

She should lay down more ground rules, but dancing cheek to chest with him made her forget all about the *shoulds* in favor of the *coulds*. Instead of talking, she could listen to that steady heartbeat of his. Never mind that the band had started ripping out some marching tune that had sent America's boys overseas more times than she cared to remember. The lights were out now over at the firehouse, and maybe that was one fewer boy for her to worry over.

Jack was settled. Evan was on his way. That left Rio. And her.

Ben's hands locked around her waist, pulling her close right there on the porch for all of Strong to see.

Tonight was her turn.

Chapter Fifteen

Outside the hangar in the late-afternoon sun, the crickets sent up a powerful whine, singing a mating song despite the brightness. It was a pretty time of day. Still hotter than Hades but with a promise of coolness later.

Looking at the man sprawled in the dilapidated deck chair beside hers, Faye *knew*. Evan Donovan was a damn fine man. Last night, she'd admitted to herself that she was more than half in love with him, which meant she had some choosing to do. She sure didn't want to love him, but there she was. Halfway to headlong in love. Strong could be a second chance, and, if the universe was passing those out, she'd grasp hers with both hands. No more regrets. No more holding back.

She could take Evan back to the firehouse and try out that bunk bed again. She could tell him how she felt. Why not?

Right now, though, she had a ringside seat to his childhood in Strong. She'd borrowed several photo albums from Nonna. The older woman had stuck the pictures in carefully with paste corners and meticulous labeling. Nonna had a whole shelf of them in her house, and Faye hadn't been able to resist the invitation to pick one or two to borrow. Sharing embarrassing photos was a future-family thing, and she suspected Nonna knew that.

With each page, she saw who Evan had been. He hadn't come to Nonna until he was ten, so there was a sad absence of naked baby and embarrassing-moment pictures. Maybe someone else had those, but her heart said probably not. Anyone who would let a child wander off and not instigate a statewide search wasn't collecting Kodak moments. Still, the album was a gold mine, with pictures of him with his adoptive brothers at Nonna's, at birthday parties, at middle and high school graduations, and in his Marines uniform. Five years of service followed by five building Donovan Brothers. College at night and on the weekends studying fire management. There was even a handful of pictures of the brothers hobnobbing with politicians at fund-raisers.

"You going to return the favor? Let me see your pictures?" he asked.

She turned another page. "I'm busy here."

His laugh was indulgent. "Busy spying. But I took all the juicy ones out already, darlin'."

He hadn't, she knew. The man she saw in the pictures was comfortable with who he was, with where he'd been and what he'd done. The other people in these photos would definitely notice if he took off, and, she was willing to bet, they'd hunt him down and bring him back.

She took a long drink of sweet tea—so full of sugar she could *hear* her fillings protest—and flipped a page. There was Evan in uniform ten years ago, getting ready to deploy. Jack was right beside him, the pair of them hauling gear and flashing exuberantly youthful grins.

"You liked the military." She looked up, and, sure enough, he was watching her.

"The military was good for me. Yeah. Plenty of opportunities to fight and earn an atta-boy."

Someone in his unit had been camera happy, filling whole pages with the same group of soldiers doing all the usual things. Training and relaxing and pranking each other while they hammed it up for the camera. Those faces were so young to be doing what they did. Keeping people like her safe. Keeping whole countries safe by putting their lives on the line.

"Let me know when you hit the end, okay?" Evan kicked back, half napping in his chair. He was humoring her, but that was okay. She liked what they were doing just fine. It didn't always have to be one-hundred-percent-pure adrenaline rush.

Humming, she turned the page—and there was Mike's face staring up at her. The world slowed to a stop around her. The day was like a hundred other hot summer days, and the ice was melting inside her glass, sending streaks of moisture down the sides, but her whole body was cold, cold, cold. She should tell herself this was a coincidence, but there Mike was. She knew that face, knew he'd spent a couple of years in the Marines before he'd decided against re-upping and come back to L.A. and the fire department.

"You served with a lot of firefighters in the military?"

"Yeah." He turned his head toward her, lazy and relaxed. "You heard the story at Ma's. We were CFR crew for the Marines. The best." He winked. "Firefighting wasn't just an Air Force thing."

Maybe that one photo *was* a coincidence.

Maybe Evan and Mike had somehow briefly crossed paths in their military past.

She turned the next page and the next. *God.* Were there more pics of Mike lurking in there, waiting to pop out at her? She hated the way that made her feel, scouting each group photo to see if her nemesis was present. Did it really matter if he'd been there? What did she think had happened?

And there Mike was again, standing in front of an open

plane bay, a dark green duffel at his feet. Evan. Jack. Mike. Three guys between them, but a CFR team wasn't large to begin with, and a football field wouldn't have been enough space for her. She opened her mouth to start asking questions, but all that came out was, "You talk to these guys still?"

He cracked an eye open. "We got shot at together. Yeah, I still talk to them."

"All of them?" Her voice sounded shrill and stressed, even to her own ears.

"Why? You want to do a meet-and-greet?" He paused, his gaze going to the book on her lap and the sea of khakis there. He sat up fast. "Damn."

"When were you going to tell me you knew Mike?"

"When I got the chance, and that's the truth."

"There has been no opportunity to mention that, oh, yeah, you and my ex-husband spent a couple of years serving together in the military? What would have come next? A line about how it was no big deal?"

"It was a big deal." He held out a hand. "You want to give me the book?"

"No." She started turning pages, scanning. "Were you close?"

"Like every other guy there, he had my back. I had his."

"When was the last time you spoke with him?"

She counted to three before he answered slowly. "I talked with Mike a few days ago."

This wasn't happening. She was being paranoid. She was reading a conspiracy into coincidence. Wasn't she? "Was this a lightning-bolt-out-of-the-blue kind of a conversation?"

"It had been a while," he said, cautious now. "We hadn't talked in a couple of years. I knew he was down there in L.A., working a firehouse. I was running around Northern California and Nevada, getting Donovan Brothers off the ground."

"What did he want?" She snapped the album shut. The fun was all gone.

"He called the day you hit Strong. He wanted to make sure you were going to be okay."

"And you came looking for me." *God.* Their first meeting looped through her head, over and over. Evan coming through Ma's doors and making a beeline straight for her. Had he called her by name even before he'd introduced himself? Maybe if she hadn't knocked back all that rum punch, she'd have recognized what that deliberate approach meant. He hadn't been a man smitten. He'd been a man on a rescue mission. For his friend. His buddy.

"Is that what all this has been? A rescue operation?" She cut him off before he could answer. "Is this the part where I look gratefully up at my big, strong hero and thank him? Because, right now, I don't feel grateful. I feel *mad.* You came charging into Ma's the night I got here, and, it appears"—she tossed the photo album at him—"you've been riding to the rescue ever since. I'm not a fire. And I'm not your job."

Evan had been the perfect summertime romance—with the possibility of something more. She'd believed Evan was her *choice.* Instead, she was being *managed.* He hadn't even chosen *her.* He'd fulfilled an obligation to "one of the boys." And wasn't that Mike Thomas all over again?

She'd shut up before. She'd sucked it up, and she'd bought into that code that said the firehouse and the job came first—and she came a distant second. Fighting fire was important, but so was she. She needed a man who had room for both in his life. And who put her first sometimes.

Right now, she wanted to kick Evan's ass.

"You're mad," he said.

"You bet." She stood up and paced toward the runway. "You need to work on this communication thing. That was need-to-know information, and you sat on it way too long."

"I'm sorry." He stood up, too, as if maybe he wanted to come after her. Wanted to take her into his arms. "Give me a chance to fix this."

Not tonight. This wasn't something more conversation or more sex could fix.

Because Evan was too much like Mike, after all. Both of them were big, silent, strong men. Mike had stayed all alone in there, inside his head and his heart, where she was supposed to have filled up those empty spaces for him. But she hadn't. And, apparently, she hadn't done much for Evan on her own, either.

"I don't need you to fix anything. I can do my own fixing. Maybe what I thought I needed was to hear how you were feeling. Right now, though, I need to turn my piece in. I have a deadline."

"You promised me fourteen days. You still giving me that time?"

"I'll give you as much time as I can." She turned away. "I won't mention your arsonist yet. You want time, I'll still give you what I can, but I have to give my editor something. He's working with white space right now, and he's practically pissing himself. I don't give him content, he's up shit creek."

"Then give him something."

"Just not the real story."

"I'm not asking you to conceal anything. I don't want lies." He ran his hand over his head. "You have to believe me on that one."

"No, but you don't want the whole truth out there yet, either, do you?"

"I don't know what's true. I need facts, Faye. Proof."

He was all-facts now. He wanted proof, wanted every-thing black-and-white, but—news flash—sometimes that wasn't possible with emotions.

"So get them." She shrugged. "Don't get them. But do it now, Evan, because I'm out of time."

Chapter Sixteen

That was one hell of a fight Evan and Faye were having outside the hangar. Rio squinted at the pair. Okay, Faye was fighting, slinging angry words around. Evan was sitting there, doing his big, silent enforcer impression. Occasionally he nodded, but he wasn't volunteering too many words of his own. *Fuck.* His brother needed to learn how to open up some. Looking at Faye's face, it didn't take rocket science to figure out she was more hurt than mad. Whatever Evan had done, he needed to *un*do it. Fast. Before he lost a good woman.

The dispatch phone rang loudly, demanding attention.

"Heads," Jack called lazily. Coin went up and down before the second ring. Tails, so Rio grabbed the phone. Ben's firehouse was strictly volunteer, with Ben as the only exception. It was easy enough to reroute calls, so Donovan Brothers lent a hand and manned the line during downtime.

The operator informed him the center was transferring a call box call, and Rio got ready to roll. "Strong 911. Where's your emergency?"

"I got me a fire out here." The man's voice on the other end was strangely distorted. Rio had fielded his share of prank calls, where jumped-up kids spoke through mouthfuls of potato chips or crumpled paper, but this was something else. Probably someone deliberately using a voice-distortion cell phone app.

He put the call on speaker, silently gesturing a heads-up to Jack.

"I got you. Where's your fire? Can you give me your exact location?" The script called for a whole lot of ma'am-ing and sir-ing, but that wasn't Rio's game. Never had been. Instead, his fingers hit the keyboard as he waited for intel.

"I'm at the call box. Route 49. Mile 34.5." Mystery caller didn't hesitate as he decoded the string of numbers on the sign identifying call box 49-345.

Repeating the route and mile numbers aloud, Rio ran the next steps in his head. Sure, there were truck drivers who knew how to read the blue-and-whites, but how many of them requested Strong's team by name—instead of asking for the generic 911 assist?

To test his theory, he pushed back some. If this truly was a citizen do-gooder, the guy would answer, and he wouldn't see the stupid in Rio's question. "Okay . . . yeah . . . I copy that. You got a building on fire?"

Right on cue, the caller snorted, as if he knew dumb when he heard it. "It's a brush fire. Nothing but fucking highway and trees out here."

"Copy you there." He switched over, calling the fire-house on the second line. "Firehouse, jump base standing by. We've got a brush fire."

Quickly, he provided the when, where, and what. In the background, he could hear Ben blasting the info out to his crew and sounding the alarm. "I have one unit to respond. One engine for a brush fire on Highway 49 at the 34.5 mile marker. Time is 4:07," Ben reported. As the engine roared to life and guys hollered, Ben signed off, promising a situation report as soon as he hit the scene.

Rio switched his attention back to his mystery caller.

The guy's patience was also more than a little suspect. As if he knew the drill. Knew exactly how long it would take Rio to dispatch the local engine and get help on the way.

"Yeah. You should get out here. Now. The perimeter's growing fast, and she's going to hit the trees." Was that fear or enthusiasm in the caller's voice?

Rio played along. "Okay, we've got an engine en route, so you take a deep breath with me, because help is coming. I'm going to have firefighters there as soon as I can."

Ben's voice came in over the radio. "Strong Fire responding. We're en route." While the caller ran through flame height and smoke sightings, Rio punched out a text to Ben: *Watch who's there. Give me names of first responders.*

The site was only a twenty-minute drive from Strong. He scrawled a note on a scrap of paper and passed it to Jack, going all low-tech because his "spidey" senses were tingling. *You thinking what I'm thinking?*

On the call box, the caller cursed. "We've got some wind out here. She isn't going to stay small, Rio."

At that tell, Rio looked hard at Jack and nodded. *Yeah.* There was proof. Guy knew who the fill-in, temp dispatcher was? Rio's mouth continued to put out the right words, acting as if all was normal, while his brain kicked into high gear. "Okay, I hear you, caller. Engine's en route with an ETA of nineteen minutes. Right now, we're getting you somewhere safe. That's the important part here. You got a name for me?"

"Sure thing." With a muffled curse, their caller abruptly hung up. If that had been a genuine civvie, Rio would have been worried. This was no ordinary Joe, however.

He looked over at Jack, itching to abandon the desk and tear out to Route 49. "That's our arsonist, right there."

Jack nodded. "That's no innocent John Doe."

Rio had coded up a software script that read the emer-

gency calls and dispatch reports and pulled out the highlights before texting them to the guys on call. He'd turn
that baby off now. The only guys in the know about this
fire would be the ones already in the firehouse.

After alerting Jack to the information black-out, he
added, "Mystery caller doesn't need or get a heads-up.
Let's see who shows up *without* getting his dispatch call."

Jack pushed to his feet. "I'll take the truck, ride Ben's ass
out to the brush fire. If our guy's flicked a Bic and waited
around, I'll find him."

Yeah. That was a bitch, because Rio wanted to be in on
the take-down, but he had desk duty. He was still nodding
his agreement when the phone rang again. *Time for round
two*. "Strong 911. Give me what you got."

The dispatcher on the other end started unloading deets,
and Rio let his fingers fly, logging the new call. "We got
incoming from the regional dispatch center as well, re-
questing backup."

Jack cursed and stopped walking toward the door. "Tell
me more."

The nearest computer flashed an alert, scrolling details.
Latitude and longitude. Elevation and a real nice descrip-
tion of the lay of the land.

It was heating up to be a busy night, all right. Those co-
ordinates put the newest fire ten miles west of the caller's
brush fire. The area was difficult territory, full of big-ass
ponderosa and gullies. If the fire got in there and made a
run for it, they could lose a lot of territory fast. There was
a high possibility of its hitting homes, too.

"Put a plane up?" Rio looked over at Jack for confir-
mation. "We got the crew we need. Joey can take over the
desk here because he's on his rest period, and I'm still
good to jump. We've got the plane, and it's easy enough
to hover and pick out any hot spots. If we need to go in,

we can, but a look-see should be enough to get the fire crew pointed in the right direction. We can play the hot-and-cold game for the guys on the ground."

Jack nodded slowly, thinking it through. "Small crew for this one. I want Mack, you, and Evan on the plane. Page Mack and Joey—get them in here stat." He jerked his head toward the unhappy couple outside. "Our boy will have to sort his love life out later, because right now I need him on that plane."

The burst of activity on the runway screamed *Time's up,* and, right on cue, Jack whistled sharply from the hangar door. "Evan, get your ass in here. We've got marching orders."

Evan glanced down at Faye. "I have to go."

Faye eyed the plane taxiing out as if she suspected Evan had ordered it up to get out of the heart-to-heart she'd instigated. Four days ago, she'd been onboard and headed out the bay in his arms. Now he was leaving her behind on the ground. A little adventure and that magazine piece of hers might be enough for her, but he wanted more. He wanted her. Today, however, wasn't his day for wishes coming true.

"And I have to stay," she said bitterly, her gaze following the plane. "I'm tired of sitting things out, Evan. You think I didn't get enough of that, being married to Mike?"

"I hear you." He did. Problem was, he didn't know what to say to her, didn't have any idea how to fix this right now. He wanted to fight *for* her, not with her, but that kind of explaining wouldn't fit into a few hurried sentences. *Hell.* He needed to go up, and he needed to stay right here. And maybe one day he'd learn how to pull the whole Superman routine and satisfy both needs at the same time. *Good luck with that.*

Jack bellowed again, and Evan pointed his feet toward

the hangar. Christ, what was he supposed to say? He opted to go with the platitude, "You stay safe now."

She shot him a glare, all feminine ire.

Which meant he'd picked the wrong thing to say. Again.

"I'm also tired of playing it safe, Evan." She wrapped her arms around her middle and stepped away from him. He wanted to drop a kiss on her, but she was mad, so he turned and jogged slowly away. When she didn't call out to him, he kept on going.

Chapter Seventeen

The plane ran down the end of the runway and popped up into blue sky. Ten minutes later, the jump team was a black smudge on the horizon, gunning for a fire Faye couldn't see. Faye turned away, because she didn't need to underscore how pathetic she was. Evan was gone. That was his job. She had no business standing there like a war widow waiting for her man to come back home.

Instead, she concentrated on unzipping her camera case and popping the cap on her lens. She couldn't bear to scroll through the pictures she'd taken so far. Too many of them were of Evan.

Still, she had a job to do. She grabbed the camera. *Click.* A pair of empty racks by the hangar doors from which the jump team had grabbed their gear and gone. *Click.* The duty roster pinned to the bulletin board in the corner that the Donovans used as an on-site ops room, a pair of Xs and Os scrawled in a masculine hand beneath the last name on the list. Joey hunched over the radio, headphones tight to his ears.

"You sticking around?" Joey looked up at her as he asked his question. That young-old face of his said he understood all too well about being left behind. He'd pulled desk duty while the others went out and up.

The words shot out of her mouth. "No. It's time for me to go."

"That right?" He fiddled with a mechanical pencil, and a long piece of lead shot out of its tip. As soon as he put the pencil to paper, though, the point snapped off. "Well, shit," he said, looking down.

"It's time to move on." There. She'd said it.

He nodded. "Right. Job's done here?"

Yeah. There was the kicker. "Yes. No. I have to send something to my editor tomorrow, and that's the thing. What do I send?"

"You got a nickel? 'Cause the doctor's in, and we've got us all evening to work this out."

He kicked back in the chair, propping his booted feet on the desk. His note got crushed beneath the black soles, but he didn't seem to care. She gestured toward the carnage. "Doesn't matter." He gave her a crooked smile. "Mack likes to play the lottery. I get the numbers for him when he's up. Thinks he's lucky. I take it you're not feeling lucky about this assignment of yours?"

"Not in the slightest." She gave him a brief recap, running through her options. Turn in a sensational photo-story about an in-house arsonist that could win accolades—but make the Donovans' firehouse renovation project take a backseat. Or turn in something more mundane and sit on a story that deserved to see the light of day.

"Huh." Folding his arms on the desk, Joey leaned forward. "Evan ask you to keep this story under wraps?"

"Temporarily. He wants to be sure before he accuses anyone."

"That sounds like Evan, all right. He likes things definite. Black-and-white. But he wouldn't ask you to scuttle your story." Joey sounded confident. "Evan's a straight-up guy."

"I need to go," she repeated.

He poured her a cup of coffee from the pot, throwing her a packet of fossilized powdered creamer. "Put the camera down for a moment, and drink that."

Why not? She took the cup, the heat soaking into her through the Styrofoam sides. "Magic fix?"

He winked. "Not really. But it's going to take you at least ten minutes to choke that down and then another ten while you contemplate chucking it back up. That gives me time to come up with something insightful."

It was worth a shot. She tore open the packet and emptied the contents into the cup. Powder floated to the top of coffee in jagged chunks. The creamer iceberg had her checking the expiration date on the packet. *Too late*. Joey's ten-minute estimate seemed highly optimistic.

The radio crackled, and Joey tapped industriously away at the keyboard.

"Bad fire?"

"No such thing." He hit ENTER, and someone, somewhere, got his update. "A challenge, sure. Our guys are playing backup on this one. Fire's mostly contained, but they want more eyes looking for any hot spots the ground crew missed. A quick flyover may be enough. If the team sees something, they'll jump in for a closer look. See what they can fix out there."

She took a cautious sip. *God*. Joey's coffee *was* bad.

He gave her a told-you-so smile. "You really thinking of leaving?"

"Yeah." Bad coffee and good company wouldn't fix her situation. "It's best for everyone. I go. I get a little distance."

"You talking about heading back into Strong—or a little farther?"

"As far as I can get."

★   ★   ★

The Corvette flew along the highway, taking the mountain curves like a dream. Faye had the windows down, and that fresh air pushed all the summer heat outside. No strange noises today. No sudden need to pull off the road. Since Evan had been under the hood, the car handled beautifully. It figured.

When the mountainside showed black, she pulled off. The site of that original brush fire was nothing more than boot prints and tire tracks now. Two minutes later, she was sitting on the hood of her car, soaking in the sunshine. The place was all peaceful and quiet, full of summer sounds and nothing else.

Flipping open her cell, she thumbed through her address book and selected the familiar name. He was still in there. Why hadn't she deleted him? Maybe for the same reason he'd called Evan. Familiarity made it hard to let go. It was easier to go with the same-old, same-old.

"Hey," she said, when Mike picked up.

"What's up?" She listened hard, but, for once, there was silence on Mike's end. Maybe she'd caught him at a good time.

"You called Evan Donovan." She cut right to the chase. "You asked him to check up on me."

"Faye . . ." Yeah, there was a defensive note in his voice. He'd crossed a line, and he knew it. "I was worried, okay? I wanted to make sure you were doing okay."

"We're not married anymore, Mike," she said quietly. "That part of your life—the *our* part—is over."

"I know." The tense note in his voice made his frustration clear. Before, she'd loved listening to that voice of his, to that low, rich rumble of sound. He could have made a fortune doing voiceover work in L.A., but he'd chosen firefighting instead. "I've seen the lawyers' bills. I get that."

"Do you?" She felt sad. Older. It was easy to imagine Mike slouched in his favorite armchair down at the firehouse, his feet propped up while he took five. She sat for a moment herself, feeling the sun-warmed metal beneath her bare legs and knowing she was finally in a good place.

"Evan said you bought a new car. A Corvette." Humor replaced frustration in Mike's voice. "I'll bet that was one hell of a drive up from L.A."

"It was." The drive had been a blur of speed, pit-stopping only for gas. Then there had been the stop after the plunge through the flames. Strong. And Evan, who'd pocketed her keys and fixed her car. She wanted to cry, and damned if she knew why. "You shouldn't have asked him to check up me."

"I need to know you're safe." His use of the present tense had her gritting her teeth.

"I'm not your wife." She said the words out loud to him. "You're not my husband. Maybe we'll be friends again someday, but that someday isn't happening for a long time yet. I'm not a responsibility you share with the guys in the firehouse."

"I was trying to do the right thing," he said stubbornly.

"And you'd do it again. I get that. Really, I do." She leaned back, staring up at the sky. All blue today. No smoke, no clouds. It shouldn't be possible for any sky to be that blue outside of a Crayola box, but this one was. "You want to hear something I realized about the firehouse?" She didn't wait for him to answer, just kept on talking. "When a guy goes down in the line of duty, all the rest of you band together and look out for his family. His wife, his kids—whoever needed him, you all step in. A firehouse widow, she isn't ever going to be alone. She'll always have guys ready and willing to lend a hand, to do whatever it takes to keep her going. That's a nice thing."

"You going somewhere with this?" Maybe he was expecting a call, or maybe all this heart-to-heart had him itching. It was a relief not to care. He could take his pick of reasons. Either, neither, she was a free woman.

"Yeah, I am. I'm not a widow. I don't need you to give the order to circle the wagons and make sure everything goes smoothly for me. If it does, great. If it doesn't, well, that's life, too, Mike. It's not your business anymore. Stand or fall, good or bad, this doesn't have anything to do with you now, and you need to let me go. And I need to let you go. We both get to start over. Tell me you're on board with that, okay?"

There was a pregnant pause. She could practically hear him hosting an internal debate down there in L.A. Argue. Don't argue. Either way, he was off in his own world. Overhead, a squirrel complained noisily on its branch, demanding she move along now because this spot was taken.

That was good advice, even if it did come from something with four legs and fleas.

"Good-bye, Mike," she said and punched END. To make it official, she deleted his number, pocketed the phone, and slid off the hood.

The grass was already coming through the burn, a layer of green slowly preparing to swallow up the black. Lifting the camera, she took a shot. In two, three more weeks, there would be no sign of the fire at all. Just Mother Nature doing her thing.

A week made one hell of a difference.

Chapter Eighteen

One truck already on the scene. One run-of-the-mill, dust-covered truck, sporting a decal from a nearby fire department on the driver-side door. One truck that shouldn't have been there yet, because Rio had dispatched a single engine, and Ben was riding it.

Another firehouse had loaned this guy to Strong when the call had gone out for more summer help. He'd lived in the area all his life, and his fire chief praised him as a nice kid.

Hollis Anderson.

When Hollis had made his pitch to join the jump team right on the heels of Jack's near-miss with death, Ben had reserved judgment; he hadn't wanted to ruin the kid's career just because Hollis had been an insensitive asshole. Now he knew that he had been right to be suspicious.

Worse, the boy had split. Hollis might not be the brightest bulb in the box—Ben Cortez had no respect for the intellect of anyone who set fires for kicks—but he'd still been smart enough to scram. When the engine had pulled up, and Hollis had gotten an eyeful of the anger on Ben's face, Hollis had leaped into his pickup and run.

But not before every man riding the engine had also gotten a good look at Hollis and his truck.

As soon as the brush fire was out, Ben went down to the police station and filed a report. He wanted to track Hollis down and force the guy to man up, but there was a procedure that needed to be followed here, and that included police reports and letting the law do its thing.

Yeah. Time had run out for Hollis, which was fortunate. If the boy didn't stop lighting up his job sites, sooner or later somebody would get hurt.

Ben put the truck into park—in front of Mary Ellen's house. Jack was doing okay, but that last fire had been a wake-up call to Ben. Or a swift kick in the ass. Either way, Ben had gotten the message. No man had unlimited time. It had been too long since he'd lost his wife. She'd been a good woman, a woman he'd loved with all his heart. No way he'd have been here, knocking on Nonna's door, if Elizabeth had still been alive. But she wasn't, and there was room in his heart for one more, if she was Mary Ellen.

He'd take this chance.

He knocked on the door.

"May I come in?" he asked when Mary Ellen answered.

"You okay?" She stood back from the door, making room for him. The way she always did. Her living room was an oasis of serenity, with plenty of throw pillows scattered on the furniture and pictures on the walls. The place looked like a catalog, with a spark of Mary Ellen. She'd picked out everything in the room and decided where to put what. Looking at that room always made him feel as if he had a little in on who she was. At the very least, he knew she liked blue.

He did, too. Blue was good. Mary Ellen had blue eyes.

She disappeared briefly into the kitchen, and, when she came back, she had two longnecks in her hand. Silently handing one over, she sank into an armchair and cracked her beer. Maybe she'd picked that spot on purpose. There was room for just one right there. Or, maybe he was over-thinking this because he hadn't dated seriously in decades. Could be that chair was the closest. Hell. He didn't know.

Since he was going all in tonight, he got the ball onto the tee and lined up the club. "I want to see you. I told you that the other night."

The beer bottle paused on its trip to her mouth. "You did."

She was buying time, but it was too late to stop him.

"And I asked you to think it over. You had time to do that, Mary Ellen?"

Her bottle hit the table with a little thump. "You really want to get naked with me?" Her eyes laughed at him. "I promise you, I don't look like I did at twenty."

"I don't want you to look twenty. I want you to look like you."

Hell. He wasn't perfect. Hadn't been when he was twenty, either, but no point in beating that horse right now.

"If I do this," she warned lightly, "I'm doing this all the way, Ben."

"What's happening here," he said thickly, because he agreed with her, "isn't just a *this*. I want us to be together."

"Second chances." Her hands smoothed the arms of the chair, and he wanted her fingers touching him like that.

"No. A first chance at us." He willed her to see what he did when he looked at her. This thing they had was special, and he didn't think he could let go of it. Let go of her.

"You want to kiss me?" There was laughter in her voice again—and something else. Something that sounded more like wonder. With a side order of doubt.

"I'd be happy to do a little show-and-tell." God, would he. He pulled her up and put his hands on her shoulders, cupping them. She was warm and feminine and wearing some kind of silky shirt that slid beneath his fingers. "Tell me that's okay with you."

She looked up at him. She'd fit right into the crook of his shoulder, and he liked that, too. God, he liked everything about her. She had him tied in knots, and now he was thinking she had no idea how intensely she made him feel.

"You want me to do that, Mary Ellen?" he drawled, and his voice came out all rough and hoarse because his body was telegraphing desperate messages to his brain. He wasn't going to make a move until she gave him the go-ahead. She smiled up at him, a smile full of mischief, and all his good intentions flew right out the window. She got to him. She did. He drew her toward him slowly, closing the small gap still between them, and she came.

She came all the way into his arms, her hands resting easily on his chest. No way she didn't feel the hard *thump-thump* of his heart, the beat that said he'd been waiting for this.

And he kissed her. He had to have that much of her. He lowered his head and put his mouth on hers. His lips brushed her lips, and they parted. Opened up to let him in. Sweet. She was so very sweet. He'd kissed and been kissed before, but this was *their* first kiss, and, Christ, it was everything he'd been waiting for. He got one arm around her waist, holding her close, because he wanted to feel her touching him, and the other threaded through that glorious hair of hers. Each breath he took filled him up with more of his Mary Ellen.

She kissed him and kissed him, and nothing was ever going to be the same again. He licked deep inside her mouth, pushing his tongue against hers, and she pushed right back. And he knew right then that there was no question about it.

She'd stolen his heart.

Chapter Nineteen

Hollis parked the truck behind Ma's and got out. It was late enough for the bar to be open, but, since it was midweek and the scanner in his truck was full of a forest fire, the place was deserted. That worked for him. The fewer people around, the better.

He'd fucked up.

He knew that, and he didn't have to wait for the police to pull up with their questions and their flashing lights to point that out to him. He'd called the dispatcher by name. Your average innocent civvie wouldn't have known who was picking up the call. And then he'd been busted at the scene.

Reaching into the truck bed, he grabbed what he needed and considered his options. They'd come for him—no question about that. If he was any kind of lucky, it would be just the Donovan brothers and any other firefighter who wanted to take him on personal-like. He'd get a beat-down, and then he'd never work as a firefighter again, because everyone would *know*. An entire underground railroad pumped this kind of intel throughout their community. Which meant cops and jail time, because he was no kind of lucky at all.

So he'd go out with a bang and make sure he had his fun first.

Hell, Strong was an all-you-can-eat-buffet, full of tar-
gets, and the only question was where he kicked off his
swan song. The old firehouse called his name, so he headed
that way; the cars parked in the side lot would make it an
easy place to start. Hit the gas tank on one of those, and
he'd have his *boom,* too.

The Corvette was up first. Shame to torch a car that
fine, but a red Corvette on fire was definitely make-you-
look. A quick swing of the Pulaski, and the driver-side
window smashed. He reached in, opened the door, and
popped the hood. Then it was around to the front of the
car, pouring his diesel oil and kerosene cocktail into the
engine compartment. He'd gone heavy on the kerosene
because he wanted to light this bitch up fast with the drip
torch he'd lifted from the hotshot supplies earlier. Really,
it was simple. Two quick turns of the breather valve and a
dip of his wrist so the kerosene soaked the igniter, a flick
of the switch, and he had flame.

No one came running out, so, moving quickly, he did a
rinse-and-repeat on the other two cars lined up next to
the Corvette. The Toyota and the minivan probably would
have caught when the Corvette really got going, but he
was aiming for certainty tonight.

Burn, burn, burn. He paused. Turned. The world was his
oyster tonight, and all he had to do was choose what went
up next. What pissed him off most in this town? He rocked
a mental soundtrack of tunes as he considered his options.

Bingo.

Next up was that goddamn historic firehouse itself that
everyone was so gaga over. Burning that would be a pleasure, all right. Climbing the porch steps, he got busy with
the drip torch.

"Choose. How hard can it be?" Too bad there was no
one there to answer her. Instead, Faye was alone, hanging

over the laptop she'd set up on the card table in her borrowed bunkroom. Two sets of images. Two different choices. She'd done the Photoshop thing, and the images were looking good. All she had to do was hit SEND and make her editor a happy man.

Two different stories.

Two different endings.

The first story was the obvious one. The arsonist stood there, back to her lens, with flames licking up around his legs. She'd pieced together what had happened next, adding the images she'd shot during the investigation. Black char covering the mountainside afterward, the investigators combing the area and finding the match, Ben and Evan's concerned faces, and that intent, focused look of two men hunting their perp. Finally she had the empty blackness with its hint of green. The mountain hadn't stayed the same. The mountain was already changing. She liked that promise. In one week, nature had started her own repair job.

The second set of images belonged to her boys of summer who manned the firehouse. The focused, determined team diving out of the plane's belly and into the flames— and the sexy, playful men who took advantage of their downtime. Evan starred front and center, but she'd shot all of them together, too. These guys were a team, a single unit with one purpose, and yet all she saw was Evan. Evan barreling toward the ground, chute out behind him. Evan manning a hose that Saturday, wet T-shirt plastered to his rock-hard stomach. Evan, peeling off the soaked cotton, then laughing as he wrestled with Mack and Rio and Joey. Jack watching from the sidelines, picking up the hose when Evan dropped it. Though bandaged and banged up, Jack wasn't down for the count. No, Jack had gotten right back up, and there he stood in the background, big and tough and watching over the others, laughter tugging at his mouth.

Evan was even bigger and tougher, a man who could and would fight for you. He wasn't polished or GQ handsome, just so very there. Until he wasn't. She scrolled through images. In the last shot, Evan looked at her, over his shoulder. Why couldn't he have cared about *her*? Just her? But, no. Mike had phoned him. Faye had been a favor from one firefighter to another, and Evan had his boy's back—this was about Mike and the team and that unspoken fucking *code* they shared. This week and change hadn't really been about her at all.

Choose. She straightened up, rubbing the small of her back. Which story did she tell?

She wrapped her arms around her middle. She'd snagged one of Evan's T-shirts, a gray cotton number sporting the jump team name. No logo or fancy branding, his shirt was as simple and uncomplicated as the bunkroom. Go out there and get the job done—end of story. The shirt was too big and slid from her shoulder, but today was a sweatpants-and-bare-feet kind of day, and she liked the sensation of being wrapped up in all that fabric. Comfortable instead of sexy, Evan's scent doing a number on her senses with each breath she took.

The window called her name, and she let her feet take her toward the glass, as if staring out at Strong and the mountains would somehow provide the answers she didn't have. There wasn't an easy call here, and the universe hadn't left clues outside the window.

Just one hell of a stink.

She sniffed. *Smoke.* Not a wood fire or how-rare-do-you-want-your-steak kind of smoke, but an ugly, acrid smoke, full of burning plastic and metal. That wasn't right. The smoke detector stuck to the ceiling agreed with that call and started to ping, a loud, strident, get-out-of-Dodge warning.

For a moment, fear froze her. This was a firehouse. Fire alarms weren't unusual, right? And yet there was that smell of smoke and the detector wailing its unhappy song. Her feet moved, closing the final yards to the window, where little wisps came in and the smell got worse.

Oh, God. Strong was on fire. The parking lot was on fire. And, when she looked down, it was horribly clear that the firehouse itself was on fire. Despite the heat raging outside, she turned cold. Her skin prickled with horrible awareness. Fire. Smoke. Either or both could kill her.

Get out. Get help. That's what she needed to do, but she couldn't force herself away from the window. Down below, flames swallowed up two cars, sheets of black smoke billowing up as the frames popped and cracked. Next to the first two, there was a third car, sparking and smoking. Her Corvette. That was *her* life going up in flames.

Adrenaline punched through her system. *Do something.* Backing up, she ran to the table where she'd been working, rummaged in her purse for her cell, flipped it open, and dialed 911. Dispatch answered right away.

"I'm calling to report a fire—yeah, in Strong. We're up in the mountains on Route 49. Yes, a fire. Actually, two fires. Three cars and the historic firehouse. Yes, I'm inside the firehouse. Yes, I'm getting out." Cradling the phone between her ear and shoulder—why the hell had she purchased the smallest phone out there?—she shoveled her laptop into her bag, then grabbed the camera and her purse.

As the dispatcher promised to send help and finished playing twenty questions, she hung up and ran for the door. She was a hundred yards from the newer firehouse and Ben Cortez. He'd help. Grabbing a fire extinguisher from the wall, she took the stairs at a run.

She'd help, too. However and wherever she could, she'd help.

With the borrowed fire truck finally pointed back toward Strong, Evan kept his foot on the gas, taking the highway's curves as quickly as he could without running off the road. As soon as today's fire was ninety percent contained, the jump team had hiked out to the pickup point after a mere ten hours. Now the loaner wheels ate up the miles while Evan tried to figure out how he could fix things with Faye. The closer he got to Strong, however, the less certain he was that he'd find the words. Christ, he wanted to. Wanted to say all the things he felt, wanted to make her understand that hurting her wasn't what he'd intended. Yeah, well, he could probably take those good intentions and shove them. She'd made that perfectly clear.

"You lost in thought there?" Mack's voice jolted him out of his unfortunate reverie. Mack had called shotgun, so Rio was jammed in the narrow backseat. Both jumpers were staring at him.

"There something you want to talk about?" Rio cradled a Styrofoam cup of coffee. It smelled bitter and strong as hell. His brother obviously wasn't worried about falling asleep that night. Doubtless he had better plans in mind.

"You think Faye can be convinced to stick around?" He put the question out there. Rio was good with women. He was never at a loss for words, so whatever secrets he had, Evan wanted in on them. He wasn't ashamed to ask. Not when it was for Faye. His hands tightened on the wheel. He couldn't lose her, couldn't imagine watching her drive away from Strong.

There had to be a way to fix this.

Rio looked at him. "Faye? Yeah. I do."

Mack rolled the window down, while Evan considered

his options. With the ponderosa crowding the road, it was pure black outside the open window, but the tease of cooler air coming in was a relief after the day's heat.

"Good." Evan cleared his throat. "Tell me how."

Mack snorted, but Rio looked as serious as Rio ever did. "It's not that complex, my man. You lay it out there, tell her how you feel. You've done that, right?"

"No." Hell. He'd screwed this up long before yesterday.

Rio nodded. "Then you've got your work cut out for you. You have to tell her. Better yet, you find some way to show her."

"That doesn't involve a bed," Mack added. "Anything you say in bed is suspect."

Rio smiled slowly, some clearly happy memories lighting up his eyes. "You have to say it right. You mean it, you can say anything you need to say in bed."

"Says you," Mack grumbled. "I try that shit, and my ass isn't *in* that bed anymore."

"Then you didn't mean what you said." Rio dropped the Styrofoam into the cup holder. "Or you said the kind of stuff that any self-respecting woman is gonna invite you to hit the door for saying."

"So there *are* some things you can't say." Mack stretched his feet out. "I rest my case."

"Give me an example." Better yet, Evan needed a list.

"You can say the nice stuff." Mack ticked items off on his fingers. "How fine she looks. How great the night was. What you like about her and what you want to do with her. That's stuff you can say in bed, but that's about it. The rest you save for when you're dressed and back in your right mind."

The hail on the radio interrupted Mack's explanations and put Evan's internal radar on high alert. No one should be pinging them. The three of them were off-roster for the rest of the night unless the entire lower forty-eight went up. The last two hours on this frequency had been general updates and chitchat—so a direct call-out wasn't good. This wasn't going to be a social call—this was going to be shit hitting the fan, and they were in the blowback's line of fire.

Rio got a finger on the volume and punched it higher.

Sure enough, Joey, the day's drafted dispatcher, was knocking. "Jump One, this is base."

"Base, Jump One." Rio acknowledged the incoming and adjusted the radio's frequency, trying for a better signal.

"How far out are you?" Distance couldn't disguise the urgency in Joey's voice. "And what's your ride?"

Evan didn't have to check the GPS to know. "Ten miles. We'll be with you in fifteen to twenty. We're riding a borrowed truck."

"Copy." Joey paused. "We've got a problem here."

Evan gave the truck a little more gas, and the speedometer crept up. "Give me deets."

"Three cars on fire and the old station house is smoking."

"Roger that. You got responders en route." Rio muted the receiver for a moment. "Fuck. That's bad. Ben lost Hollis—how much you want to bet this is his work?"

"Point fingers later," Evan growled. He shared Rio's reaction, so he'd save his breath. All that mattered now was speed—and his boys were about to find out how fast this truck could fly. His boot went down, and the speedometer shot up. Fuck careful. Any second he shaved was one more he had to give to Strong.

He guided the truck around a tight turn. Mack was busy rolling up the window because they were gaining speed now and the wind threatened to drown out the radio. He didn't say anything, though—just got real quiet. Whatever needed to happen back in Strong, Mack was all over it.

"Copy that." Rio spoke into the handheld, bracing himself on the radio console with a hand as the truck picked up more speed.

"Yeah, but most of the guys are out on the wildland fire call. I got the two reserves and not much more. Faster you get here, the better."

Rio eyed the speedometer. "Not a problem. We're there as quick as we can. Jump One signing out."

The truck ate up the highway. Heavy with gear and not designed for speed, though, the rear end skipped roughly when Evan took the next curve. Sixty miles per hour was usually the maximum recommended speed.

And Evan was already ten miles over that.

Rio cracked first. "You think you should slow down there, Evan? We're not running the Indy 500 here."

"I know how to drive." Which didn't exactly answer Rio's question.

Evan downshifted on the next curve to make his point, pushing the truck, smooth and easy, into the straight stretch. He forced his fingers to relax on the wheel, but he wasn't backing off. No way. Instead, he hit the gas and started praying as the road bent again. "You don't have your seat belts on, you'd better put 'em on now."

"Not SOP, Evan. You know that." Rio pointed out that little truth calmly.

"Then you might want to shut up so as not to distract me."

Mack snorted, reclining in his seat. "You make it back in half the time, you can explain the moving traffic violations.

"I don't care." It was all black night outside the windows, and the truck's headlights barely carved up the road in front. Slowing down was a no-brainer. One deer out for a late night stroll, and he'd roll the truck.

And he *didn't* care. That was the truth. "The sooner I get back, the sooner I slow down."

"You think Faye's in trouble." Rio fiddled with the channels, hunting for the local airwaves. That was smart. They'd get more details that way.

Evan did think that. "I hope she's not," he said grimly.

"But she could be," Rio pointed out, all Mr. Logic. "It's late, and she's bunking in the firehouse."

"I know." *Christ.* He needed to be in Strong. He needed to see Faye and make sure she was okay. The next curve came up, fast and tight, and he pushed the truck through it.

Mack closed his eyes. "Then you drive this thing as fast as she'll go, okay? No one here wants to hang back."

"No worries." His foot was permanently down, the gas pedal sandwiched between his boot and the plastic floor mat. Before too many hours it would be dawn, the first pink and orange fingers of light spearing up from the dark horizon. He'd be home long before then. Or in a ditch. "We're going to fly."

His head ran a dozen different scenarios. Faye in the firehouse. Faye trapped in her car as fire shot up around her. Before he took the next bend in the road, he'd imagined a dozen hideous endings to the night.

"Evan?" Rio stared out the windshield at the road. "When you get back, when you see her face and know that she's safe, you just tell her what you feel, okay? That's what you tell her."

Chapter Twenty

The beer was real cold, a Budweiser pick-me-up while Hollis waited for the show to get started outside. Mimi hadn't asked questions when he'd come in, so he'd ordered up the Bud and waited. Nothing unusual about banging one back at Ma's. Still, Mimi was watching him. He'd ditched the drip torch outside her door, but he definitely smelled like kerosene and smoke. That happy little stink could be on the up and up, though, so she was hanging back right now. She'd put two and two together in the next five to ten, however.

Right on cue, fire alarms blared to life outside the bar's front doors. *Showtime.* He started pulling money from his pocket, because he might set fires, but he paid his bar tab.

"On the house," Mimi growled, and she ran for the door. She'd definitely gotten the 411 on fire safety, because she felt the knob before she decided the metal was cool enough, and she flung the door open. Yeah, he'd lit up the firehouse parking lot good.

A car horn went off, singing a swan song, accompanied by small pops like bullets firing. Two of the three cars were fully engulfed now, and smoke shot up in black streams that faded to gray as they became airborne. The stink was bad now, because something plastic had caught, and there was plenty of orange. The added bonus was the wind lending a helping hand, spreading fire from A to B with each hot breath of air.

Yeah. He'd set a real good one here.

Mimi cursed, whirled around, and came right back inside, grabbing the land line beneath the bar. As she punched buttons and placed a call, he grabbed a bowl of peanuts and another beer. Popping the top, he headed for the still-open door. Shutting it on her return trip would have been a smart move for Mimi, because now his fires were pouring smoke into the bar, and she'd have one hell of a Febreze job on her hands.

Behind him, Mimi slammed down the phone. "What do you think you're doing, Hollis Anderson?"

He gave her the truth. "I'm getting me a ringside seat."

She grabbed a fire extinguisher from the wall and a handful of dishtowels. "You're a fucking firefighter!" she yelled over her shoulder as she ran for the door. "Fight that fire, Hollis!"

"Right behind you," he agreed, to shut her up. Taking a sip of the beer, he followed her outside. It was that Coors Light shit but in a bottle, so that was one step up from a can. Plus, it was real cold and free. On the house was a definite bonus.

The parking lot between Mimi's and the old firehouse was ringside, all right, and he had a good view, despite the sheets of smoke plugging up the sky now. Mimi was giving it the old college try, dancing in and out with that no-use fire extinguisher of hers. That much flame needed a fire hose. His professional assessment as he parked his ass on the smokers' bench outside the bar was that she should forget the cars and worry about her bar. A little wind and the fire would hop from those cars to her building in no time at all.

He lined up his beer and bowl of peanuts. What he should have done was grabbed a third beer. It wasn't as if he'd be driving home tonight.

It was like the Fourth of July out there, all lit up with the smell of smoke and shit going off. Sure, it was kind of strange to hang back, but he was done. So very, very done with trying to prove he fit in fine. He'd started this, and now someone else could finish it. That was a message right there.

He swallowed beer and peanuts and watched.

The doorknob was hot. Faye let go fast, thanking God for mandatory school fire education. If she opened that door, all the air on her side of it would feed the flames on the other side—and she'd be dead, dead, dead. After a really bad barbecue.

God. That door was her out to the street and the parking lot. The fire alarms shrilling around her warned that getting out fast was still number one on her to-do list. Smoke was filling up the downstairs, and, now that she eyeballed the door more closely, smoke curled visibly through the hinges and edges. The cars were definitely not the only thing on fire.

Mind racing, she tried to remember what Smokey the Bear had to say about fire safety. But Smokey was an outdoor bear working his thing in the forest. She was inside. This fire was trying to get to her. So she'd have to find another way out, on a different side of the building. She could do that, right?

And help had to be on its way.

Even now, she could hear the long, hard wail of a fire engine approaching fast. The dispatcher knew she was inside. He'd tell the guys riding the truck and . . . what? They'd come for her, maybe, but she needed out *now*. The smoke swirled and eddied around her ears, and she bent over, getting herself as low as she could without actually hitting the ground.

There. The bay for the trucks. The large space was empty now except for the painting and building supplies, stacks of lumber and ten-gallon buckets of paint. Yeah. That was an arsenal of fuel, but there wasn't much smoke there yet.

So that was where she needed to be. Moving quickly, she punched the button to open the bay doors. The doors started rolling with a loud rattle and roar, and outside air swept in.

That air was also full of smoke and trouble.

She didn't wait for the doors to go up all the way, simply ducked under and out as soon as she had enough clearance. The muscles in her legs burned as she straightened up with all the damned stuff she was carrying, but she couldn't bring herself to abandon anything.

The stink of burning rubber and plastic hit her first. A minivan had gone up completely in the minutes she'd spent getting out of the firehouse, and her Corvette was all dark smoke and sheets of orange, with more flames coming from the undercarriage. As those flames hit a sweet spot of combustion, the fire surged up until only the rear bumper was clear—and everything else was fire.

And the fire wasn't limited to the cars. The nearby foliage caught, flames shooting up the bushes. Those pretty flowers were the icing on some dry, dry branches, and the fire consumed it all like some kind of party snack.

This was out of her league. This wasn't something she could fix or stop.

Right on cue, an engine roared, the long, slow wail of the siren warning Strong to stay alert as the big vehicle stopped somewhere between the firehouse and the bar, air brakes hissing. Firefighters bailed out. Nine-one-one had come through. *Thank God.*

Not in time, though. Her car was way beyond rescuing.

Men shouted, pulling hoses and working wrenches on the fire hydrant. And yet the seconds ticked by, all slo-mo, and still there was no water. Her car burned and burned, and all she could do was watch. The big fuck-you to her ex. The freedom of tearing up the highway, going just fast enough that she wasn't completely safe. It was going up in smoke, and all she could do was watch.

No. The Corvette was only a car, and the damage was done there. Dumping her load on the sidewalk, she man-handled the fire extinguisher and pulled the pin. Running to the edge of the parking lot, she squeezed the trigger and swept the flaming bushes, dumping a load of foam.

The Corvette couldn't be rescued, but Strong could be.

Strong was a war zone. With fire hoses unfurled and water streaming, men hollered directions and Mimi worked a fire extinguisher while the long, deafening tones of the engine's siren woke up any sleepers. Evan pulled the truck up just outside the burn zone.

Before the truck stopped completely, Mack was out, booted feet tearing up the ground as he alternated be-tween cursing a blue streak and bellowing Mimi's name.

"Mimi's gonna be a dead woman if she doesn't back off," Rio muttered. He paused to grab gear from the back of the truck, and then he was hot on Mack's ass.

Evan didn't care where they went. All he needed to know right now was where Faye was. The rest of Strong could burn to the ground as long as the little piece hold-ing Faye came through intact. So, until he laid eyes on her, Rio and Mack and the rest of them were on their own.

Spotting Faye turned out to not be much of an im-provement, however. She'd evacced the firehouse—thank God—but she was too close to those damn car fires. A sheet of black smoke shot off what had been someone's ride until maybe a half hour ago. Minivan. Honda. And the Corvette. *Christ.* Of course, that was her car on fire, and undoubtedly that was why she was heading right toward the flames. The fire extinguisher in her hands didn't pack enough power for that kind of trouble, and ten seconds or so of foam was hardly worth the effort of yanking the pin. She'd be out of juice before she got started.

Worse, the volunteer engine had already turned its hoses on the minivan. The stream hit the burning vehicle hard, water fighting the flames for possession. That wasn't the problem. No, the problem was that Faye would soon be directly in line with those powerful hoses, and with all the smoke and flame, the men probably wouldn't see her.

Her name came out as a bellowed roar, his feet hitting the pavement hard. Christ, he wasn't going to make it. The fire crew repositioned the hose, aiming for the Honda. Forty yards. Thirty. He pumped hard, eating up the ground. If Faye got hit with that stream, it was about the equivalent of getting hit by a freight train. Faye wouldn't stand a chance.

The Corvette was going up. Sharp, popping noises peppered the air as the frame slowly bent beneath the fire's pressure. White-hot heat danced around the burning car, and the fumes were a thick, toxic wave.

"Get back!" he roared, catching her arm and yanking her backward as he tore off his Nomex jacket.

Her face, when she looked up at him, was a mask of anguish and indecision. "I have to do something."

Throwing the Nomex around her, he grabbed her upper arms and put her behind him. He wasn't going all PC here. Not when her life was on the line. "Go. We've got to go."

A fresh column of black smoke billowed from the cars behind them. Fire had found something else to burn and was going to town. Burning embers and debris rained down around them, but the smoke was the real killer. He yanked the Nomex over her head and shoulders, scooped her up in his arms, and ran like hell. Embers struck his back and shoulders, but he was big and used to the sting of the burn, and he hadn't been all that pretty to start with. All he had to do was get Faye where she could breathe and where the air was clean. His legs pumped, desperate to get her to safety. Twenty feet. Forty.

But, Christ, it was too late. He looked over his shoulder to gauge his distance from the cars, and the sound caught up with his eyes. First the tires blew out in a mini-explosion, and then the fire finally found the gas tank. The back end of the Corvette went up and came back down, slamming burned-out rubber and rims against the asphalt. Wrapping himself around Faye, he dove forward, taking her to the ground beneath him. Cradling her. Covering her.

She said something, but the fire's noise ate up the words, and he simply pressed her Nomex-covered head deeper into his chest. What wasn't exposed couldn't burn, so his hand cupped her, keeping her down.

"Man down!" he yelled, but he'd need more than luck to be heard over the fire and the jet-blast of the hoses. A thick, black wave of smoke hit, and he closed his mouth, choking on the fumes. *Hold on, hold on.* The blast would die back in a minute, and he'd have a window of opportunity to move.

Faye felt small and fragile trapped beneath him. That he could still lose her ripped through him in an unwelcome wake-up call far more painful than the burning debris hitting him. Nothing mattered more than this woman. *Nothing.*

He wasn't losing her.

Not as long as he could still fight for her.

★   ★   ★

Evan had her tucked beneath him, shielding her with his body and his coat. The hot wind blew over and past them as the fire flared greedily and the remaining bushes on the side of the parking lot went up like birthday candles, flames sheeting straight up.

"I've got you." His rough voice rumbled close by, his arms crossed over her head. "No worries."

She opened her mouth, closed it. She'd worried about *him*. A second, smaller explosion drowned out his next words. Startled, she twisted in his arms, trying for a better view. He held her effortlessly in place.

"We really, really need to go," she bit out. The ground beneath her shook hard, water coming down over her head in a dense, wet sheet as the hoses unleashed a salvo at the flames.

She felt rather than saw him shake his head. "Better to stay put, stay low. Give it thirty seconds, darlin'. The boys have the hoses up, and we don't want to get in the way of that. You had a close call there."

"A *hose*?" He'd thought she'd been about to get hit by a stream of water? When she glanced past his shoulder, the water was definitely headed in their direction now. Spray hit her as the water smashed into the cars and bounced back.

"They couldn't see you." His voice sounded anything but calm. "Goddamn it, Faye. You know what a hose like that can do to a body? Imagine someone driving a pickup truck right at you." His voice rose. "You don't run toward a fire. Not any fire."

"You do."

He cursed hard and low, his next words shocking her, as blunt as the man himself. "You scared me. I thought I was going to lose you, Faye. That hose came around, and you were in its line of fire, and I didn't know if I could get there in time."

He'd worried for her. "I'm okay." Freeing her hands from his Nomex, she slid them up his chest, finding the sides of his face and cupping them gently. "I'm okay."

"Yeah," he said gruffly. "You are, darlin'."

He lowered his head and covered her mouth with his.

His kiss was unexpected and exactly what she craved, as if he'd crawl right inside her and stay there if he could.

He smelled like fire. The rough five o'clock shadow on his jaw chafed her fingertips. Nomex and smoke and man. Her very own, bona fide hero. She'd never been so glad to see anyone in her life. Time to choose, once and for all. She looked at that hard face, turned away from her now to watch the fire. Assessing. He was a firefighter to the core.

When he scooped her up and carried her to the perimeter, she didn't protest. She simply put her head on his shoulder and waited for what came next.

"You got her? She okay?" Rio hollered, concern flashing on his face.

Christ, he hoped so. "She'd better be."

He didn't know who or what he was threatening, but those words were a promise he'd do anything to keep. He prayed some, too, as he got her behind the perimeter. Plenty of action remained out there in the parking lot, but that was none of his biz right now.

Faye was.

She moved in his arms. He put her down, and her hands shoved at the suffocating folds of his coat, pushing the heavy Nomex away. She sucked in fresh air, coughing.

"I'm getting the EMTs over here," he said grimly. He wasn't taking chances. "Have them check you out, give you some oxygen."

"I'm fine." Her fingers clutched the folds of his fire coat, pulling the heavy material around her shoulders like some kind of a blanket. She stared past him at the thick cloud of black smoke and the car burning down to its frame.

"It's all gone."

What did he say to that? That car was more than a car to Faye. He knew that. Whatever she'd been running from in L.A., that car had been her ticket out. So handing her platitudes about filing insurance claims and it-was-just-a-car wasn't a good option.

He cleared his throat. "That's true, Faye." He thought about her face when she was taking the Corvette down the highway to the hangar, the windows down and her foot on the gas pedal. She felt free when she was in that car. Kind of her version of going out in the jump plane and into the air. "We'll make it okay, though, Faye. I promise you."

Her snort of laughter was unexpected. "Evan, you'd promise me we'd be okay if I'd lost both legs."

"True." An answering smile tugged at his mouth. Yeah. He'd do that. What she didn't get, though, was that then he'd *make* it okay. These weren't empty words he was giving her. "But you work with me here on this. We'll figure out your car, Faye."

"Sure." She looked at him as if she was trying to read his face, and he wondered what she was looking for. In another minute, he'd give in to temptation and pull her into his arms. "It really is just a car, Evan. Even if it was a really, really expensive car."

"Faye—" He should hang back. He should give her space, not crowd her. But he wanted to touch her and hold her and whisper promises into her ear. She didn't look as if she wanted to run back to L.A. right now, either, though. She was staring at him, all brown eyes and something else. Hope? *Christ. He* hoped so.

He was still searching for words when a shout went up

behind them, loud enough to be heard over the pounding of the water and the wailing of sirens. They both swung around.

The guys were wrestling Hollis Anderson down to the ground. Mack and Rio belted out curses and angry words while they got busy with their fists. Hollis looked as if he wasn't quite ready to throw in the towel, but he wasn't fighting too hard, either. He knew he was busted.

"They've got him." Faye didn't step away, but she hadn't closed up that little distance between them, either. She simply stood there, waiting. Evan looked back at the fight. Not much of a fight, since it was two-on-one. Mack and Rio had Hollis good and pinned on the ground outside Mimi's now. He should go over there, should make sure no one took a swing and that Hollis ended up secure in the back of a police cruiser, but his feet weren't moving.

Faye Duncan looked at him as if she *needed* him.

"Good," he rumbled. "That means our arsonist is done lighting up Strong."

"You think they can hold him without you?"

Hollis Anderson was one man, and he was no superhero. And Evan knew exactly what Rio and Mack were capable of. They had this. Sure, he should be over there with them. But this woman standing here, watching him— his Faye—she needed something, too. And she came first. Something unlocked, clicking into place inside him. Faye came first.

She always would.

"They're going to have to." He threaded his fingers through her hair. She didn't resist, just stood there and let him cup her head and hold her tight. "You come first, Faye. You do, darlin'."

Chapter Twenty-one

Evan could have held Faye like that for a week, but there were words that needed saying. Words that counted to Faye. He should have brought flowers or made up a poem—which was a ludicrous thought—anything to dress up what he wanted to say here. Anything to make her understand she was his L.Z., his landing zone, the one woman he'd make for when everything else heated up around him and the whole world was on fire.

Instead, he just said it. "I love you."

Her eyes got wide. The fire was still like the Fourth of July and Chinese New Year rolled into one around them, so, yeah, his timing was off.

He should have waited. Picked a better time—

She wrapped her arms around him, though, and that had to be a good sign. She was hanging on to him, and he had her covered. Or, rather, he had her pinned in a bear hug in the middle of the street with what had to be half of Strong looking on. It didn't matter. He was okay with that. He loved this woman. He loved Faye Duncan.

He picked her up. It didn't take much—a quick slide of his arms underneath her—and then he cradled her to his chest and breathed in for one long moment because she was safe and she was right there with him. And, yeah, because he wanted to kiss her so bad, it hurt.

"You feeling the déjà vu here?" He'd carried her out of Ma's like this, that first night. "You remember the night we met?"

"Evan—" She inhaled, and he knew the argument was coming.

"Hold that thought," he said, "and let me get you out of here, okay?"

She nodded, and he tucked her closer to his chest, shifting her so he could see her face clearly. The fire and smoke had done a number on her—plenty of black soot, and her skin was pink from the heat. He carried her to the fire truck because he didn't know where else to take her. The firehouse was looking more than a little scorched, and her poor Corvette—well, he hoped like hell she had insurance on the thing, because there was nothing left. Only a burned-up frame.

Dropping the tailgate, he sat her on the lip and put himself beside her. The engine had made a dent in the car fires, but it was still kind of like having a ringside seat at a fireworks display. Plenty of flames and smoke and popping noises every time something new went up.

She looked up at him, and there was all that hope again in her eyes. He pulled her into his side, while his hands petted her hair, her back, her arms. Checking her out for injuries while his mind raced, trying to put together something romantic. Hell, even a sentence. All he came up with was more of the same-old, same-old.

"I love you." He gave it to her again. "I wish I knew another, better way to say that, Faye. Something poetic or pretty. Something real special."

"You're doing okay," she said. He followed her gaze to the burning leftovers of her Corvette. Someone had finally run a second hose, and the shooting flames were under control. "So say it again. And again. That's something I can never hear too many times."

He needed her even closer, so he settled her on his lap, swung his legs up onto the truck bed, and stretched out. She settled right in, and he whispered the words into her hair over and over.

"I love you, too, Evan."

The words punched him hard in the gut. He hadn't dared hope.

"You mean that?" It was hard to unlearn years of caution. "I'm no prize," he warned.

She dropped her head onto his chest and looked up at him. The impact of those brown eyes had parts of him stirring underneath all the denim, too. Ruthlessly, he punched those feelings down. *Words.* This was the talking part, and, this time, he was getting it all right.

She snorted that half laugh of hers. Maybe he'd get to hear that laugh for the next fifty years or so if he was lucky. "Too late to take it back. You put the words out there, Evan. Tell me now if you don't mean them."

His hand smoothed her hair back from her face. There was a little shakiness there, as if both his body and his head knew what was at stake here. Yeah, he was nervous. This mattered. This was his forever and their happily-ever-after.

"I mean all three words. I love you. You want more than that, I'll give you whatever I've got. I'm going to be right here for you if you want me to be. That's my promise to you. I may not be much, but I'm all yours if you'll have me. You just give me a sign."

Her warm smile heated him up somewhere inside where he hadn't known he was cold. "You're a good man."

"Not so much. I'm no hero." He'd done plenty that hadn't ended up right. He'd screwed up often. He didn't know much about where he came from. He'd spent time living hard on the streets and, even though he'd been a kid then, he'd still done things that didn't make a man proud.

He'd fought for what mattered, though, first in the Marines and then for Donovan Brothers. He had something here in Strong, a home with Nonna and his brothers. Maybe that counted for more than he thought, because she was looking up at him, and even he couldn't miss the hope shining in her eyes.

"I don't need a hero." She shifted on his lap, turning around. Her legs pinned his as she straddled him, planting herself on the erection that hadn't gotten the message that this was emo time. "You want to kiss me?"

"Hell, yeah, darlin'."

"Then kiss me real good, and let's get started on that happily-ever-after."

Epilogue

Six months later

"Smile for the camera." Faye framed Evan in the lens of her camera. She looked happy, perched beside him in the cab of his truck. She'd been looking forward to tonight for a long time. Now it was showtime, and she was ready to go. Shaking his head, he got out of the truck and came around to open the passenger-side door and help her down.

"Darlin', smiling for your camera got me into a world of trouble." He slipped a hand beneath her elbow. "I can't show my face anywhere in Northern California without the hoots and hollers starting."

"Baby." She nudged him with her shoulder, and he scooped her up against his side. Faye fit well there. The black jersey number she was wearing hugged her curves in all the best places, and she'd picked out some killer heels. The heels lent her inches, and he liked the sexy sway those shoes gave her walk. He had plans for those shoes later tonight. Lots of plans. Rio wasn't the only one living out his fantasies.

She bounced up the steps next to him and then came to a dead stop when they hit the gallery's front door. The gallery was front and center on Main Street. The jump team had brought over the leftover paint from the firehouse renovation and gone to work with paintbrushes and hammers. Even he had to admit, the old building looked real good. Faye claimed that all that old wood and beams paired with plenty of windows so you could see the art from outside on the street was what made Strong's shoppers stop in. Evan knew better. Faye's pictures did that. She was amazing.

Her fingers tightened on his arm, tugging. "Look at that . . . We did it."

He looked down at her, and he couldn't hold back a grin. "You sure you don't want to trade it in for another Corvette?" She looked like a kid on Christmas morning. The insurance company, which had paid out one hell of a lot on the burned-out Corvette, had played Santa for Faye. Unsalvageable, they'd called the car. Well, Faye had sure salvaged something. She'd taken that check and bought this place, and tonight her gallery was having the grand opening she'd been dreaming of.

"Absolutely not." She poked him. "This is way better than a Corvette."

"Uh-huh." He tipped his head back and eyeballed the sign: JUMP SPOT ART GALLERY. "Sign's still crooked."

"It is not." She made a sound of feminine exasperation. "It's perfect. You hung it."

He had. He was good with a hammer and nails, and that part had been easy. It was tonight's shindig that he'd been dreading for weeks. The gallery was all lit up, with rent-a-waiters passing out bubbly on silver trays. Yeah. It was one fancy scene. A low buzz of conversation spilled out onto the street, warning him they weren't the first to arrive tonight. Through one of the big windows, he spotted Rio and Jack. The rest of the jump team seemed to be there, as well. Everyone had come out to support her. He tugged at his shirt collar.

Which was fine. She hadn't shot *them* naked.

"You can't do it again," he demanded.

"Do what?"

"No more photos," he said. *Damn it.* He sounded desperate. He could hear himself losing ground. He needed to hold his line, or she'd overrun him.

Although maybe it was already too late. He was head over heels for her, so he'd already lost his fight against love. Her mischievous grin as she looked up at him, her fingers stroking the strap around her neck, did something to his heart, and speech temporarily deserted him. He knew that seductive rhythm. She touched *him* like that.

"Tease," he said roughly.

"You like it." She didn't sound apologetic at all.

"It's not too late to turn around and go home." He'd make it up to her. For hours. She'd like that.

The look she shot him said she wasn't buying, and he still had to go in. *Well, hell.* Escape had been a long shot, anyhow. Dropping a kiss onto her forehead, he held the door for her and followed, watching the sexy glide of her ass beneath the black jersey because he really didn't need an eyeful of what was hanging on the walls.

Before they got ten feet inside, well-wishers pried Faye away from his side, and the guys started in, ribbing him over starring front and center in that damned smokejumper calendar Faye had shot. Ungrateful bastards. The proceeds from that calendar had more than paid for fixing up the firehouse.

"Hey, Evan, looking good." Zay hailed him with a low wolf whistle.

"Yeah, don't recognize you tonight, man," another jumper chimed in.

"That's 'cause he's dressed," Mack shot back, and, Christ, Evan hoped he wasn't blushing. This shouldn't be such a huge deal. It was just a couple of pictures. No biggie.

Mentally plugging his ears and rearranging his face into a mask of big-and-silent, he eyeballed the pictures on the wall. His Faye was damned good. The photos were a mix of sexy and serious, playful and deadly. That was smoke jumping, and she'd captured it perfectly. The DC-3 lifting up. A jumper coming down, chute out behind him. Soot-blackened faces with face-splitting grins because they'd held the line. Jack pulling Lily into him for a kiss because he was home. *Hell.* He frowned. How come Rio had pulled the PG moment?

In the center of the gallery, right at the heart of the talking and chitchatting, Jack launched smoothly into his speech. He welcomed everyone and then acknowledged how Faye's smoke-jumper calendar had raised a truckload of money for the firehouse restoration. Everyone raised a glass of California bubbly, agreeing that Faye was a talented photographer and the firehouse was lucky to have her on their side. That was no news flash. Faye was fucking amazing, and what she'd accomplished had him bursting with pride.

He didn't need Jack or a cocktail party to tell him that.

Rio strolled up to him, and the look on his brother's face said the teasing meet-and-greet at the gallery's front door had been merely the warm-up. Rio was here to serve the entrée.

"You seen Faye's masterpiece?"

"Don't remind me," he groaned, taking the champagne flute his brother offered. He shouldn't have let her coax him into it. But, damn, she'd looked at him, and she'd asked, and he . . . he hadn't been able to resist her. Hell, he hadn't even tried. Much.

Rio laughed. "You've seen the calendars—wait until you see this." Yeah, there was mischief all over his brother's face. Of course, he was Mr. December, and he had been wearing part of a jumpsuit. *He* had nothing to worry about.

"It gets worse?" He'd jumped into two-thousand-acre fires with less trepidation.

"She had the pictures blown up," Rio said cheerfully. "Twelve by twelve."

"Inches?" *Yeah. Definitely desperate.*

"Feet," Jack confirmed, coming up behind him. "Congratulations. You're a sensation. A *huge* sensation."

Evan looked for Faye, but she was surrounded by a knot of people spouting congratulations. She deserved every minute of that, so he couldn't pull her away now. His big plans would have to wait until later. Instead, he followed Rio and checked out the photo Rio was teasing him about. *Christ.* It was huge. There was no missing it—she'd put it front and center.

She'd taken that picture right after he'd come home from a call. She'd pulled him into bed, and he'd gone willingly. Afterward, she'd grabbed her camera and told him to smile.

"She didn't tell me it was a trap."

"Crybaby." Rio laughed. "For those of us not off the market, Faye's calendar is excellent advertising." A slow, sexy smile tugged his brother's face, and Evan did *not* want to know what Rio was thinking. "You're the only man complaining."

"I'm the only man *naked*," he emphasized.

He eyed the photo again, as if maybe something had changed there, or someone had passed out fig leaves. No such luck. He was still bare-ass naked, sprawled on their bed. The sheet didn't begin to cover said ass, and they were going to have more words about that. Faye had heard of Photoshop—but she'd refused to cover him up. Her lens had captured his boots, kicked off by the side of the bed, and the jumpsuit on the floor. Yeah. He hadn't been following any SOP there. He'd been too eager to get her into his arms.

He was smiling right at the camera, too, because on the other side of the damn lens was Faye. A great big come-hither smile, as if he enjoyed what she was showing him. Which he had. And did. Which was the whole point of tonight's operation. He patted his jacket pocket, checking.

"No worries," Rio said quietly. "You've got this."

Yeah, right. And his certainty explained the herd of manic butterflies rampaging around in the pit of his stomach. There was nothing certain except how he felt about Faye.

"Man of the hour!" Mack handed him a cold beer, and Evan didn't ask where the other man had gotten the bottle. The flute felt awkward and fragile in his hand, and he gratefully palmed his off on one of the passing waiters. The beer bottle—that was familiar.

"Sleeping with your photographer." Mack winked. "Didn't know you had it in you."

The whole calendar-buying, gallery-visiting, magazine-reading world now knew what he had in him. Watching Faye walk toward him, those high heels drawing his eyes to the feminine sway of her hips, he didn't mind. Not one little bit.

"You look handsome." Her arms snugged around his waist, and, for a long moment, he simply enjoyed the delicious weight of her pressed up against his back.

"You set me up," he growled.

"Get over it." She sounded delighted. "You know how many pictures I've sold tonight? You're the man of the hour and the best calling card ever. I should print you up and add you to my business cards."

"Don't," he warned. He didn't really care what others

thought of him, but teasing her felt good. One of many things that felt good, that felt *right,* about having this woman at his side.

He tugged her closer and steered her out of the crowd. This was it, the moment when he jumped from the plane and hit the air. He was on his way down. There was still plenty of foot traffic in the gallery's small side room, but it was slightly quieter and away from the conversational roar. The only other available place was the narrow hallway leading to the restrooms, and he didn't need a consult with Rio to know that *that* wasn't romantic. And it was probably busier than hell, given the volume of bubbly the gallery's guests were downing.

He braced himself, looking for his L.Z. "I need to talk to you."

Her lashes flickered down, then shot back up. "Something wrong?"

"Yeah." Stick with the script. He'd thought this out. This once, he knew what he wanted to say. "You have naked pictures of me."

Her mouth curved. "I have more. You haven't seen them all."

Hell. He stared at her, the script flying out of his head. "You do?"

"Absolutely. No way I'd miss such a"—her eyes slid down his body and fixed right on his groin—"*big* opportunity."

He slapped a hand on the wall beside her head and leaned in. "No." Her eyes widened, so maybe he needed to tone down the growl. "You've got 144 square feet of me on display in there. Anything else you've got, that's for the two of us. You got me?"

"That sounds like a challenge." Her teeth worried her lower lip, but her face didn't look anxious. No, his darling looked flushed. Aroused. She was playing with him, and she liked the growl just fine. "You going to make me behave, Evan?"

He liked hearing his name on her lips. Leaning in closer, he put his other hand on her hip. Tugged her body flush with his.

"Let me tell you what you're going to do." His mouth was on her throat now, nipping and kissing the sensitive skin. "You're going to make an honest man of me, darlin'."

"Evan?" It was her turn to look uncertain. He liked the dazed look in her eyes. Good. She'd turned his world upside down, so it was only fair he returned the favor. "What are you asking here?"

"I'm asking you to marry me. Will you?" Threading his fingers through her hair, he kissed her, soft and deep. Not giving her a chance to answer because, if he was wrong about how she was feeling, he wanted this last kiss.

He pulled his mouth off hers and repeated his question. "Will you marry me?" Her lips were swollen and wet, and he tasted cherry lip gloss. He wanted to kiss her again, but he needed to hear her answer more. Slipping a hand into his jacket pocket, he retrieved the small box. Flipped the top open and showed her.

The ring was an antique, and he'd made two trips to Sacramento before he'd discovered the fire opal hiding in a jeweler's tray. The stone looked as if it was on fire, all orange-red in the gold band. Two other brides had worn it, and their names and the names of their husbands were inscribed on the band. There was just enough room to add theirs.

"If you don't like it, we can get something else." Hell, he'd buy her an entire jewelry store if that was what she wanted.

"I love you." A high-wattage smile lit up her face as she spoke the words he wanted to hear so badly, and the butterflies in his stomach abruptly landed. That was not a last kiss. She stared up at his face, watching his eyes, with worlds of emotion in her own. "Yes. Yes, I'll marry you."

"Good thing," he said gruffly. "Seeing as how you've exposed me to the entire world."

"Shut up." Standing on tiptoe, she brushed her mouth over his. "Put that ring on my finger before I decide you need to go down on one knee."

"I'd do it." Picking up her left hand, he slid the ring over her finger. "That's what this means. Whatever you need, whatever you want, I'm all yours. I want to come home to you every night for the rest of my life. I want to find you there, waiting for me, or, if you're not there, I'll wait for you to come home to me. And when you're ready to hit the road looking for those adventures of yours, you take me with you. Because I love you."

"You're all mine." Delight colored her voice, her body arching into his as her hands reached for the back of his neck to urge his head closer still. And her mouth—her mouth kissed him and kissed him right there in that gallery where everyone could see them. "And I'm yours," she whispered against his ear.

Love was risky business. As risky some days as a fast, hard jump with the chute snapping you up and back. Other days, it was a slow, smooth glide down to earth. His hands pulled her to him, holding on because the heart was the sweetest jump spot of all, and now he knew exactly where he was headed in this sweet, hot ride. Straight to his woman. Straight to Faye.